Spider's Kiss

Book 1 of the Drambish Contaminate

Jesse Sprague

PART ONE

Spider's Kiss

CHAPTER 1

YAHAL BROTHEL

Hot, stale air clogged Henri's lungs as he approached a metal chair built into the wall. A servant wearing the Brothel's black uniform stepped out of the shadows. He approached Henri and pressed several buttons on the arm of the chair, causing the metal wrist restraints to retract. Seven of ten chairs along the wall contained restrained men, all of whom had paid massive sums to be in this room, most sweating profusely. Unlike the others, who quivered with nerves, Henri grinned.

His right eye twitched with excitement when he looked at the restraints that awaited him.

Sinking into his seat, Henri placed his thick wrists on the armrests, and metal bands emerged and closed, tightening around his wrists and ankles. The attendant walked over to the entrance and closed the metal door, settling net-glasses over his eyes. Once the metal bar clanged into place, no one else could enter. His work complete, the attendant stood by the door, arms folded. His net-glasses fogged over with black so he couldn't see the room.

The sweat, a product of both fear and heat, dripped into Henri's eyes.

From the chair, a final restraint slid forth and encircled his forehead, holding him in place. He didn't object to the restriction of his movement.

I didn't come here to see the other men strapped helplessly in their chairs, he thought. *I bet none of them even knows what the show contains. How many of them will scream? I love shows with screamers.*

After a few moments, the lights extinguished. The heat remained, swelling, filling each of Henri's senses. The thick, sweltering air and the straps pinning him in place overrode all else. One man began to whimper. The sound sent licks of anticipation down Henri's spine. This would be an exceptional show. The scrape of boots against the floor joined the whimpering to create an irregular beat beneath the silence.

As the seconds ticked by, his eyes grew accustomed to the dark. In the nearly lightless room, he saw Silvia's slender form, the darkness holding her close. At first, all that showed was a curvy silhouette against the back wall.

Silvia moved among the shadows with no more substance than a muffled scream. A small flame bloomed on a candle clasped between her hands. She stood in its flickering light, hands circling the tall, white pillar. Even in the grotesque shadows of the candle's flame, her face was cold and perfect. Black hair streaked with red hung to her waist. Her eyes glowed in the darkness, the black eyes of a beast. Silvia took a few silent steps toward them. The gold tassels of her belt rustled against the russet robe encasing her body.

The shadows partnered Silvia in a sensual dance. Hands as pale as smoke against the night sky caressed a jungle of dark shapes. A sigh parted her full lips and rippled in the silence. Six candles blared to light along the side walls even as the one in her hand dropped.

Those pale fingers twitched at the fabric, and her tasseled belt fell. The russet gown slipped like a creature forgotten to the floor. Beneath it, she wore only the tissue-paper-like undergarments customary in brothels. Her black eyes inspected the restrained men. Running one finger down the center of her chest, she cut through the undergarments, which flared to ash.

Lust brought Henri crashing back into his body. This was not a woman he would ever touch, but the thought of her taloned fingers on his body brought a moan to his lips. Those were foolish dreams. No sane man would ever permit himself to be strapped to a chair across a room from Silvia, the Spider Queen.

As she posed, a shadow entered the room behind her. Henri watched its skittering movements and waited with bated breath for the others to see the beast. The spider was huge, standing as tall as Silvia's waist, and its eyes stared back unblinking. Then one man choked back a scream.

Silvia smiled and began to dance, her movements fluid. The spider approached her. It came up and stopped inches from her white body. With infinite care, it caressed her shoulder with one long, hairy leg. Her face leaned against its leg in an instinctive lover's gesture. Feelers touched her hair, and she reached up to hold the spider's arm against her.

Silvia turned away from the viewers and danced for the spider. Her hands fondled its body, and she caressed the twitching maw. She glanced over her shoulder at the men, and her mouth moved, forming a chilling smile. Withdrawing her limbs from the spider, she walked toward the viewers. When she reached Henri, her long, dark nails scraped across his chest. The spider retreated to the back corner, its eyes glowing.

Silvia was gone again, walking down the line of men.

"Come. Bring me my gift." Silvia's voice was deep and colored by the dark.

Henri's breath came in bursts as he stared at the growing sliver of light emitting from the back door.

Two pretty girls dressed in trailing gauze and fogged net-glasses entered, carrying a scruffy man between them. Each of his feet banged into the floor with all his weight but without intention, as if he were in a trance or drugged. The girls let him go, and Silvia beckoned to him. On tottering legs, he stepped forward. He grabbed at her. She eluded his grasp, feet skipping to the side and hips swaying. The chase that followed was one-sided, embellished with her laughter and his stumbles.

Silvia raked her hands across the air, and the man's clothes fell in shreds to the ground. Naked and shivering despite the heat, the man stood in front of her.

Henri couldn't have spoken if he wanted to. The air around him hung heavier. Lust ate at him, but his desires would remain unsatisfied and he tried to ignore the urges. Ridden by fear, this was the most exquisite form of lust he had encountered in all his years.

Silvia did not turn to the restrained men but stared at the scruffy man as she ran her hands along her body. He stumbled to her and pulled her against him.

The Spider Queen grabbed the back of his neck and pulled his lips to hers. With the brutal kiss completed, she shoved him back. Every inch of her was revealed and yet remained forbidden to Henri. As she lay back on the ground, her hair spread out around her. The man crouched and then crawled to her. Meanwhile, the spider began his slow movement out of the corner and into the center of the room. Silvia crooned, one hand beckoning the man and the other motioning the spider closer.

Henri's fingers scraped into the chair. He panted, his breath creating a rhythm his body longed to follow.

The monster approached the man's back. The man's empty, drugged eyes turned in Henri's direction. Somewhere in the vague depths of those eyes, terror lurked buried beneath the hunger of desire. Silvia's long hair writhed on the ground, and her mouth glistened as it parted in a sigh. Her intricate dance threaded the air with rhythm.

The instant the man's hand touched her, the spider ripped him from her body and threw him back against the wall. It sprang after him. Like a wisp of smoke, Silvia rose, a laugh blooming on her mouth. The spider pinned the man to the wall, and he screamed.

Momentarily, Henri's eyes closed, but the image of the spider, the victim, and the sorceress remained etched in his brain. When his eyes opened again, blood splashed across the floor and spurted onto Silvia's giggling face.

The spider spat and left a long burn on the man's cheek and neck. Silvia's hips swayed. The light moved through the room, dancing with her. Following the command of her slender body, the illumination fell like a spotlight on the carnage. One of the restrained men began to scream as another retched.

Henri giggled despite himself.

The spider bit into the man by the wall. The man struck out at the spider's face and flailed his legs. Its gaping maw snapped shut again, pulling away a bloody chunk, and then it impaled the man with one hairy leg. After jerking for a few moments, the man slumped down. The spider dropped him to the ground and began to rend him apart.

Silvia turned to the other men. The shadows danced for her. Silvia didn't move; she only smiled. Then the spider came to her, and they embraced. The dying man's blood dripped over her, streaking her white skin red. She licked blood from the spider's prickly body.

A moan of pleasure escaped her lips, and a similar sound escaped Henri's lips. One man to Henri's right whimpered and began to mutter prayers to his gods. Silvia's dark eyes flew to the praying man. Slowly, she disentangled herself from the spider.

Since Henri's head remained fastened in place, he pictured her approaching the whimpering man. Henri enjoyed the jump of adrenaline that came with imagining Silvia's movement and ignored the twinge of fear.

Screams filled the air. Henri imagined he felt her soft fingers on his forehead. At her touch, his airways would freeze. The screaming stopped. What would his death look like reflected in her eyes? It might be worth it to feel Silvia's kiss.

"Remember," Silvia said. "Once you leave this chamber, tonight's entertainment never happened. To speak a single time of the contents of this show will earn you a place center stage and guarantee your loved ones a messy death."

When Silvia returned to Henri's line of sight, the room was silent. She tapped the side of her head, where most net-chips were implanted—as if any of them needed a reminder of the programming installed in the devices before they'd entered the room.

She caressed the spider's side as she passed by it and left.

Henri relaxed in his chair. His eyes drifted closed. Sight wasn't the only sense he could use to enjoy the finale. The spider was hidden from view as it consumed the corpse of the screamer, but he heard the snapping of bone and the rending of flesh. When the spider finished, it followed Silvia out of the room.

The attendant turned on the light and stepped over the blood and body parts. He freed the men. One by one, they fell from their chairs or ran. One stopped to vomit. Henri looked at the dead man. A mix of jealousy and pity welled up in him. He quickly discarded both emotions and whistled as he walked out.

△△△

Silvia waited in the hall outside of the chamber. Behind a curtain, she watched the men leave. Some ran, one cried, and some were silent. Each and every one revolted her. Paying customers to a snuff show for their own species. Silvia stroked the palm-sized spider that rested on her wrist and waited. Then came the smiling man.

Henri Trehar—an average-looking wealthy man who wore his expensive suit like it added value to his person. An unremarkable man on most accounts as far as she could tell. Nothing in the bio he'd submitted to The Brothel stood out to her. Except, of course, his family connections.

"Mr. Trehar," she called. Her voice was as smooth as velvet, a lovely alto. In her industry, awareness of those details mattered.

He turned to her, his smile fading for the first time since she had noticed him in the show. She raised one black eyebrow at him.

"Follow me. I'll not make a second request." The blood had all been wiped off her, and a crisp tunic hid her modestly from the eyes of the world. This was how she preferred to converse: clean, with the stench of death and fear lingering. Henri Trehar looked up at her like the little troll he was. It was nothing new to be taller than the cretins who came to watch her dance, and the height variance effectively reminded them that she was always in charge.

The spider's prickly hairs slid under her fingertips as she turned and walked deeper into the hall. Henri followed. He stunk of sweat.

A smile played over her lips, never wide enough to show the gleam of her white teeth. Maybe if bathed properly, he'd be less revolting.

They walked down a long corridor containing many curtained doors. Other wings of The Brothel had more modern accouterments, but Silvia preferred the elegance of the old-fashioned décor, even if it meant a sacrifice in technology.

Silvia lifted one of the cloths and strode into a large chamber decorated in red and black. She seated herself on a red leather chair with a black quilt thrown over the back. Henri's eyes immediately went to her darling tarantula, and to maximize his discomfort, she began to pet this spider even as the other scampered off her arm.

He sat across from her after checking for any arachnids. This was good. She didn't want to work with someone who killed one of her pets. He already had a strike in her opinion as someone who attended her shows. The spiders were the only things in The Brothel she loved. The objects that filled her chambers all belonged to the Yahal Brothel and as such were tainted, decorations in a jail cell she'd endured since she'd been a toddler. The rest of The Brothel was vile, an elaborate parade of the worst of humankind, showing their most monstrous faces.

"My lover recognized you," Silvia said. "I rarely note a

face among the chained who come to play voyeur. But he has an amazing memory."

"Your lover?" Henri asked.

"The arachnid," Silvia said. Each word dripped out like a separate sentence. He should feel stupid for such a statement.

His ensuing silence was encouraging. He might be useful after all, this compact, hairy man. A spider crawled across the floor and onto the toe of her boot. Her soft, full mouth curved up in a smile.

"I'm called 'Silvia.' As a meeting place, my rooms leave much wanting. I'm not akin to the harlots here, who keep their rooms friendly to male visitors." *I'm not a whore.*

Mr. Trehar made no response, and Silvia expected none once she heard the *click, click* of Halis' eight feet coming up the passage behind the bed.

Halis didn't pay any heed to their visitor. He was still sticky with blood. From the look on Henri's face, he found Halis hideous. She pitied some humans when confronted with Halis but had no tenderness for the breed of monster who came to watch one of their own species slaughtered for no purpose except entertainment.

You're more a monster than he. She pursed her lips, studying Henri's pale face.

Then her eyes slid over Halis. His body was covered with hairs as thick as copper wire and his eyes, blacker even than her own, observed them.

"*Soon, my love, soon,*" Silvia said in a voice carried over the air's shadows. The web that wound between them, connecting them to not only each other, but also the guiding force at the center of the internal network, allowed them telepathic communication.

Halis' chuckle reverberated in her mind, covering her thoughts in delicious darkness. "*There is an ancient parable about a soft-hearted woman who takes in an injured snake. When its needs have been met, it acts as nature dictates. Let me know when I can eat him.*"

"My partner, Halis," Silvia said. "You're going to do us a service, Mr. Trehar."

"Any-Anything," Henri stammered.

"I've a little voyage planned. We intend to leave this backwater planet."

CHAPTER 2
THE COUNT'S SON

Wind whipped through the grassy meadow, making the yellowing grass ripple like waves. Darith stared at the movement as he rebuckled the belt around his waist, trying to hold on to the pleasantness of the moment. The conversation to come would be distasteful, and the taste in his mouth was foul, knowing he should have talked with her before their clothes ever came off.

Gretta arranged her skirts and picked bits of grass from the small, tight curls of her free hair. She was a remarkable creature, and Darith allowed himself a moment to admire the dark, hickory brown of her skin, especially where her bust met the white of her low collar.

Why did I believe she'd prove any longer-lasting than the other village girls? They always ask too much.

Darith fingered a small clip of cash in his pocket, but, no. She hadn't done anything to imply she was one of those girls. Some of them secretly liked having cash tossed their way as a consolation prize. Gretta's family wasn't poor, though, just lower-class.

"Next week?" she asked.

"No. It's been lovely," he said.

"Lovely? I don't understand."

"I didn't take you for dim-witted." Darith turned and walked back to his car. The black vehicle was parked as to block them from view of the road.

"Why?" came her breathy reply at last.

Darith looked at her reflection in the tinted windows of the car. Tear-filled eyes stared up at him, not yet angry, but that would come next. As his mother always said, the truth liberates and heeding those hurt by it is a pointless endeavor.

"My father is the count. My wife isn't going to be some sweet-faced shop girl. You're not going to be the mother of my children. What is the point of continuing once you start bandying around words like love? I can't love you. Call that accountant you keep laughing about—he wants to hear your confessions of love and earns enough. Haven't you wasted enough time chasing dreams?"

"You're heartless, Darith Cortanis. You—"

"No, dear. *Heartless* would be to discard you, and some bastard child, only after I found a woman I intended to marry. This is pragmatism."

Gretta threw a tuft of grass at him, the dirty roots brushing his calf.

"I never asked for more than ye can give. Never," she shouted.

Darith rubbed his forehead, wondering if the money wasn't a good idea after all. He'd enjoyed this one. The tears rolling down her cheeks shown in her reflection in the car windows touched him where her words failed.

"But you would have," he said. "Would it be kindness to continue this a year or two until your other suitors are gone? How long before this affair gets out and you're considered sullied? Any other planet than Yahal, you might be fine, but here? No decent man would have you. I'm too young to commit to a lifelong mistress, and you deserve a husband."

"Why start if...?" Her words choked off in a sob.

"Because you are lovely, and I'm ending it because you want love. Call me heartless if the word consoles you."

He'd thought Gretta had more common sense than this. Sometimes village girls understood intuitively what his attentions meant. He granted them some patronage, and they both enjoyed the dalliance. If they wanted a more liberated society, more options, then all they needed was a passport off of Yahal.

Darith opened the back door of the car and slid into the seat. Closing the door, he blocked out the sound of crying. The silence of the cab soothed the fresh pounding in his head. He tapped the glass dividing the front from the back to let the driver know he was ready to depart.

Where had this strange idea that she could win his undying affection come from? *It spreads like a plague. It didn't used to be like this. When I was younger dalliances were so simple.*

"To town. Park at the outskirts. I don't want to fight with carriage traffic," Darith said through the speaker. The encounter with Gretta had left him with a sensation of slime over his skin.

They sped down the smooth black pavement of the motor road until at the edge of town the black merged with the packed dirt of the carriage path. Inside the city, there wasn't enough space for cars and carriages to have separate roadways.

The car slowed entering town, catching up with a carriage. Darith rubbed his temples to ease the ache. But at this speed someone could see into the car, so he dared not use his gift. Even for a count's son, it was wise to contain his aptitude for energy-bending or "magic," as the lower class called it.

Traffic wasn't likely to let up. Carriages always got right-of-way on the road since their occupants tended to be the rich. Darith didn't really want to be seen in a car in town anyhow. All the wealthy folk had cars, but using them for anything but long-distance travel was looked down upon.

If I found a few black-market contacts, maybe in Brothel City, where it's legal, I could have a hovercar and just fly over traffic jams. The idea of his parents' faces if he were to go past the import restrictions on such tech and be seen in a hovercar lifted his mood.

"Park here." Darith pressed the intercom button and on

release, he waited for the driver to pull up to the curb. The location was a good one, close by one of the pharmacies with a little "herb" shop in the back. The illegally engineered smokables would keep his driver busy while Darith ran his monthly errand.

The door swung open, and Darith stepped out onto the pavement. The walk wasn't far. Still, he risked tugging at the energy on the air.

Tufts of grass sticking up from the cracks in the sidewalk withered, browning and wilting. He wove their energy in his fingers, which he stuck in his jacket pockets. This one spell he allowed himself in public since its entire purpose was to remain unnoticed.

The energy curved around him, blurring his features and hovering around him like a voice whispering, *Look away. There is nothing here worth your time.*

He didn't want his visit to the lower quarter getting back to his father. No, it was better if no one from the nobility ever witnessed his steps.

Darith brushed back his black hair. At nineteen, Darith knew his place in the world. As a noble, there were many advantages, but a handsome face offered its own set of advantages. The two together opened every door. There was nothing in the world Darith couldn't obtain. But could and should were not the same.

I will not be my father.

Darith picked up his pace with a glance to the now-empty street. He turned off into a thin offshoot alley fit only for foot traffic. The clutter of shops narrowed the passage, making the entrance to the alley a flurry of color, but past the vivid displays, the area darkened. Lights in garish colors flashed from the sides of the buildings. Signs stated the types of sexual acts offered within.

Has Father ever seen this place? Has he actually stepped foot here? Seen where the flesh he buys comes from?

A pang of guilt followed the thought. His father's appetites were more of concern now than usual due to their houseguest. He'd protected Little Marim from his father since her mother died, and although she'd now reached the cusp of womanhood, she wasn't quite old enough to lose his father's interest. All the more reason to hurry and get through his errand.

One task at a time.

The alley reeked of piss. Darith was alone but for the eyes behind the frosted glass windows, some shining wordless signs in neon. A few servants rushed by him to fetch what their masters wanted, enduring the stench of excrement and the undertone of drug-laced smoke so that the nobles they worked for could wait in a starched hotel rooms. The idea of renting a hotel room made Darith's gut tighten with anger.

All the proprietors and dealers of flesh knew him. No one catcalled him or stepped from the doors to try to entice him. In one of the doorways, a seated drunk leaned against the doorjamb, moaning in his sleep. His pants were folded neatly in his lap. Darith averted his eyes, not wanting to recognize the man on the off chance he was from the nobility. He had little enough respect for his father's generation as it was.

Toward the end of the alley, Darith approached a tall, brick building. They would wait until he walked up the stairs to open the door. Darith didn't ever enter the establishment. Just as he only came in daylight. There were rules. Rules helped. Once he reached the top, a boy slid out, opening the door only as much as needed for his thin body.

"Timmy," Darith said. It was not a name, more like a title. It represented boyhood to the patrons. If you asked for Timmy, you knew what you got, someone between eight and thirteen.

This Timmy was new and offered a bright hopeful smile. As he aged, he would grow silent, sullen. But for now, Darith still saw the gleam of hero-worship in the boy's eyes.

I can't rescue him. He couldn't change a damn thing about Timmy's life for the next handful of years. Darith averted his gaze from the boy's eyes. There was a hope there that Darith couldn't answer.

Timmy lowered his eyes and shuffled his feet, making Darith distinctly uncomfortable. He did not come here to witness a child in pain and floundered for any vaguely adequate words to give the shirtless child.

"It doesn't last forever," Darith said.

He handed the boy a large fold of bills. He almost cautioned the boy to split it with the master of the house, but that was a lesson Timmy needed to learn on his own. *I hope he's saving the money. He could have a future, escape his current existence, but I can't live his life for him.*

It wasn't enough. The last Timmy had been found strangled on a hotel-room floor. The only comfort Darith had was that his father had been at home the night before the body had been found. His father might pay to sleep with the boys, but he hadn't killed any. The hotel staff never spoke of who'd occupied the room, though they must have known. It had been a few days before the kid's eleventh birthday.

"Thank you," Timmy said softly.

Poor kid. How did he come to this? How does any child? The parents—it's always the parents. There should be restrictions on parenthood.

"Don't thank me. Follow the rules. Never cheat the boss, and get out of this place the moment you can."

Darith turned and left the alley. Eyes bore into his back. It wasn't enough. Money solved nothing, but it was all he had.

No one looked at him when he reached the shops, and on the main road, he avoided eye contact. He brushed his fingers over his pants as if he could wipe the stench of the alley, the slime of existence from him.

A pounding ache taunted his temples.

He was relieved to reach the black Town Car. The driver sat on the hood smoking, but on seeing Darith, he dropped the burning, drug-laced paper, opened the back door, and moved into the driver's seat. Darith pretended he hadn't seen the drugs. The guy was a good driver, and Darith's mother would never tolerate such a thing.

Darith slid into the backseat. He closed the door, blocking out the town and encasing himself in the expensive interior. The silence of the cab soothed the fresh pounding in his head. He let the driver know he was ready to depart.

As they drove, Darith glanced at the tinted glass that obscured the driver's view of him. Unsanctioned magic was more illegal than the drugs he pretended not to see. No one would keep that secret for him if he got caught.

Still once outside of town with only the long stretch of tree-lined road between him and the Cortanis estate, the pounding in Darith's head demanded he take the risk of exposure.

Darith lifted a finger, a pale glow forming at the tip. Placing the finger at one temple and sweeping it to the other, he let the power trickle from his finger and loosen the pain in his head. The steady beat of pain slowed, dimming into a dull ache. A sigh escaped his lips.

The encounters of his afternoon had spoiled his mood, and when the car pulled into the Cortanis estate, he welcomed the known pitfalls of his parents' home.

Out the window, his father sat on a lounge chair in front of the heated pool—some modern conveniences were not looked down on even on Yahal. A glimmer of red hair and white flesh from the water alerted him that their house guest, Marim Cortanis, was out there with his father. He smiled thinking of her gliding through the water until he realized that it was his father sitting there watching her.

Sick lecher. Darith lifted his hand to tap on the glass but never made the motion. He didn't need to stop the car. Marim didn't need his protection, as she had when she'd been younger. Being the daughter of the count's best friend should be protection enough during the daylight.

Darith had puzzled over the two men's friendship since he'd been old enough to understand the difference between the chief of police and the count. The only possible conclusion was that Berrick was a complete moron who had managed to be fooled for upward of twenty years by the count's empty charm.

Both men shared the same staunch, old-fashioned, anti-tech values and had chosen to return to Yahal after attending a university on another world. But many people on Yahal clung to those values. Marim's father could do better, keep her away from here.

Darith bit his knuckles as they drove by the pool. If she'd still been a child, if he had been, he'd go out to her, but things were different. Marim was one of the only pure things in his life. He wanted her to continue to see him as her white knight, to hide from her the slick, poisonous secrets. How selfish his reasons really were for helping her or how wicked the soil he sprang from was. It wasn't too much to ask for one person in all the world to believe in him.

And Father wouldn't hurt her.

The car stopped at the end of the drive, and Darith got out in front of the stone façade of his parents' mansion. His mother stood in the doorway, her back as stiff as a wooden board, her gray hair pulled into a severe bun. Despite the hair, dour expression, and lack of any discernible cosmetics, the countess remained an attractive woman. Darith had inherited her sharp, strong features and pale, blue eyes. Though his hair was still a healthy black, not faded and tortured to gray by years dealing with the friendly, social, voluble, and utterly adored count.

"Mother," Darith said, stepping up and kissing her cheek.

"Walk with me. The evening air is pleasant, and we must speak."

Darith took her arm, which was as stiff and unyielding as her back. They ambled back down the drive next to fragrance-free roses in exotic colors.

"You stink of village girl," the countess said.

Darith laughed and patted his mother's arm.

"Will this require paying a family off?" she asked.

"No, by the Gods' Mother. I don't want a bastard child any more than you do."

"The time has come to put aside these childish encounters."

"And marry little Marim? She's all of sixteen. With how you've felt about the family in the past, I counted on you to support me. She has the body of a boy. I know Father enjoys it, but I have no desire to bed children."

The countess gave his cheek a sharp slap. Her cheeks moved as if to smile, but her mouth never twitched. His father's activities were a closely kept secret and not to be spoken in the open air. However, the countess seemed to take a vicious joy in hearing her husband judged. After she reclaimed his arm, they started walking again.

"You needn't choose her, though the merger with the chief of police's family *is* what your father wants. Her mother was a moron, but I have no issue with the girl's family. I only wish she weren't such a fool herself. You'd think her mother's death would have lent her some wisdom."

An image of Marim's small cherub mouth smiling came to Darith. Such warmth. *What would it be like to kiss those lips? No point in wondering. I'd only hurt her. I can't ever let it happen.*

"I never fail to be amazed at your tact, Mother dear."

"Yes, my kindness is matched only by yours. Nevertheless, the girls all seem to like you. Cecelia Birch sends you love letters and Taria Midland twitters every time your name is mentioned. You have the face of an angel, boy. Perhaps you should choose a bride before your personality gets in the way and you're left with only dregs. Marim may wind up your only option."

"Maybe I want a girl who likes my personality."

"We all have our dreams. I wanted to be an opera singer."

"Get on with the point, Mother. Why did you ask me out here?"

"Eliza's ball is in three days—"

"I'm not going to that farce."

"You are taking Marim. Her father is away, and she needs an escort."

"No."

"Don't say *no* to me, boy. That girl's life has been rotten and the least you can do is allow her to attend the party of the season while her idiot father is doing gods know what." His mother paused, then drove on. "And if you desire a bride who likes you for who you are, that little ball of fluff is your best gamble. She's been sweet on you since she first came to stay at our house after the deaths in her family."

Darith remembered that. He remembered Chief Trehar sobbing over his wife's coffin. He'd looked over at his mother, who'd had this little smirk on her face. Like she was just barely holding back an "I told you so." Everyone knew she'd never liked Polly Trehar. The chief's wife had been a plain, simple woman who'd only wanted to see the good in things. The countess had often wondered aloud if the woman didn't have some mental deficiency and continually stated that Polly's trusting nature would get her in trouble. Anyone else would have regretted their comments, staring at Polly's husband in tears beside her coffin. Not the countess.

So Darith had done the only thing he could do to prove to himself he wasn't his mother. He'd walked over to Marim, ten years old at the time, shaking with silent tears in her seat, and he'd sat next to her and held her. He'd held her for hours as she'd cried, and when she'd stopped crying, he'd brought her outside, away from the black-draped room, and helped her pick a bouquet of flowers for her mother. He'd promised her that day he'd protect her. A simple vow to make—though it hadn't been simple to keep—but so far, he'd kept it.

Marim could do better. Implications that she agreed with their fathers about the wisdom of them marrying only complicated things. The idea of telling her his own views on the matter, hurting her feelings, shredded his insides.

He might not be willing to marry her to indulge her whims, but he could take her to a party, no matter how insipid.

Darith patted his mother's arm. "I'll take her."

CHAPTER 3
THE CHIEF OF POLICE

C hief of Police Berrick Trehar watched as his brother, Henri, entered the restaurant with a svelte gentleman. The man was tall and ebony-skinned, a color that labeled him as an alternate humanoid. Since splitting to multiple worlds, some races had departed from the original human strain, and skin the color of smoke crossing a night sky was a mutation. Reddish-black hair fell to his shoulders.

Every female eye in the dimly lit restaurant traveled to him with hunger. The reaction struck Berrick as extreme, another mutation along with the skin tone perhaps. As it was, Berrick became even warier. Even women who had not been facing the cad turned as if sensing his entrance.

The chatter from the other tables died. In the stillness, the clink of a single glass and a knife hitting a plate rang like claps of thunder. The cessation of sound lasted only a moment, but when noise returned, voices throughout the restaurant remained hushed.

Where did my brother come across that man, a con artist no doubt?

On seeing Berrick's name, the hostess had seated him by the bay windows, the best seat in the house. He'd almost asked for a privacy curtain, as once it got around that the planet's chief of police was in residence, he tended to receive more attention than he desired.

Seeing his brother and this man approach him, Berrick was thankful he hadn't obtained the curtain. He didn't want to be out of public view with them. In the years since he'd seen Henri, his brother had become pudgy around the middle, and many of the thick hairs over his body had gone gray. The look in Henri's eye was the same base hunger as always with a twist of fear.

Berrick stood, jostling the table, so the glasses clinked against each other.

Henri reached the table first and strode up beside Berrick. The other man moved with a shuffling walk that didn't fit with the graceful look he presented. He positioned himself on the other side of the table, leaning one smoke-black hand on the lacy tablecloth.

Berrick wished he was back home with his daughter. Family was family and so he had come. *Learned my lesson. Does no good trying to let family sort out their own messes when they cross the law. He'd let his wife do that. Never again.*

"Berrick, this is Halis," Henri said.

Berrick guessed he outweighed both the other men. Which might be important, as the stranger resembled a villain from one of Berrick's son's old superhero comics. Even in his forties, Berrick's muscle had not translated into fat. Berrick prided himself that he'd kept both his mind and body free of sloth.

"Halis?" Berrick asked. He wanted a last name to put with that frighteningly handsome face. A name he could plunk into his computers back home and find out what foul deeds had caused Halis' dark eyes to simmer.

"Just Halis," the man said, his voice a gentle baritone. "Exchanging first names is the custom among friends. Is it not? Surnames are for acquaintances and business deals."

We're not friends. Berrick fingered his badge inside his jacket pocket. Brothel City made his authority mean little, but the badge still calmed him. The city had its own law. He dealt with crime from all over the world, but here only one power held sway. The Yahal Brothel. Its shadow covered the whole city, protecting the depraved fiends within from any outside law.

One thing was evident: Berrick didn't want this smiling gentleman to think he was on a first-name basis with him. "I'm Chief Trehar."

Halis' smile broadened at the slight. He sat across from where Berrick stood and motioned for the others to sit. Henri put a hand on Berrick's arm, encouraging him toward his chair. Berrick returned to his chair but kept it pushed well out from the table.

"Well, Trehar," Halis said. "Your brother informs me you're the one to solve a problem I've been having."

"I'm not." Berrick glared at his brother.

The little man squirmed in his expensive suit jacket.

"That's hardly something you can know, given you're ignorant of my dilemma." Halis' black eyes had a predatory gleam.

"Let's not discuss business here," Henri said, looking at Berrick. The message was clear. Whatever Berrick had been called here for was not above board. "This is a fabulous restaurant, Berrick. Everything is delicious, but the seafood is especially so."

Halis stretched his smile until the white gleam of teeth overshadowed the smoke of his skin. "Recommendations, Mr. Trehar? Seventy-nine percent of adult humanoids have a major dietary restriction that is entirely voluntary. Me, I choose to avoid food products that have synthetic bases. I prefer my meat to drip red."

Henri swallowed. Berrick tensed as his brother's mouth flapped like a fish deprived of water. Despite Henri's red face, Halis relaxed back in his chair, one arm thrown over the back and a feral glint to his eye. The scene reminded Berrick of when Marim's fishbowl had fallen off the table and shattered on the kitchen tile. While Marim and his wife, Polly, had run to find a fresh container, the cat belonging to their son, Petyr, had crept up and then sat motionless as the goldfish flopped in the remaining puddle. Occasionally, the predatory kitten had batted the fish with its front paw until the fish gave one last shuddering flop. Then daintily, the cat ate the goldfish.

Polly had given Berrick hell for just sitting there. Berrick had hated that fish, but Polly's admonishments had been true. That silly fish had been family and regardless of his feelings, as Polly had said, "A decent man doesn't sit by and watch a family member, any family member, get tortured and killed."

For this reason alone, Berrick made no attempt to leave. Whatever skin-crawling business and moral decisions Henri had built his life upon, all that mattered now was the danger looming over Henri's head. Family. He only had Marim and Henri left, and he wasn't going to let one of them down without trying to help.

"I have no intention of sitting through a meal with you." Berrick shoved the napkin-wrapped silverware to the center of the table. "I came to hear what Henri needs to say, nothing else."

"Do you drink?" Henri forced his voice out in a squeak.

"Sometimes," Halis said.

A waitress sauntered up to the table and Halis' attention slid over to the slender brunette. Free of Halis' gaze, Henri wiped at his sweating brow. Berrick used the moment to make careful note of the exits. Chances were they would walk out without incident; even criminals didn't come to restaurants with crystal drinking glasses intending to shoot at each other. But an exit strategy hurt no one, whereas the reverse could not be said.

Halis smirked up at the waitress, who beamed back at him. Not sparing a glance for the brothers, she leaned closer to Halis.

"What can I get for you? Anything to drink before the meal?" She blushed under his steady gaze.

"We will not be having a meal," Berrick said.

"Ah, Alita," Halis said. "Fetch me a glass of your finest red wine."

Berrick glanced at her nameplate to find her name typed in bold black. Yet Halis didn't appear to have looked away from her eyes. Even for a con artist, the caliber of showmanship he displayed implied he belonged to a selective elite.

"Of course." She didn't look away from Halis. "Anything else for you gentlemen?"

"Bring the bill with the wine. We won't be staying long." Berrick glared at his brother.

The girl hung about for another few moments before hurrying off.

"Why am I here?" Berrick asked.

"Berrick, hush," Henri said.

"Tut, tut, my friend." Halis shook his head, the leer never faltering. "I wonder why someone with your cut-to-the-chase attitude came to Yahal. Of the seventeen worlds, none have a dance of manners as intricate as this backwater you oversee."

"Why am I here?" Berrick shoved a finger onto the table, in a forcible point.

"Simply put, because Silvia and I wished it." Halis sipped the glass of water in front of him.

"Who is Silvia?" Berrick asked.

"My sister. We're very close, she and I."

"An amazing woman, Berrick," Henri's words poured out, blending into one long word. "You'll get to meet her later tonight. Amazing, beautiful as a goddess, I tell you. I've never met anyone like her."

Something flashed in Halis' eyes, and Berrick wondered if his brother wasn't being too forward about his admiration. In many parts of Yahal, it was a tricky thing to admire a woman without insulting her honor. Of the seventeen core worlds, Yahal was the most restrictive to female sexuality. Berrick thought that came from having a large portion of their wealth and fame coming from a brothel. No one wanted women of standing to have any doubt attached to them lest they be delegated to the same strata as the whores by the public eye.

The drinks came, and while Halis flirted with the waitress, Berrick laid several bills on top of the check. They probably used net transfers of money in Brothel City, but Berrick didn't care. *I'm not here to fit in. The sooner I get out, the better.*

Henri babbled about his practice and the latest big cases as they drank. A sheen of sweat accumulated on his brow and caused damp spots on his shirt. Halis was mostly silent, but with a word or factoid he struck out occasionally. The comparison to the cat toying with the dying fish resurfaced repeatedly to Berrick. Halis rubbed him as the worst kind of criminal, a charismatic sociopath.

When they finished their drinks, the other two men escorted Berrick to a waiting car. Berrick didn't have a chance to rethink getting into their car or insisting on taking his own before he was ushered into the sleek vehicle that had pulled up to the doors for them. He felt more like a prisoner than a guest. Sweat caused his thick button-down shirt to stick to him. Halis reclined in the back of the car while the two Trehars sat up front.

Berrick went through a list of the horrible things that Henri could have called him to Brothel City to help mediate. As they drove and he pondered, he flipped his badge over and over in his fingers.

They drove to a rich-looking property and parked in the cobbled drive. By the time they arrived, sunset had preceded them by a good hour, and Berrick could see little of the home but its lofty size. They all got out and went inside.

"I'll alert my sister to your arrival." Halis departed.

Berrick watched him go.

"This is my house, Berrick," Henri said. "I've been trying to get you here for ages. See that rug? Do you know how much that cost?"

"Henri," Berrick said, for the first time addressing his brother by name. "Screw how much your rugs cost. What is going on here? Who's Halis?"

"Why don't you come into the study?" Henri wiped his

brow.

Berrick followed him because there was no other option. The study was a tidy little room, done up in imported leathers and abstract paintings. Despite an attempt with potpourri, the air stank like a showroom. Probably the room had been designed and decorated by a professional, and all Henri ever did there was shuffle papers. The brothers sat across from each other on brown chairs made of soft animal hide.

"Henri, what trouble're you in?" Berrick asked.

Henri stared at the floor and crossed and re-crossed his legs.

"Damn you," said Berrick. "I shouldn't have come. I should've let you rot in your mess."

"But you cling to a moral code that would not allow such abandonment." The voice was female and sultry. A figure moved silently into the room, her large black eyes not looking at either man.

Berrick's pulse raced, his eyes slipping to the neckline of her gown, where her soft white flesh, whiter than nature allowed, swelled. Like something crawled from his dirtiest fantasies and made flesh, she leaned in his direction, her red lips parting. His mouth was dry and formed no words in response.

"I, for one, am glad you came." She turned to Henri and stroked his cheek with one slender finger.

"Silvia," Henri said. "This is Silvia, Berrick."

"Berrick," she said, turning to him.

"Mr. Trehar," he corrected her. His fingers dug into the arms of the chair. He understood what the women at the restaurant must have experienced at Halis' arrival. Her presence affected him like an aphrodisiac. *This woman won't get the best of me.*

"No formalities between friends, Berrick," she said.

"Why am I here?" Berrick growled. They didn't look like brother and sister, what with his tar-black skin and her white flesh, but by the gods, they played the same games.

"I'll divulge my intentions in time. First, you need a

modicum of history." Silvia turned her back to them. "You see, Mr. Trehar and I established a variety of acquaintance a year ago."

The succubus has no problem calling Henri by a formal name. How firmly do they own him?

"I didn't know then that he had friends of your caliber, Berrick. My *brother* ferreted that out. My *brother* is a font of wisdom and possesses a memory that knows no equal. Mr. Trehar and I got along straight off, and when I broached the subject of a meeting with his brother, he accommodated my desires."

"Answer my question. Why am I here?" Berrick asked.

Silvia turned to him and smiled a quick, cruel smile. "Such impatience. Has no one ever told you the voyage is worth more than the destination? I thought we might be friends."

"This is not a voyage. This is a trap. One more time—what's all this about?"

"My *brother* and I work together." Silvia tapped her finger on the ruby hanging against her collar bone. "And have been contained here for many years. The confinement grows tiresome. We'd like to leave Yahal. The lure of other planets grows too strong to ignore. You see, we came from one of the unclaimed worlds and were brought here as children. I crave new sights and different sorts of people. Halis' research implies that now is the perfect time to leave. So we found someone who could help us get off of Yahal. We found you, Berrick."

Berrick stared at her perfect mouth as it shut. Her eyebrows lifted, waiting for his response.

"I'm no pilot."

Silvia laid her hand on Henri's shoulder. Henri flinched and then his head tilted toward her hand, like a beaten dog craving the caress of his mistress.

"There are pilots in plenty, Berrick. Space-trains leave hourly. However, first, we must obtain the papers necessary for such a journey. You can find us names, valid IDs, and anything else we need to get off Yahal. And you have the power to strike the whole trip from records, so we cannot be tracked. We must be untraceable."

"Find someone else," Berrick said.

"No. We won't do that." Silvia smiled again, and her teeth were sharp. Henri stared up at her face, a goofy smile on his own. "It'd take little effort for you to do as instructed. Pull a few strings and talk to a few people. I was told you were intelligent. Don't be blind to the benefits of aiding us."

Or the veiled threats of what happens if I don't.

"No," Berrick said.

"Now, Berrick," Henri said. "Be reasonable. Hear the lady out. She has a proposition."

Propositions, trades, and bargains were part of Henri's makeup. He thought in neat columns. This had been true since their boyhoods, but it had never made Henri seem so soulless to Berrick as it did in that instant.

"I do indeed." Silvia stared at both of them with her dark eyes. "We need your services, Berrick, and we're capable of paying exorbitantly for them. Perhaps even enough to fund you leaving this backward little world for your own fresh start. I'm willing to pay off your honor, though there is little that's dishonorable about helping two people who are down on their luck."

"If you're not allowed off the planet, there is good reason," Berrick said.

"Ah, one would think so. In a perfect world that would be the case, but this is not a perfect world, as I'm sure you've noted. After the tragedy your family has undergone, I thought you might understand that sometimes the law stands in the way of what is right. In the way of happiness and contentment. We are simply another family in dire need of aid."

"Really, Berrick, what could it hurt to help them?" Henri added.

"And the papers you have now?" Berrick said.

"We have no papers. According to the law, my brother and I do not exist."

Berrick stared into her face, into her dark, empty eyes and

grew cold. His mind was made. Whatever line she was feeding him, what she was asking for was wrong. He was only getting part of the story and whatever she was withholding was what made him feel cold at her gaze. This was not a woman he wished to aid.

"I won't help you," he said.

"Poor, deluded man. You've no other option."

She sounded sad, and Berrick shivered.

"I'm done with this. I won't help you. Look elsewhere." Berrick stood.

"I haven't the time for your temper tantrum," Silvia said.

Berrick turned his back to her and began to walk away.

"You'll reconsider for Mr. Trehar's sake and for your daughter, Marim."

Berrick stopped walking. If they'd done enough research to know his family tragedy, they would know about his surviving daughter. Whatever doubts he had about Silvia's general wickedness were dispelled in the breath she uttered Marim's name.

He turned back to her.

"Ah, now I have your attention. Next, shall we discuss desecrating your dead wife's bones? And your friends—I can have their heads torn from their bodies. Maybe the count and his wife, maybe their handsome son. Though I might have to sample him first. I could have them all. I've no desire for any of that death or pain, but I'll use any means to my end. Nothing will keep me from freedom."

Many people bluffed threats in the cold metal of his interrogation room or when cuffs first touched their wrists. But he believed *her*, trusted the intensity in her sparkling eyes. Henri just sat there mesmerized beneath her hand while she threatened his life. So he trusted she both could and would follow through.

Her smile faded, and she stroked Henri's head. "So why don't the two of you talk the matter over? Mr. Trehar can answer any questions you have."

She left the room as silently as she had entered. Her hair drifted behind her, unbound, and her skirts rippled across the floor. Her image seemed infused into the walls. She burned her way into Berrick's brain.

"What have you done?" Berrick asked.

"All they need is papers. It wouldn't be hard for you. No inconvenience at all."

"And your cut is worth risking our lives?"

"I'm not risking my life." Henri looked at him with a cold lucidity.

"You're a fool."

"Beautiful women make men weak. Theirs is a power that few of us can battle. Not even you could've resisted her."

Was Henri philosophizing? Berrick placed his badge in his pocket. Despite what Silvia said, even after his wife and son's deaths, he still believed in the law. Had to. That was the life he'd chosen, and Polly was already gone. The laws she'd broken already paid for in blood. Letting go of the law would leave him with nothing, no reason however tenuous to rationalize her absence and that of his son.

"They'll kill you right along with the rest of us," Berrick said.

"I have a feeling I'll be dead before any of you." Henri smiled.

For a moment, Berrick remembered how it had been when they'd been kids, back when Henri and he would play in the yard. Henri would sit under the big elm in the backyard and read his books while Berrick climbed in the branches. He remembered how much he'd loved his brother.

ΔΔΔ

The light flared on with a sharp word, and the illuminating glow of rows upon rows of candles flared up, granting the room a soft glow. In the center of the bedchamber reclined a giant spider, limbs thrown out across a huge bed. The spider lifted its empty shining eyes to the door. Silvia entered, her hair dancing in the candles' shadows. Then the spider skittered off the bed to her side, its hard, black body absorbing the light.

Silvia knelt and pressed her head against the spider's underbelly. One long, hairy leg wrapped around her. Face pressed against his spiny hide, she pulled on the web that traveled out from them, gathering energy. Once her hands filled with blackness, Silvia twisted the energy into a new form.

As the darkness danced from Silvia's hands, a picture appeared before the two of them. In the wavering magic image reclined a pretty girl of about fourteen with red curls. The girl was having her hair done, and she pouted her mouth and batted her eyelashes into a silver-rimmed mirror.

"Marim," Silvia said in her voice of velvet.

The girl in the picture looked up, startled. The servant let go of her hair and then picked it up again. Marim's face froze. Wide eyes searched for the voice that had said her name from the ether. Her face was pale and ashen.

"Yes? Did someone call me?" the picture said in a youthful voice. She sunk into her chair, trembling. This was a child already terrified of dark places—ripe for their message.

The spider and Silvia watched with identical gleaming eyes. Silvia closed her fist, letting the energy strands unwind, and the picture dissipated.

Once more, Silvia gathered the web's strands close to her, forming them like a new gown. Her dress split in two and fell to the ground at her feet. She stepped away from it, and coaxed by the black strands of web, the pale lines of her body faded into eight long, white legs and a striped spider's body.

"She has no part in this. I hate to tangle her in our machinations." Silvia's voice trickled through the web.

"For you, my queen, perhaps I shall leave her alive."

"Berrick had his chance to protect her. Yet her innocence stings me. Does it you?"

"*No. Her blood will be sweet.*"

"*Was I ever that? Innocent, pure... helpless.*"

"*You were always a thorn ready to cut.*"

The two spiders intertwined and rested on the floor by the bed. One long, hairy leg caressed another but otherwise, they were still.

CHAPTER 4

A STOP ON THE ROAD

The hired car stank of grease and perfume, leaving Berrick to be thankful not to be exposed to whatever those odors might be covering up. Berrick stared ahead of him at the road as the driver tried to chat with him. He kept his hands in his lap, away from the stained seats—this city was disgusting, and the sooner he escaped it, the better.

"No special plans in Brothel City? I know lots of places." The driver turned right. They were only a few blocks from the restaurant he'd eaten at with Halis, where Berrick had left his car.

Berrick shook his head, hoping this time the sweaty, strung-out driver would leave him to brood. If it had been any other city, Berrick would have called in his license. Yahal didn't need trash like this working in any public capacity, but Brothel City was independent. Even getting information from anyone here via polite request sometimes took work.

He had bigger concerns than a drug addict hired driver.

When they pulled into the nearly empty lot, Berrick tipped the driver and hopped out, ignoring what the other man called after him. If he never heard another word about this disgusting city, he'd be happy.

Half a dozen cars dotted the lot—it was long after the

trendy restaurant closed for the evening. Only one other person was in sight, a woman sitting on the hood of a car smoking. Berrick looked for his vehicle. He didn't drive it often. Preserving the reputation of his title took using the horse-drawn carriages that the nobility preferred most of the time. Even so, after two sweeps, he realized the car the woman reclined against was his.

He checked for his sidearm, and having reassured himself that his gun was prepared if this night continued to deteriorate, he strode up to his car. The woman didn't flee at the sight of someone approaching. Probably not some drugged-out teen, then.

When he was close enough to recognize her, his glare deepened. Alita, the waitress who'd served them drinks, her eyes wide and vacant as she puffed smoke into the already thick city air.

"What're you doing on my car?" Berrick asked.

"Your friend asked me to keep an eye on it." Alita blinked as if clearing her head. Standing straighter, she flicked her dark hair back over her shoulder.

"My friend?" Berrick tried to keep his voice from falling into a snarl, but any patience he had with the current situation was fading.

"Halis." Alita breathed the name, reminding Berrick of how Henri had spoken of Silvia.

What sort of power did these people have?

"When did he ask you to look after my car?"

"He called." She sighed. "I gave him my number, and he called."

"Is there a phone inside?" Berrick ground his teeth, a habit that had always bugged Polly. He stopped himself when he realized.

"Yeah, suppose you could use it. Don't you have the money for a net-chip? You don't seem the sort for public phones."

"Not a Yahal native, are you?"

Alita shook her head, her brown ponytail bouncing from

side to side.

"Leave Brothel City and you'll find no one messes with that tech." He rubbed at the tiny lump behind his ear—a deactivated net-chip, gotten in his college days. It would be useful to have instant access right now. He could always use his net-glasses, which he kept for emergencies in his glove compartment. But the whole point was not to use the advanced tech when there was an easier option.

"I'm not really supposed to let people in."

"You know who I am?"

"The police chief." Alita didn't sound impressed. Foreigners never did. They heard the title and thought of some hairy detective sitting behind a desk in a small town. They didn't get how different things were on Yahal.

"Chief of what?" he asked, leading her toward the true meaning.

"Some city, right?"

"The whole planet."

"How does that work...?" She crinkled her nose. "You investigate every crime?"

"No. I advise the local chiefs when they're in over their heads or when they're dealing with the nobility or the rich and famous. But I promise you, your boss won't mind me using the phone." Was that even true? Would a restaurant owner in Brothel City even care? Probably. They wanted him to stay out of their city's business. It was a mutual relationship of avoiding each other's toes.

Alita shrugged and waved him to follow as she headed back up to the restaurant. It looked different with all the lights out. More sinister. Or maybe everything looked sinister to him after meeting with Silvia and Halis. The whole situation gave him a bad feeling.

He waited out in the dining hall while she retrieved the glasses and returned with a phone. She dropped the phone into his hand.

"Hurry," she said. "I need to lock up."

He waved Alita back. The last thing he wanted was some-one who knew Halis overhearing anything he had to say. Alita wandered into the back room, and he dialed his secretary at home. She picked up after six rings, sounding like she'd risen from a deep sleep.

"Sue-Ellen," he said, in greeting.

"Boss? How's the family?"

"Having issues."

"Sorry to hear it. It's nearly midnight."

Good point, get on with it.

"I need something."

"Boss." Sue *tsked* with her tongue. "You're meant to use your family leave without calling in. Everyone needs a break."

"This isn't a vacation."

"All right. I've got a pen. What do you need?"

"Silvia and Halis Black. Run them through the system. They're in Brothel City, so you may have to call in a few favors. Do it. I want any information you can find on them."

"Anything else?" Sue-Ellen had something more to say; it lingered in her voice. A hidden accusation.

"Yeah. Can you have a local unit stationed outside Count Cortanis' place? Had a threat on Marim—nothing too invasive, just keep an eye out for anyone suspicious. Make sure Marim doesn't go out alone, stays in public places, that sort of thing."

"Should I be worried? We could call the threat in."

"No. Just get the unit out there and get me information on the names I gave you."

"Got it. You coming back early?"

"No. In fact, extend my leave. I want to do a personal investigation, and I don't need red tape. Keep the office away. I don't need The Council of Five complicating my life or tying my hands."

"If it's serious, you shouldn't be handling it alone." Sue-Ellen would have her hands on her hips at this point. He could see it perfectly in his head. Her gray hair up in a tight bun even at night.

"Thanks for worrying, but family matters are best kept that way."

"What happened to Polly—"

"Sue! What happened was I let my job title get in the way of family. I'm not doing that again. Just do as I ask."

"Good luck, sir." She heaved a sigh to tell him what she thought of his plans. "Give me a call when you get home."

"Have everything on Silvia and Halis ready. It isn't more than a few days' drive."

They hung up, and he nodded to Alita on the way out, handing her the phone.

"Don't know why you needed the phone. You *had* net-glasses," she said as the door closed. She'd flipped the lock by the time Berrick processed the words. He stared at her for a moment, feeling a new surge of dread.

How did she know that? Shit.

He ran across the deserted lot and opened his glove compartment.

The net-glasses had been neatly snapped in two. *Little bitch.*

I'll have her looked into too. But first, he had to get out of here. More than ever, he needed to get home. He could assume that if Halis had called her, her little vandalism was to make a point. He was lucky it was nothing worse.

He stuck the key in the ignition and turned, holding his breath. The car turned on, and he sighed. First thing to go right all night... at least they hadn't sabotaged his car. He'd have it looked over once he got home, but for now, he had to get on the road. Get back to Marim.

The sun shone down from overhead, blazing on the country backroad—the fastest way back to Count Cortanis' place unless he'd used a hovercar. But only off-worlders ever used those, and he wouldn't even know how to drive one. There was no direct route from Brothel City out to the major cities of Yahal.

Yahal Mainers, as the rest of the world was labeled, didn't travel to or from Brothel City and didn't want residents of Brothel City infecting the rest of the world.

He heaved a sigh as he saw the sign for unincorporated country that bordered Brothel City. He was almost out.

At the sign, a crack emanated from the engine. The car sputtered to a stop.

Berrick beat his fist against the steering wheel and cursed himself. Polly had always said his biggest flaw was that he just ran headlong ahead without bothering to plan, to consider the variables. He'd known they could have tinkered with his car. That was the worst part... he'd known and ignored it.

"Planning ahead saves you time in the long run," Polly had said.

"I get shit done before you are even through planning."

"Except when you don't."

Well, this seemed to be a severe planning issue. He should have known the moment the glasses were broken that something bigger was happening. Silvia and Halis hadn't seemed like the go-small type. *What would have happened if I'd taken the car to the shop before heading off? Or hired a car to take me all the way?*

Too late for what-ifs. Time for solutions.

The sign that proclaimed he was heading out of Brothel City was back a few yards, but even from the distance, he could see the electric box that topped the pole. Designed to keep Brothel City citizens from smuggling forbidden tech into the country, those boxes had been instituted a dozen years back. They interacted with any tech that didn't have a Yahal passcode by initiating a destruct sequence.

All the bastards would have had to do is wire in a piece of off-world tech...

He got out of the car and stared helplessly at the smoking hood. He knew less than nothing about the interior workings. So the only possible thing to do was find help. Find a house and a phone. Sue-Ellen would lay into him, but he could get a bigger detail put on Marim.

The road was lined with trees, and the thick greenery covered anything that might have been on the other side. Berrick walked for nearly an hour before he came to the edge of the trees. The fields implied a farm, so he turned off the road and headed back until he saw a farmhouse over the fields.

How long would it take Silvia and Halis to reach the Cortanis estate if they took a hovercar? Every minute he was delayed made the possibilities worse. What a fool he was. He had to assume Silvia and Halis were planning something with the time, and all he could do was try to keep the delay as short as possible.

If he was wrong—great. But for now, he'd plan for the worst.

A little girl with thick, black braids and brown skin pelted down the path toward him.

"Hey, mister!" she called, grinning at him and planting her feet—in boots much too large for her—on the path.

"Your mom around?"

"Nah. She left. Dad's at the house, though. Who're you?"

"Berrick." His title was more likely to hurt him than help him out here.

"I'm Risa." She pointed to her chest with her thumb.

"I'd like to speak with your father, Risa. I'm in need of some help, a telephone at least."

"We ain't got one." Risa motioned for him to follow and started to walk back toward the farmhouse. "Papa says phones are as bad as any of that other off-world tech."

Extremists. Didn't surprise him, but it was inconvenient. They were all over the country.

"Does he feel that way about cars?" Berrick asked. She seemed willing enough to talk. Might as well find out what he was up against.

"Nah. He likes engines. Why?"

"My car broke down."

"Oh. Daddy'll help. Don't matter none. Daddy'll give you a tow into town. Always does."

Berrick forced a smile but inside he cursed himself a thousand times over. That sort of help would take far too long.

CHAPTER 5

THE PARTY

T he lights of the house beckoned from a great distance, lining the drive like fairy lights. Marim looked at Darith through the silk lashes glued atop hers. If they were fairy lights, he was the untouchable fairy prince. His ice-blue eyes were fastened on the road, nose slightly curled.

Look at me. I can make you happy—I swear it. Just look at me.

Darith's eyes flicked over to her. For a brief moment, a smile twitched on his mouth. Marim glowed inside her skin. Even when his glower returned, warmth suffused her. She leaned across the seat and brushed her lips across his cheek.

"Thank you for coming. I didn't want your mother to escort me."

"Were those your only options? You're old enough for suitors," he said. His sneer looked charming on him.

I know you, Darith Cortanis. Glare all you like. You're the only suitor I want.

"Yes. Old enough, perhaps, but I've no need to sample the nobility's eligible men," Marim said as the car pulled broadside in front of the wide double doors into the mansion.

The driver emerged and opened their door. The dark outside seethed, and an all-too-familiar clutching contracted in her chest.

Anything could be out there in the dark. Waiting for me. The police car trailing them did nothing to assuage her fears. Why did her father have men following her everywhere? The officers hopped out of the car in the drive, and then one leaned against the hood as the other crossed to the gardens.

Darith took Marim's hand and helped her out of the Town Car. She could walk safely through any night if he guided her. Her fingers tingled at his touch, and she left her hand in his before she stepped down. Her green-and-gold dress fluttered around her legs, clinging briefly to her thighs. Maybe even Darith would see her as more than a child tonight.

He met her hazel eyes.

She hoped he noted what a dashing couple they could make, the red-haired girl and the black-haired boy. Both slender and graceful, he made of the colors of the night and she of sunshine bound in flesh.

If he observed anything of the sort, he gave no indication. He took her arm and led her inside; she clung a little closer than necessary, relishing the heat of his body. This warmth slipped through her skin to cradle around her heart and flutter like a sigh in her mind.

Inside, a servant took their coats, and another led them through a tiled hallway into a ballroom. Marim took in a breath at the splendor of the room. Girls in ballgowns spun on the floor. Men both young and old escorted them. Crystals drooped from the chandeliers and their phantasmal reflections sashayed over the room. There were punch fountains and layered cakes. From the corner of her eye, Marim saw Darith's thinly veiled boredom. The curl of his nostril.

He ushered Marim in through the velvet-draped doorway into the maze of perfumes and colors. She looked up at him and smiled.

"Will you dance with me please, Darith?" she asked. If she could get him away before the other girls crowded in, perhaps tonight would be the night he remembered she was there, the night he realized she wasn't a child who needed protecting. Tonight, the rogue was hers.

Darith nodded to her and led her onto the dance floor. Marim closed her eyes as the dance started. She tried to trap the sounds and the smells inside her head. She wanted to keep the throb of music safe inside. When her eyes opened, Darith was looking down at her. He was more than a head taller than she was, so she had to tilt her head to meet his eyes. Her feet knew the steps, even if she had forgotten them. The weight of his fingers and the warmth of his body intruded to her core. He was so close to her.

Darith smiled, his eyes crinkling as the grin spread over his face.

The song ended, shattering the smile. Darith broke away from her. He bowed to her slightly and kissed her hand, his breath tickling her knuckles.

"You're not a child, Marim," he said, a slight smile touching his lips. "When did that happen?"

She blushed at his kiss and looked away. "Under the sun for all to see."

"My father wants us to marry." He didn't sound utterly repulsed by the thought, and Marim dared to take his hand in hers.

"A new song is starting," Marim said, not daring to push the marriage discussion further.

"May I cut in?" The male voice was full of humor.

Marim and Darith turned and looked. Encased in charcoal silks, the couple that greeted them had a sobering beauty that Marim couldn't avert her eyes from. The woman had upswept hair in a deep red-black color and eyes just as dark, but her skin was whiter than lace. The man had the same red-black hair, but his skin was as black as a moonless night.

"Of course, you may," Marim said automatically. Her eyes were wide and startled.

She glanced to Darith, her protector. His face was stern, but he nodded her on.

"May I ask your name?" Marim asked.

"My name's Halis, ma'am." The man bowed to her and

took her hand.

"I'm Marim Trehar."

Halis smiled—his teeth too plentiful and sharp. Marim glanced for the officers, but it was an idle fancy. They never would have been allowed in the party, would still be lurking outside, looking for suspicious characters.

For a moment, Marim's instinct was to run from this handsome predatory smile, but what was the point? Running didn't save anyone—it hadn't saved Marim's family. Neither had the elusive protection offered by her father.

No one could protect her from the monsters. And now Marim had nightmares every night but had learned to wake silently. Except when she could hear Darith's breathing outside her guestroom door at the Cortanis estate. She'd never asked why he spent certain nights settled against her door. The why of it didn't matter. It only mattered that those nights she slept a dreamless sleep.

Marim glanced back over her shoulder to see Darith dancing with the lady in the black gown. He was already enchanted and Marim wouldn't let him face a creature of the night alone.

Halis swung her into the dance, and she tripped at the suddenness of the movement, leaning heavily on his arm in order not to fall. When she glanced up, she decided he wasn't any sort of monster, not with that smile beaming at her clumsiness. He moved stiffly but well, and his eyes never left her, nor did his smile falter on his face.

"You dance beautifully, Marim." Despite the slight shuffle in his gait, Halis moved her across the floor seamlessly.

Older than me, but not too old. Perhaps there are merits to sampling men other than my white knight. Her thoughts seemed to float on a cloud and doubt was too heavy to remain in the fluffy cumulous filling her mind. After a while, she forgot all about Darith. Halis danced like the steps flowed in a current from mind to feet, and he carried her with him across the tide. The steps she'd so carefully memorized drifted away forgotten, and she found new ones. They found a dance that was theirs alone.

She spun and dipped and stepped and then did it all over again.

His hands were hard and hot. He didn't hold her at all as a gentleman should. Though he didn't touch her in the wrong places, the way his hands rested departed from decorum. It wasn't a difference she could have named, but she knew it instinctively. He pressed into her flesh just a little too hard. He was careless and wild with her as he pulled her in and out of turns.

He does not see me as a child lost in mourning.

Then they stopped. A moment passed before she realized the song was over. The two of them stood staring at each other. Marim's breath came in bursts. For the first time, Halis broke eye contact.

"Shall I get you a drink, Marim?" he asked. He said her name like he was tasting the syllables but wasn't sure if he found the experience pleasurable or not. He sampled, and he considered.

"Yes, please," she said.

Halis led her across the room and got two cups of punch. He handed Marim a glass, and she sipped the syrupy, red liquid. The dancing went on behind him in a whirl. Marim glanced around for Darith but didn't see him.

"A breath of fresh air? You are flushed," Halis said.

Her stomach knotted up, and her hands grew cold. The last thing she wanted was to step onto the balcony. She reached a hand up to cover her neck, where her jugular vein pulsed. Then the feeling was gone, and she touched a finger to the sweat on her forehead. "Yes, a stroll amid starlight would be pleasant."

He guided her across the floor onto the patio. There were plenty of couples standing out there. Among them stood Darith and the woman Halis had come in with, but there was no sign of the officers. Marim headed automatically to Darith and the strange woman. Halis did not try to escort her anywhere else.

The woman in the black dress turned as they approached. Her lips were red as fire, but she did not smile. She curtsied slightly toward Marim, then leveled her gaze on Halis.

"Silvia, this is Marim Trehar. Marim, this is Silvia," Halis said as he took Silvia's hand and kissed it. Silvia smiled as she regarded Halis.

They are married. Her heart sank. Dimly, a small voice said the stranger's union was the best news possible. *Darith will dance with me.*

"And this, dear *brother*," said Silvia, "is Darith Cortanis. Darith, this is Halis."

Brother. They are siblings. Marim sighed. They did look alike, aside from their skin tone. And Marim tried not to focus on the inflection in Silvia's voice when she said brother, almost as if it were a joke.

"Good to meet you, Halis," Darith said.

"You as well," Halis said.

"Darith and I were contemplating a stroll through the gardens," Silvia said, raising one eyebrow in what seemed like a challenge.

"Tonight is a very pleasant night," Marim put in, trying her best not to seem like a sixteen-year-old girl. Halis' hand rested on her waist, and her heart beat faster. His nearness slowed her thought and cast everything into a dizzying spin. Her body reacted so strongly to him, her mind raced to catch up, the two never meeting, leaving her dazed and out of control.

"Why don't the four of us take a stroll together?" Halis suggested.

Darith's hand lay over Silvia's on the banister. Marim's eyes caught there, and the spinning stilled. What did it feel like to have Darith's touch?

"Shall we?" Darith asked.

Silvia laughed and took his arm. "Roses smell better at night."

Marim took Halis' arm and gazed up at him. He cut such a fine figure. She was sure there was no man in the entire ball that rivaled him. His white teeth caught the moonlight. She wanted to find something to say but couldn't think of a word that wouldn't place her as exactly what she was: sixteen. He seemed content enough to stroll along with her silently.

In front of them, Darith and Silvia conversed in low voices. They walked through rows of flowers heading away from the light of the party. Little stones crunched under their shoes, and occasionally, a torch flared on the side of the path.

"Yahal roses have a fainter scent than any others on the seventeen core worlds. Did you know that?" Halis asked.

"No," said Marim, drifting easily with the harmless subject. "Why is that, do you think?"

"The genetic modification to allow them to grow here affected their smell. Before humans messed with them, roses had a rich, potent smell. They grew wild once and their smell could help people identify them from a distance, but then humans changed them, and their smell grew weak. Though their blooms grew larger and of far more varied colors."

"That's sad. I wonder why we'd change them."

"When the world was first founded, the ladies grew disappointed with the lack of smell and would pour perfume on them. It's why literature from the early years here is littered with references to roses smelling like vanilla or cloves."

Marim bit her lip and glanced up at the moon. He was right that she could hardly smell the roses, but had it ever been different? What a strange conversation.

Marim broke the silence. "I haven't seen you or your sister before. Are you from around here?"

"Not from around here, no." His dark eyes met hers. "It is wonderful. I should spend more time here."

Marim blushed and dropped her gaze. The closer she stood to him, the more her mind reeled, as if she'd downed far too much wine. What would his dark hands feel like on her skin?

"When did you arrive?" she asked. Questions kept her from blathering about herself.

"Tonight. We came to town for this." He motioned around. "It's a one-of-a-kind party."

"They have it every year." Marim bit her lip. What a stupid thing to say. She managed not to tell him that this was only the second year she had received an invitation.

"Ah, but it is not the same every year. No two nights are alike." He moved his hand to her waist again.

Dizziness swept over her. His body was so close to hers. Coldness twitched in his black eyes, a creature from the deep uncurling.

"I can't recall having known a night like this one," she said.

"Neither can I."

The night made noises around them, and Silvia's laugh traveled across the air. Silvia blended in with the evening and was lost in the landscape except for the white slivers of her arms. They had somehow gotten quite a distance ahead of Halis and Marim. Surely, they should have reached the end of the garden. Were the grounds really that extensive? Marim's stomach tightened. Something wasn't right. She glanced back for the house, and sure enough, the mansion shone like a beacon behind them.

"Perhaps we should head back." Her voice quavered.

"I hate to relinquish you to the rest of those gentlemen, but if you desire to return, we shall." The warmth in Halis' voice comforted her. It did not reflect the monstrosity behind his eyes.

"We're just getting so far from the house," Marim explained, but she no longer cared.

"Would you feel safer if I called Darith and my sister to walk closer to us?"

Marim tittered. Her laugh sounded young and light to her ears, lacking the depth of Silvia's mirth. "No, no. I quite like walking back here with you. They aren't so far away. I'm sure it isn't improper for us to wander with all of us together."

Halis picked a flower and handed the tight rosebud to her. The colorful petals seemed black in the night. She touched the bud's velvety surface. Her glass of punch was empty, and she set it carelessly on the path. Someone would find it in the morning.

"You're not engaged to Darith, are you, little one?" Halis'

voice was husky, and she leaned into him.

"No. Our parents are friends, so he was asked to escort me." Her mind grasped at fleeting thoughts, trying to connect with her emotions from earlier in the night. The fog of Halis' nearness made it impossible to feel more than a flicker of concern.

I should. I should be running away. Running to Darith. If only Halis would step back, I could clear my head.

"I'm glad." He chuckled. "I'm sure my sister is delighted as well."

"Halis is a name I've never heard. Is it foreign?"

"My parents hail from one of the unclaimed worlds."

"What world?"

"You've never heard of our birth planet. Silvia and I are a variety of orphan. You know, I know the name Trehar from somewhere." He paused.

"My father is the police chief. He looks after security for the whole planet." *How like a child I sound.*

"That must take away from the anonymity of the name. Is it hard to get out with a father like that?"

"No, he's not strict with us."

"Us?"

"Well, just me now. My mother and my brother died six years back."

"Ah. I'm sorry to hear that, Marim."

Marim twirled the rose between her fingers. "You know, you never did tell me your surname."

"Silvia and I were given one, but it lacks meaning. So we've dispensed with it. A family name is a mere formality. How often do your friends call you Ms. Trehar?"

"Not often," she admitted. Their gazes locked, and he angled his body toward her. They stopped. His chest was hot and firm under her fingers as her hand settled on him of its volition. Her fingers moved up his chest over to his muscular arms, hidden inside the dark shirt. Would all of his skin prove as dark as his face?

Deep inside her, she knew she should stop. But the morning waited at the end of time, an eternity away.

"Marim," he said, "that's what I'll call you. That's who you are. You aren't your family. You're Marim."

"And you're Halis."

"Yes."

He kissed her, his lips softer than the petal of a rose, his mouth warm. Her eyes fluttered closed, and she tasted the night on his breath. His hand moved to her shoulder, and his lips hovered over hers, mere breaths between them.

"Marim."

Now he liked the taste of her name, and she soared.

"Halis." His name felt solid on her tongue. He was contained in those two syllables. "Please, kiss me again."

He kissed her again. The rose fell from her fingers. She had never been embraced by a man. His kiss traveled to every secret place on her body without his lips ever leaving her mouth. She leaned her body against his, her limbs conforming to him. She felt him right through their clothes. She had been taught all about the male body in school, but now the muscles moved under her fingers. For the first time, she knew what the male body was. For the first time, she knew her body. His hand traveled down her side, and she sighed into his mouth.

"No, stop," she said, something stirring in the back of her mind. This wasn't right. This wasn't what she wanted.

"Yes," he said.

The feeling of wrongness drifted away with his word. "Yes," she said.

He kissed her, and she allowed him, welcomed him. Her lips parted and his tongue slid across hers, and she shivered. He held her close, and she tried to get closer.

"You've bewitched me," she said.

"We shall make music, you and me."

"Silvia..."

"Is with Darith."

"It isn't right." *But it feels good. Life is so short... so very short. I want this. Why say* no? A fog of desire covered her brain, making further ruminations drift away into the thrum.

"Does it feel wrong?"

"No, but it is. Isn't it?"

He drew back. "Ms. Trehar."

"No, don't call me that." Marim's hands gripped his arm. Her body called out for his, yearning as if the inches between them were miles and the distance tormented her.

"Marim." He pulled her close again, his hands sliding up the front of her dress, resting on her breast.

"Yes, yes." Her eyes closed, and she delved deep into the feelings within her.

"We're making music already. You can feel the song in your bones, can't you?"

She could. "It's a dream and nothing can be wrong in a dream."

Somehow the ground wasn't hard, but soft and warm. He was heavy on top of her, and his kisses slipped inside her. Her dress slid up over her hips and his fingers stroked and explored the exposed flesh. She leaned her head into the ground and experienced the feel of him without burdening the experience with names. The straps of her dress slipped off her shoulders, and he kissed her there.

She moaned. His hands played her body, and she held him to her. Then his mouth warmed her as her skin was revealed to the dark heavens.

The night's eyes saw her, and she saw the night in him. She knew him but was not afraid. Her fear hovered in the night waiting to swoop down but couldn't get past the spell he wove. His next kiss was forceful, and she moaned and moved her hips against him.

Then he was inside her, and she cried out in pain. The pain didn't last. The feeling of the night did. The night slid into her with him, like velvet. Her fingers dug into his back as she clutched him to her. He was the hungry void, and there was a hidden cruelty beneath his charm, but for now, she was his.

Nothing else mattered.

Bark scraped against Silvia's bare back, and she turned her face up to the moon. Drunk on her aura, Darith's mouth traveled down her neck. No sense of triumph came with the conquest. With one so young, the natural pheromone lure of her breed rarely failed.

Her fingers wound through his hair, stroking softly. She took this moment, after coupling, to touch the web inside her, drawing power from it. Conception was a foregone conclusion —the pheromone and hormone mix also ensured that. Mating with a human, without proper precaution, always led to a child, just as she and Halis could never create a child together.

If only I could bear a child for Halis. But being made as they were, that was impossible. And now that they would have their freedom, the idea of offspring appealed to both of them.

"I didn't intend this," Silvia said. It was true, but something about the boy called to her. His beauty had tempted her, but there was something deeper, something inside him that she could not name.

Darith leaned back on the tree beside her and smiled.

"When I came here tonight, it was for one purpose only." Teaching Berrick a lesson on how easily they could break him using little Marim, but Halis had clearly been as impressed with the girl, as she had been with Darith. Did Halis even realize that coupling with the girl would be worse in her father's eyes than any physical harm he could have done? She doubted it. Halis saw bearing a spider child as an honor. "But you were surprisingly impressive."

"Purpose?" Darith's eyes narrowed.

Clever boy to have picked that out. She doubted she could enthrall this one as fully as she had done with Henri. *Too bad, a message was needed.*

Silvia gathered the web of energy around her and drew on the currents, forcing her body into her spider form. No matter how she wished the transformation was natural for her, it wasn't. Unlike Halis, the change took effort for her. Long, white legs thin as spears thrust from her sides as her body fed into its new form.

All of her spider eyes fastened on Darith. Despite her expectations, he didn't run. After leaping to his feet, he spread his arms to the side, and a glimmer formed around his fingers.

He was an energy-bender like her. Interesting, the mutation was rare, especially in a form powerful enough to give him any practical aid. Yet clearly, he was strong. The plants around the edge of the clearing drooped, the flowers dried up, their petals either falling or shriveling. He knew how to pull on the surrounding energies.

Silvia gathered venom in her jaw. She needed to incapacitate him, but he was too beautiful a specimen to destroy. This would require a gentle touch.

Darith's hands ignited, and he took several steps away from her. His glare had widened into something more akin to what she had expected. Fear.

"What are you?" The energy in Darith's hands crackled as he brought his palms together, gathering it.

Too slow. He may have ability, but he wasn't trained properly. That's what comes of having to hide your strengths as if they were perversions.

Silvia leaped, and he released his energy to form a wall. A light shock ran through her as she collided. Tumbling back, she released the venom she'd gathered, burning the ground and Darith's flimsy protection.

This time, she circled more carefully. Darith's eyes darted around for something to protect himself with. When his gaze strayed from her, Silvia pounced.

Darith crashed to the ground under her weight. The tips of her legs, razor-sharp, pressed against him, but she eased back, avoiding slicing the lovely body. This time the venom she gathered was not so deadly. She swirled it with the energy gathered inside her.

Her maw broadened, and she darted down, sinking her fangs into his stomach, several of her legs holding his upper body down. She released the venom aiming for a spot on his spine. Sitting there, the contaminate would cripple him until he accepted the Drambish gene that her venom carried.

His scream echoed out into the gardens, a song that should have been sweet to her ears. As soon as he'd received the full dose, she darted off into the trees. His cries reached her as she allowed her body to change back into its human form.

She wanted to tell the boy that he'd be whole again, in time. But he couldn't know that some of the damage was temporary, if he knew, he'd tell Berrick. And she needed Berrick seeing as much harm as possible in this attack.

I could have killed him. That would have been even more terrifying. But no matter what they see, I'm not a monster I've never killed by choice, and never will. Why did that feel less comforting than it should?

CHAPTER 6

CONSEQUENCES

T he drive from the shop in the boonies back to town had been completely silent. Berrick leaned against the passenger door, watching the country go by, cursing himself for not being more vigilant. Sue-Ellen drove, tapping her hands on the wheel and occasionally glancing at Berrick.

When the vehicle crunched up the long drive to the Cortanis estate, Sue-Ellen gave a little gasp. Berrick lifted his eyes from the rose-lined walk to the house.

The count's house was decked in black.

"I'll send someone to retrieve your car from the city. Don't you worry none," Sue-Ellen said. The car came to a halt. She laid a hand on his arm and gave him a reassuring squeeze.

"Thank you, Sue." Berrick climbed out and waited until the sound of gravel under tires faded away to approach the house.

For a moment before he knocked, he imagined that the black flag on the door bore no relation to his adventure with Henri. After a few days off the grid stranded in the country, anything could have happened. *It may have nothing to do with Marim.*

The fabric flapped heavily in the wind. Each *flup, flup* sounded like an accusation. The huge oak door swung open, exposing a dark entryway and behind that the cavernous black of unlit halls. With the steward's sad, sallow face, hope dissipated. Halis and Silvia kept him in their control as surely as if they'd tied him up until he did their bidding.

"Mr. Trehar, come in." The steward bowed and stepped aside. Berrick grabbed his arm and stared into the house passed his head. No answers leaped out from the dim entryway.

"What happened?"

"The young master was attacked." The steward looked away. "Go in and talk to the count, sir."

As uninviting as the house was, Marim was inside. Berrick strode in and focused his gaze, determined to get to the count as quickly as possible. He didn't want to talk to his friend. Getting to Marim mattered exclusively. By the gods, if they had hurt her... his wife's bloodless face in her coffin swam in his vision. Marim looked like Polly had in her teen years. Berrick wanted to see Marim's face immediately, to ensure that she was filled with life and health.

He couldn't and wouldn't lose her, but the count must come first no matter what the instincts of a father told him. Any planet but Yahal and formalities might have been dispensed with, but not here. That was why he'd chosen to move his family here in the first place. No good would come from questioning those choices now.

The first person who met him was the countess, her face swollen and red from crying. She clutched a handkerchief in her hand. The tight line of her mouth and too-wide set of her eyes formed an expression Berrick knew. That look of grief had lived at his house over the past six years. Berrick turned away.

"He can't walk, can't even move his legs. My little boy, my angel. I never should have let them attend that party. Why should he have gone? He didn't want to go. He went to keep your daughter happy."

You're the reason, her voice accused him. *You're the reason my son is hurt.*

Why did you let them go? Had she not guessed that he'd put a guard on Marim for a reason?

Then the count entered, and Berrick tried to look any-where but at his friend's tear-stained face. The count ran his hand through his hair, a nervous gesture he'd had since they'd been in college together. "What have you been told?"

"Nothing."

"The kids wandered off at the party, and..." Count Cortanis' voice trailed off. "Darith took Marim to the ball, and when they got there, they took a walk in the gardens with two unknown guests. Marim came back with the man. There wasn't a scratch on her. No one suspected anything was awry until Marim left and the guard unit wasn't there. Both guards were found dead in the bushes...they'd still been searching for Darith. They thought he was... They found Darith in the morning." His voice choked to silence; he lifted a half-filled glass of whiskey to his lips.

The countess slapped her husband's hand. A sob escaped her lips before they pressed back together. The glass crashed to the ground, scattering glass and little amber droplets over the pale carpet. The couple glared at each other before the count-ess lifted her hands to her eyes and sobs wracked her body. The count turned from her to the wall, his shoulders stiff.

The nearly silent tears tore at wounds hidden deep within Berrick. That hopeless grief waited under the surface for him, never more than a thought away. In those little gasping breaths, he saw Polly, cold, gray, and ugly in death. Only her red curls pretended to life. Blood had splattered from several holes in her chest. Berrick had witnessed Petyr as he must have been before he died, alone, terrified, and splattered with his mother's blood. Suffering for a crime he hadn't committed. Petyr's exist-ence had been the crime.

"Gods, I'm sorry. We'll find whoever did this," Berrick said.

I'll kill them. They'll pay for touching Marim, for crippling Darith. Since Darith's birth, Berrick had been there to watch him learn to write and hunt. Darith had been a rock for Marim when Berrick broke down after they found Petyr's body. And now someone had taken that prideful young man's future and shredded it. *What kind of monster harms a kid?*

He couldn't pursue the ones who'd hurt Petyr. Even knowing who they were, he could do nothing because they'd only been executing the directive of The Galactic Council. But these, the ones who'd dared to accost Marim, he could exact revenge from.

"I think you know who did this, Father." Marim emerged from the shadows of the doorway.

Her words slipped through Berrick's ears. The countess' flare of anger also swam by. Nothing took root in his mind except for the frail, changed child in front of him. A contagion corrupted her and left a black streak creeping down her once fiery-orange locks. Marim's altered hair tumbled over her bony shoulders. Clear as day, Halis had left his mark.

Marim wore her nightdress, but despite being dressed for sleep, her eyes were rimmed with circles as dark as kohl lining. He had only stayed away for a short while, but his daughter was a different creature. Her eyes made him shiver, and then Marim's legs crumpled, and she toppled to the ground in a pool of white lace.

The countess screamed, and everyone else rushed to Marim.

Berrick sat by her bedside, silently watching as Marim came to in her borrowed bed. If he could have helped her open her heavy, drugged eyes, he would have. Instead, he put his hand on hers. Alive, she was alive, but the dark in her hair was a calling card that things could have gone differently. He turned his badge over and over in his hand—useless. After all he'd sacrificed, all the anger and pain he'd buried, his title was useless to help him once again.

Marim pulled herself to a half-sitting position and fixed him with an imploring stare. From many investigations over the years, Berrick knew that look. His sweet little girl didn't think he would believe her. Possibly, she didn't believe her own memories.

That was easy to understand. From what he could gather from the count, everything Marim remembered about the night was implausible, vague, or both.

"Please, have they found the people who hurt Darith?" Marim asked.

"No. Who are they, Marim? The count says you don't remember." According to the police report, she remembered things, just not anything that made sense. But if he said that, she would shut down and tell him nothing. He wanted to believe her.

"I recall dancing." She closed her eyes. "You'll believe me, Daddy. Won't you?"

Berrick winced. Once she'd turned ten, she'd stopped calling him "Daddy." From then on, he'd been "Father." She'd begun to call him "Father" as they'd stood over her mother's coffin.

"You'll listen," Marim said. "I danced with the devil..." She cried out and sat up, her eyes wide open. "She didn't kill him. The roses have no scent. They're monsters, Daddy, Daddy!"

"She who, Marim?" Berrick asked, though he already knew the answer.

"I don't know, Daddy! I don't know!" She turned to him and buried her face in his jacket. He held her, stroking the back of her head until she grew calm again. Then she pulled away and looked at him with her soft brown eyes. "Where's Tyr?"

Berrick paused and looked into her eyes. If she referred to her little brother, she always called him by his full name. The nickname died with his little boy. The amber eyes that stared at him were wild and scared. "He's fine."

"He's not hurt?"

"No."

"I've had weird dreams where he wasn't safe."

"I'll keep us safe, little one."

"Please do, Father."

Berrick relaxed when she called him "Father." He looked

in her face and saw nothing but Marim.

As the sedative the countess gave her kicked in and she fell back into a heavy, drugged sleep, Berrick watched Marim. He stared at her pale eyelashes lying against cheeks that were just beginning to lose the freckles of childhood.

Those creatures came here, and they touched her. They hurt my little girl. And they could have killed her. I couldn't have stopped it.

The clock on the wall ticked away the minutes, and after an unmeasured length of time, Berrick got up and left his sleeping daughter. The other victim of that night might have answers.

Darith's room was in another wing of the mansion, and as Berrick walked the halls, he couldn't help but wonder if he had missed something. He would expect with a sick child in the house that the area around the room would be bustling. The parents would remain within earshot, lest their child called out, but the hallway that contained Darith's bedchamber was empty.

Was he hurt worse than implied? On the doorways hung black mourning cloths covered with the family crest. What was the count thinking? He had a living, breathing son in agony behind one of those doors. How was it that Berrick was the only person in evidence?

The door swung open at a touch, and Berrick looked across the room at Darith. The boy lay in bed with a sheet covering the lower half of his body. His hand lay over a book.

"Come to ogle the cripple?" Darith asked. The look he leveled at Berrick was full of pride and disdain.

"I'm doing an investigation, Darith. I need to know what happened to you that night."

Darith watched him with a blank hateful stare from his bed. His face was pale when he spoke.

"You aren't going to believe me. No one does."

"Give me a chance, kid. Marim was out there too. She never had secrets from me, told me the promises you made her. You were her white knight, and now someone's hurt her. Are you going to let that stand?" The words were a risky ploy. Berrick had never seen much evidence of altruism in Darith, but Marim thought the world revolved on Darith's shoulders. She believed he would protect her. Time to test the theory.

Darith paused. "They led us out there, a man and a woman. They were brother and sister, or that's what they said."

Berrick's teeth ground together. That described Silvia and Halis.

"She was gorgeous but cold," Darith continued. "If Marim hadn't been there, I wouldn't have had a second thought, but despite her beauty, I kept expecting... I didn't know if it was more likely she'd take off her dress or gut me. I should have cared, but I didn't. They led us out into the garden. Marim and the man walked behind while the woman, Silvia, and I went ahead. At first, we walked very close together, then Marim and the man drifted farther back. She seemed happy. I had no logical reason to believe she was in danger."

Berrick waited for him to continue, but he seemed to have stalled. "I know you didn't. Tell me what happened."

"Silvia and I, well..." Darith averted his eyes. Was he blushing? "We moved off the path, and..." Darith motioned emphatically with his hands. "She was very beautiful, sir. And more than willing. Eager. She was eager."

This kid had gone off to dally with a woman when he was supposed to be watching after Marim? That thought wrestled with pity for how much trouble the young gentleman was having telling Berrick about his exploits. Both emotions were wiped clean when Darith leaned forward, his impetuous motion stopped by the dead weight of his legs. He was just a kid.

Only nineteen. And where were his parents?

"When it was over, something happened to me. She bit my neck, and I got very tired. I just lay there in the trees. I couldn't."

"She didn't hurt you?" Berrick asked.

"She bit me. Nothing more. But she changed into a beast. You won't believe me, will you?"

"A beast?" Berrick said.

"A spider. A giant spider." Darith stared at him with a challenge in his dark eyes. "As big as a man."

Berrick looked beyond Darith's head. Stories like this one were rare, but not unheard of. Sometimes victims of violent attacks had no other way of processing than to victimize their attackers. He had heard retellings of trees that moved and of rats as big as dogs. Something about this story unsettled his stomach. Silvia and her brother had come, and now both Darith and Marim spoke about demons.

Berrick stood up and turned away from the bedside. He stared at the wall and shoved his hands deep into his coat pockets. Darith began to laugh behind him. It was a cold, lost laugh. Darith didn't care who heard him. He might as well have been crying for the desperation and sadness in the sound. There was mirth there as well.

"Don't believe me?" he said. "Cops never listen, especially to kids. I thought maybe I was old enough that one of you would bother to listen. I overestimated you. Try to catch them—you'll see."

"I *will* catch them, Darith," Berrick said. Once his word was given, he never broke it. Not only would he not be helping those siblings, he'd see no one else could, either. "I'll make them pay."

Darith continued to laugh.

CHAPTER 7
MAGIC & A GUN

The garden outside the fluttering curtains was dotted with color. Flowers lined a cobbled landing and a walkway that stretched out of Darith's view. From composition and beauty alone, the spot would have been a perfect strolling place for lovers, but no one ever walked the path but for a gardener. Trees stood in a line behind the flowers, forming bright green bars that locked the outside world from him. The noonday sun pounded onto the stones, causing a glare to warp the view and burn like probing fingers into Darith's skull.

He lifted a hand and tried to call the power to soothe away the throbbing, but nothing responded inside him. The web the spiders had left had locked that part of him away. Yet when he reached down, a voice thrummed in the distance, its words indistinguishable, and thousands of eyes stared into his mind.

Darith smacked his skull into the bedpost and the flash of sharp pain dimmed the relentless headache for a moment.

Crippled. They've not only taken my legs, but the only power that was mine.

The door opened and the curtains around the floor-length window billowed at the change in pressure. He refrained from looking since only silent servants came and went. His mother's single visit had only reinforced for him that he could expect to remain a leper. It was not until tentative steps entered the room that he paid attention.

"Darith?" The whisper from the entrance accosted him, driving into his solitude, making demands.

Darith gripped the sheets in a hand and turned. A neatly dressed girl with skin the color of molasses and full, red lips wrung her hands as she approached. He assumed she had been cued by his mother's investigation into finding an heir among the village girls. On any normal occasion, Gretta would never have thought to visit him here. Even while their short-lived physical relationship had thrived, she'd never come here.

A questing smile formed on her painted lips. Their last encounter had not ended well, and he waited for her to gloat. Last time she'd lacked a potent weapon and had hurled clods of grass from the field at him, accusing him of exaggerated cruelties. Now he was certainly at a disadvantage. But there was no triumph in her brown eyes, just sorrow.

"I'm surprised the servants let you in. Am I so fallen in their eyes?" Darith asked.

Gretta smoothed her dress, an expensive creation, funded by the profits of her father's store. Yet having money did not make her noble, and even the servants on the Cortanis estate could spot a peasant, no matter how finely dressed.

"Hush. If ye talk cruel to me, I'll go."

"Why did you even come? Just to reassure yourself that you achieved a stroke of luck escaping being tied to me?"

"Has nothing to do with that. I heard of yer misfortune. I wanted to see how ye were."

"You've seen."

"Darith." She stepped farther in, and her cleavage rose and fell inside her tight bodice. Her breath was fast, nervous. "I came because I care."

"Came to gloat."

She didn't lower her eyes and blush as a noble girl would, but her eyebrows creased and her hands plunked on her hips. "You stop that business. Gloat over what? I don't want bad things fer you. When ye discarded me like some piece of trash stuck ta yer shoe, I was fit to strangle you. But ye were right about our future together and a stern manner does not change noble intent. Can't ye let me be concerned?"

"Why concern? Concern implies there is some chance I'll avoid disaster. I'm done. Nothing left but a slow rot, and I don't need voyeurs... especially pretty ones."

"Who says yer done? Your parents maybe." She shook her black curls.

"You talk to Mr. Dent?"

"No. Not every girl is just out to land a man. I wasn't turning him down because of you, but because I had no interest. Don't worry about me. I'll get along. I'm more worried about you and it's not the accident, more that you're trapped here. Afraid ye'll lose yourself."

Darith gritted his teeth. Now, this reeked of pity.

"Tell me, Darith, and gods' own truth, I'll leave ye be. Now that ye can't escape them and this place in the village, tell me there's something else ye love. Something that means something ta you?"

"I've got no use for girls now."

"Not everything is about sex. Lots of folks in the village have accidents, can't do what they did. Some of them get bitter and mean. Some of them find a way to move on, love life for what it is. You're already bitter and mean, but that doesn't mean ye can't find joy. You ain't dead. Not everything ye ever did was with yer legs, was it?"

Darith stared at his fingers and tried to feel the tingle of magic inside, but nothing came to him. *That's gone too.* He didn't speak his thoughts. Her interest touched him. It felt like true concern. He didn't want to burden her heart further.

"You're a good woman. I'd assume you'd still be angry."

"I was, but you were trying in yer own pigheaded lord-y way to look out fer me. I just want to do the same fer ye. If ye need something, something ye can't get here from the servants and lord types, just ask."

"Don't let my mother see you here," he said. "She's bent on finding a bastard child. If she knew we were having contact, she'd be certain you were the girl."

"I said I was here for Marim."

"You know her?"

"We all grew up here. Yes, I know her, not well, but I know her."

"Don't tell her you know me."

"You think I'd brag? Not exactly a selling point for a girl to have slutted around. Why do ye care anyhow?"

"She's one of those things you were talking about," Darith said. "Things I care about that doesn't require anything I lost."

ΔΔΔ

Berrick thrust the door open. Henri, who must have heard Berrick barreling up the walkway, bustled the remaining few steps to the door. A large smile spread over Henri's sickly face. The hallway behind Henri was covered in spiderwebs, giving it the appearance of a house long abandoned. The showroom feel he'd noticed days before had been swept away.

"Out of my way," Berrick said.

"Berrick! Come in, come in. I'm so glad you're back."

"Where are they?" Berrick entered. His boots crunched on the stone floor. The dirt under the heels made little crackling sounds as he moved.

"I'll tell them you're here. Would you like a drink while you wait?" Henri's smile faded. With distaste, he looked at the dirty trail Berrick had made. That he did not admonish Berrick for the mess told Berrick all he needed to know about Henri's state of mind.

Berrick grabbed his brother's arm and pressed his gun into Henri's stomach. "I'm not here to play games. Where are they?"

"You're making a mistake!" Henri shook in his grasp.

"Where?" Berrick's thumb pulled back the safety.

"If you just give them what they want, they'll go away," Henri pleaded, his forehead damp with sweat. He looked up into his brother's eyes, then winced.

"Where. Are. They," Berrick said. He dug the muzzle of the gun into Henri's gut.

"They're upstairs. I don't know where," Henri squeaked.

"You do, and you'll show me." Berrick shoved Henri toward the stairs.

Henri stumbled up the web-ridden steps in front of him. He began to whimper, and Berrick jabbed the gun into his back. Henri led his brother back to a room, then stopped in front of the door. His entire body shook.

Either way, the game ends here. Either they die or I do.

Berrick took a deep breath. He opened the door and strode inside. A perfectly normal bedroom awaited him. Normal except for the dark-skinned man, dressed in black silk, whose black eyes drank the light of the room around him.

Halis leaped to his feet from his reclined position on the bed. Berrick pointed his gun and pulled the safety. Halis smiled, an odd, shimmering field rippling around his body.

Berrick pulled the trigger.

The bullet crashed into the wall, behind the spider.

"What the…?" Berrick leaped back. His arms dropped. He held on to the gun by force of habit and swore. The spider scuttled toward him, its legs covered in hairs as long and thick at the base as Berrick's fingers. Berrick stumbled away from the huge creature, colliding with the wall.

The spider struck at his arm with one bone-thin limb, knocking the gun from Berrick's hand. The mandibles encasing its massive mouth clacked loudly.

One of the spider's long, sharp-tipped arms came flying at Berrick. He dropped to the ground out of the way and rolled to the side. The coarse hair on the spider's legs brushed his arm as he moved past.

Where's the damn gun?!

One of the spider's massive legs drove down into Berrick's thigh. Berrick screamed as blood welled from his leg. His vision blurred under a haze of agony that threatened to pull him under its waves. Another leg drove toward him. He kicked into its underside. The spider jerked back, and Berrick pulled himself out of the way.

The gun lay a few feet from Berrick. He dove and grabbed for it. A spider leg tore the fabric of his shirt, leaving a burning pain down the side of his back. His fingers met cold metal.

He pointed and shot. He shot again, and the spider fell back.

The spider let out a high-pitched scream. One of its legs hung limply at its side, and blood dripped from the right side of its body. Berrick hoisted himself up against the wall and lifted the gun.

The creature before him was huge, and it had Halis' cold, laughing eyes. He steadied his arm and aimed at the thing's eyes.

A word exploded in the air and caught him.

He tried to pull the trigger, but his finger wouldn't move.

Silvia moved into his line of sight with Henri slumped behind her. Her finger pointed at Berrick and the whites of her eyes swirling with black.

Berrick struggled to scream. Struggled harder to pull the trigger.

He knew magic, but this wasn't in the scope of reason. This went against everything he'd ever learned about the mystical arts. For her to wield power so extreme wasn't possible.

Henri's face was pale as death, and he stumbled. His hair was entirely gray and his skin a shade that nearly matched. Silvia gripped Henri's shirt and threw him in front of her on the ground. Henri crumpled, giving no resistance.

The sorceress stepped toward Berrick with her teeth bared. She struck the gun from his hand and the pistol spun across the floor. She hissed another word, and the gun melted.

Henri twitched behind her, his body sinking inward, his

skin shriveled and colorless.

Then Silvia slapped Berrick. Her ring dug into the flesh of his cheek and ripped a bloody patch out of it. Berrick struggled to move again, and the spell rippled around him. She shoved him back against the wall, and he drove against her. She had amazing strength for a woman so slender. And then Halis was by her side. A line of blood trickled from his mouth. He punched Berrick in the face, and Berrick slammed into the floor.

Silvia pulled her foot back and kicked Berrick in the ribs. Berrick's eyes clouded and his brain struggled to overcome the agony in his leg, to fill his aching lungs with air and find some explanation, any explanation, for what had just happened.

When Berrick's vision cleared, Halis leaned on Silvia's shoulder. The darker man's arm dripped blood, and a crimson stain spread across his shirt.

"You'll make the calls needed to get our papers ready. Now," Silvia said. Her black eyes broached no argument.

"A spider... Darith said he was attacked by a spider." Berrick gasped in pain.

"Get up and call them," Halis said, a sneer in the place of his characteristic smile. "We need you alive, or you'd be dead right now. We don't need your daughter."

Berrick pressed his back against the wall and forced himself up. Silvia's eyes flickered. Halis held on to her, but he recovered his smile.

How much did he trust the count? On leaving, he'd provided instructions to take Marim and the boy to another planet to hide them if he didn't return. He looked into the cold dark eyes of Silvia and Halis.

"Give me a goddamn phone," Berrick said.

Halis let go of Silvia's shoulder, and she walked across the room. Halis held his side and smiled.

"No one has shot me before, you know," Halis said. "Be proud of that. You'll have scarred me. Silvia won't thank you for that."

Berrick spat at him. Halis laughed.

Silvia returned with one of the old-fashioned phones favored on Yahal. She held the receiver out to Berrick. "No tricks, Berrick. The only ones who get to play games are Halis and me. This is our gambit, and we'll succeed."

She took Halis' hand and led him back to the bed. Berrick considered running, but he still remembered the power of her stare.

Berrick looked over at Henri on the ground. His hand was gray, as if he'd been drained of all his blood. He didn't move, and he didn't breathe. Berrick felt nothing looking at the corpse. Brother or no, Henri had opened the door that had put Marim and Darith in harm's way. He'd earned his end. But to die like that... and they knew where his Marim was. They'd marked her.

He'd left his badge behind. What difference was there between this illegal deed and the one he intended? As long as it kept Marim safe? But a queasy churning competed with the blinding pain at the thought of using the badge he'd built his life around to betray that system.

"Make the call," Silvia said. She was looking at him again as she perched on the edge of the bed. Her hair fell down her back like a black flame.

"Whose life'll you drain for your next spell if I don't?"

"I have more reserves than you could dream. Make the call. I'm tired of your games."

Berrick lifted the receiver and dialed. His fingers were numb. He made three phone calls, talked to numerous people, and chatted with a good number of them. He did all this with her eyes on him. The cold crept out of her gaze and drained him. When at last he hung up the phone, she dropped her eyes.

"When will we have our papers?" Silvia asked, using one long finger to prop up her chin. The bracelets jangled on her slender wrists. Their gold shone on her pale skin.

"A week, maybe two," Berrick said.

Silvia stood and walked over to him. "Then that is how long we will stay with you. Or more accurately, how long you'll stay with us."

"I'm not staying here," Berrick said.

"You'll not be out of our sight until we're on that ship, Berrick," Silvia said. "We could come with you to your home and sleep in your bed... but that puts us under the same roof as Marim."

"We'll stay here," Berrick said through gritted teeth.

"Didn't you have a son once, Berrick?" Halis said from the bed. "I read about it, I think. He died a while back in some tragic accident. It was all over the papers."

Berrick glared at the grinning man on the bed.

"Ah yes, a shooting, it was." Halis continued. "The boy was shot twice in the head, once at point-blank range, after he was already dead, then dumped off a cliff. Two days until your police force found his cold, broken body. Wasn't that the story?"

"Yes, dear. You have such a wonderful memory. I never would have recalled that." Silvia glanced at the bed. Her white teeth flashed in a smile before she turned back to Berrick. "Was there ever an investigation?"

"No," Halis said. "Odd thing for the wife and son of the police chief, no? You'd almost think you already knew who'd committed the crime and chosen not to accuse them."

Berrick glared at both of them.

"Wasn't your wife with your son?" Silvia asked.

"During the attack, she was," Halis said when Berrick stayed silent. "Pretty thing, very like her daughter. They have the same eyes. They didn't shoot her in the head, though, would've been a pity to destroy that face. I'm glad they didn't. They found her—"

"Shut up," Berrick said. How they'd found Polly shone in a bitter cold cutout across his mind, bloody, three gunshot wounds and numerous stabs. The coroner had said she'd been alive for all but the final shot.

"Hmm, actually, I think he's right, my darling," Silvia said, taking the phone from Berrick. "We must fetch a doctor, or one of you will bleed to death."

CHAPTER 8

TEARS & BLOOD

T he darkness crept into every crack of the room, kept at bay
by a single bedside lamp. Darith stirred in the semi-dark-
ness. He felt the night in his bones. It called to him in the same
way he'd been called as a child to leap into the lake's deep water.
Only he didn't want the pleasures the night offered him. Warm
blood and screams. He felt Marim's fear riding the air, drew the
shaking of her hands into his lungs. Her nearness spoke to him
past walls and doors, and the closer she came, the more urgently
he felt her confusion.

Like a wraith, Marim entered, red hair strung with daisies
from the garden, and her face as pale as the moon in the darkness. A nightshift covered her body, offering little in the way of
modesty. She stared at him with her eyes huge and frightened
and reached her arms out, a daisy chain hanging from her fingertips. The promise of her dangled in front of him, so different
from the promise of the dark.

Darith tried to go to her. Then he lay back with a short,
harsh laugh.

She went to him and laid the flowers in her hands on
his head, a child's summer crown. Darith ripped the carefully
twined stems from his hair and tossed them at the wall.

"Outside the funeral parlor, your hands twined in mine,"
Marim said, her eyes stripping his anger away. "You sat in the
grass with me and braided flowers to lay on Petyr's coffin. I

loved you then, and I love you now."

Marim clasped Darith's hand and laid her head on his chest. Her body was soft and warm. Her breasts flattened against him, and every breath pressed her body into his. The promises her flesh made were well-crafted lies.

He shoved her away and stared at her face. There was a time he would have enjoyed having a well-bred woman come half-dressed to his bedchamber, but what was he now? He was nothing. Even the shadowy magic he'd practiced for years had left him. He was powerless. She knew it, or she wouldn't come.

"You didn't come in here to offer me love I can't use."

"Something is wrong," Marim whispered. She let her voice drift off into the hungry arms of the night before she continued. "I hear the voice inside me and there's nowhere for me to run. No one believes me... but you, you were there. Please, tell me you feel the changes."

Fear. That was all he saw in her pretty face. Had their wickedness not tempted her as it had him?

She sat up by his side. In the dim light of the moon, he watched her move. She took his hand and pressed it to her heart. It beat, pulsing against his hand.

"My blood is telling me there's something wrong," Marim said. "I'm not mad. I'm not."

"You *are* mad, and so am I."

At the trembling of her lip, Darith pulled her against him. He held her there. Her hand curled into a little ball on his chest. They took a breath.

"They say I went back to the party, and that I danced. I don't remember that. All I recall is the night, and now... tonight has the same pulse. My blood sings and I'm scared."

"They're morons. They say a man did this to me." He smiled into the night; he knew the night understood the joke. The darkness heard him. "The funny thing is, there isn't any pain... I don't remember any pain the whole time. Pain would be something real. Something to hold on to. Otherwise, it's all a dream."

"Oh, if only it were all a dream. And we'd wake up among the roses. And it would have been only us out in the garden." She smiled as she shivered against him. "We'd wake up in the sunlight."

"Don't." Darith turned his head to the side, away from the woman who lay against him. Her leg rested on his, but he couldn't feel her silky skin. Her entire body draped carelessly against him, and that couldn't mean anything to him. Marim slid up his body, and her thigh rested on his stomach. She cradled his head against her small chest.

"If we wake, we'll wake together, Darith," she said, "and if we sleep, we'll do that together as well. Even if I could leave you, I wouldn't."

Tears slipped from Darith's eyes, but before he could stifle the well of emotion bubbling up, Marim's lips brushed the tears from his cheek.

"Please, let me shelter you for once, Darith," Marim whispered.

"My loving mother has visited me *once*. I suppose I should be thankful for the consideration. Do you know what she asked? She wanted to know what lovers I'd taken in the village, in hopes she could locate some bastard brat. She said it like I ought to be grateful to her for taking the time."

Marim held him as he wrestled back self-pity. Her hair fell against his face, and it smelled only of her. He remembered darker scents that came with the night.

Inside his mind, the lurking image of a spider moved, mandibles quivering. She gasped.

"You see it too?" he asked.

"In my mind, but it's so real, like it's touching my thoughts. Will it eat me, Darith, and leave only my body?" Her fingers clawed at her face.

Darith gripped her wrists and stared at the tiny scratches on her cheeks, more lining her neck. Whatever she was feeling, it was not the same as it was for him. He longed to go into the night, but there was a wild terror in Marim's hazel eyes.

Neither of them moved or breathed as the web spread and the spider crept forward. Darith tightened his hold on her, and she clenched her fingers as she held him. Then Marim hissed a deep, guttural sound.

"Leave us!" she cried. "You are not welcome here."

The image stayed, and Marim wept.

"Why won't they go? They want to consume me... they whisper, whisper all night long. Only the daylight drives them from me."

Darith pulled himself up with his arms and held Marim against him. He glared at the wall, poured all his anger out against it, and the stones shook. A shiver of power woke in his body.

"Go," he said, releasing the tiny spark of magic into the word.

The spider melted away like wax. Marim lay in his arms, quivering.

"I will go insane," she wept. "I will be lost to this terror growing inside me."

"If anything comes for you, it must face me," Darith said. He pressed her to him until it hurt. She cried softly but did not try to push him back. His hold loosened, and his hand slid down her back.

She tilted her head up toward him. Her eyes were full of tears, and her mouth parted. Inside her was blackness. Darith kissed her, and she shied away from him for a moment. Then she kissed him back, her small mouth pressed to him. He felt everything then, experienced parts of himself they had told him he'd never feel again. He took her in and drank her pain from her lips. She gave freely.

The night sighed outside the window. They held the night from each other, intertwined till morning. They lay there until the first light of dawn streaked the sky. Then, without a word, Marim stood. She didn't look at Darith. It took her only a few steps to get to the door and then she was beyond his world. Even had he desired, Darith couldn't follow her. But he wasn't watching her—he watched the morning come.

△△△

The morning light, a flare of cheerful orangey-red, caught in Silvia's hair and was doused there. She sat at a vanity table with her long, red-black hair piled on top of her head. Next to her familiar reflection was the image of a bespectacled man. She rose and swirled toward the door where the doctor she'd called for Halis and Berrick waited. Her starched black dress clung to her waist, and her hips swung.

Dr. Trarsius hovered in the doorway, his eyes riveted on her slender form. It was hardly a triumph for her to entice men. To use them. They were easy and seduction was not an art she wished to pursue. With a lowered gaze, perhaps a demure hand resting on her chest, she could have changed the doctor's hostile gaze into something different.

The power is mine. The idea repelled her. That was the only difference between her and the whores who groveled for coin in The Brothel. How could she retain any pride if she stooped to their level?

"I've bandaged them up. I've done all I can, but you need to get them to the hospital," Dr. Trarsius said.

"So you instructed yesterday." She raised one hand and held it as if to block his notion from reaching her. "I don't intend to."

"Ma'am, your brother may very well be in danger of losing his life. A wound to the side like that..." Dr. Trarsius stared plaintively into her eyes, and his voice trailed off.

"My brother will live," she said. She placed her hand on the doctor's shoulder and looked directly into his eyes. They were of a height. He broke the gaze and stepped back a pace. Silvia allowed herself a smile at his discomfort. "I do not wish for official attention to this little fight. The two parties are amicably inclined now, and we have no desire to deal with any legal proceedings."

"Yes, miss," Dr. Trarsius said.

"You'll come again just before supper time and see to them. You'll be compensated."

"So you keep saying," Dr. Trarsius said. "But this has gone above my standard fee."

Her lips parted and she could practically taste his blood filling her mouth. That wouldn't do. They needed him and there were other solutions to his impatience outside physical harm. It was hard to remember that. Since childhood, she'd been expected to help Halis kill. Now that she was free, unless she willed it, she never needed to kill a man.

Her hand slid down her side, and he followed its journey. "A retainer for your silence? Follow me."

She stepped deeper into the chamber and walked around the bed. From a small bedside table, she picked up a wallet. She withdrew a single bill, running her fingers along it. The taint of her pheromones would follow him this way. She lifted the bill and brushed her lips over it. She might not want to seduce him, but for their safety, she needed to have some sort of hold on him. After the contact, she placed the bill in his palm.

How she longed to be on a civilized world, where they didn't cling to nostalgia for paper money. Somewhere… clean. But for the moment, Yahal's backwards values served her purposes.

He looked down at the cash.

"Enough to cover your pains, and it's only a token of my appreciation." She moved around him, her skirts dancing on the floor. She had him cornered between the bed, the wall, and her. How odd to corner a man, look at the fear in his gaze, and know she didn't have to play bait until Halis pierced the man's heart. Without Mr. Ymel ordering her, she could let him live. "I thank you for your time."

She moved back across the room, freeing him. He walked past her out the door.

Silvia watched him leave through halls lit with sun. It poured through the open drapes and traced over the walls with its carefree fingers. The morning paraded across everything, but when Silvia walked by, she held darkness close around her like a shawl. The web that stretched out from her created shadows that, though unseen themselves, seemed to dim the light. When the sunlight slid over her, it made no difference.

She entered the master suite and shut the door. Halis lay in the next room on the bed, his eyes closed, his face abnormally pale. With a casual glance to Berrick where he lay propped up among pillows on the chaise lounge, Silvia lifted her skirts in her hands and ran to Halis. She kneeled as one in prayer by his bedside and took up his hand.

"My darling." She sighed.

"It's just blood, Silvia."

Her gaze accused him of lying, but her mouth said nothing. The morning light cascaded over her now. There was too much of it for it to be held off even by the web of darkness that clung to them both. The brightness found no fault in her face, no blemish on her skin. Tears slid down her cheeks unheeded; except for the droplets, there was no sign from her that she wept.

Halis lay in front of her, his arm wrapped up tightly in a new white bandage and beneath his shirt, there was another wrapping for his side. Her hand slid over the bandage on his arm and then she touched his side. The tears continued to travel from her lashes down her flawless skin. Halis sat up with a wince, propping himself up on his good arm.

"Stop wallowing," Halis said.

She wiped the tears away just as casually as she had unwittingly shed them. "I'm sorry. It was my foolish game. You never should have gotten hurt."

"You cannot steal a spaceship, nor can you fly one. Your games, as you call them, were necessary. I shouldn't have been so careless with the gun. Be lenient with both of us, my queen. This is one of few real interactions with the world you've had. How were we to predict, without any experience, how our actions would ripple out?"

"Soon we'll be free. No one will own us. We won't have to be the creatures they've made us. No one but you will ever have to touch me again, Halis. All of our acts will be free. They will be ours."

Silvia moved up onto the bed and sat by his side. They leaned together with their foreheads pressed against one another. They did not speak or move for many long moments. She placed her hand over her stomach as she spoke. It was not the human language she used, but the language of Halis' birth race. "*Soon.*"

He pulled back and looked at her, then touched her stomach as well. His usual smile returned to his face. And he spoke a word to her in the same tongue. "*Yes.*"

She laughed, and they embraced, their mouths coming together.

In the corner, she heard Berrick whisper his daughter's name.

Yes. Do it for Marim. Hold your tongue and swallow your pride. There was an honor in Berrick she approved of. For his sake, she hoped Marim could be saved. But after encountering Halis, Silvia wondered if the web and the mind-voice of Halis' fallen people wouldn't eat her sooner rather than later.

△△△

Count Cortanis sat in his study. He sat with his back to the door and put on every appearance of being busy. His financial papers lay out neatly on the desk, and he held a pen. A box of open envelopes sat by his right elbow. He stared at the desk; he stared right past the papers without sparing them a thought.

"Uncle." Marim's voice was as soft as a sigh, but he knew it instantly. He didn't turn or move. "Uncle, my father went to find the couple that hurt Darith, didn't he?"

"Go play, Marim," the count said.

"Please," she said, and her hand brushed his shoulder.

The count turned to her. She had lost weight in the past couple weeks and it made her appear both younger and older than she was. She no longer resembled a woman, but at the same time, she was one now. Dark ringed her eyes, and he guessed she'd had little sleep.

"You look so like your mother," he said, staring up into her sad eyes. The only eyes he saw anymore were depressed. His wife was half-crazed with mourning, and the servants crept around with their eyes downcast. He looked in the mirror in the morning and saw hollow, sad eyes.

"Please," she repeated.

"Yes, child. He's gone to find them."

"But not as the police chief." She held Berrick's badge in her pale fingers.

"No, he went as a man." The count settled his head against the soft leather of the chair. They both knew what that badge meant and if Berrick had left it, then there was no denying his goal. "He went to avenge Darith."

Maybe to avenge Polly too. He never had that chance.

She placed the tips of her thin fingers on his hand. "Darith isn't dead, Uncle."

The count moved his hand away from hers quickly and stood. How dare she presume to understand, this slip of a girl? How could she comprehend what Darith's condition meant? All those years wasted, all the times the count could have acted differently if he'd known Darith would never come to anything. Darith was better off dead.

The count was a good deal taller than her. Yet she looked up at him unperturbed, her pointed chin thrust out. *Willful child. I should teach her her place. Berrick always did let his family run too freely.*

"Darith isn't dead," Marim said.

The count hit her across her face. The blow toppled her to the ground. She lay there for a moment with her face inches from the carpet. Then she sat up, propping herself up on her hands. Her curly hair fell across her face. It was as red as blood. She didn't cry, but she turned her sad eyes back up to him.

Pulse racing, the count forced himself to step back from her. Regardless of her mouth, she was still Berrick's daughter. Visions of teaching her what a man was bubbled up in his mind, ripping that flimsy dress from her and showing her how weak her flesh was.

"Please. He needs you, Uncle," Marim said. "He doesn't need to be avenged. He needs his father, and I need mine." Her voice was still soft, and tears brimmed in her large eyes. Her cheek was red, and a small line of blood crossed her lip where she had bitten it. A tear spilled out of her eye and traveled down her unmarked cheek.

The count turned his back to her. He clenched his fists at his side. He heard her stand up. He tried to clear his mind again, but it wouldn't empty. It was filled now with all the plans that could never come to fruition and the dreams of a future his son could never have.

How life had changed. He recalled those early days away at university. Berrick and he had stuck close together as the only Yahal natives. No one else understood why at eighteen they were both married or accepted that their wives were both under eighteen. Enduring those years had seemed a trial that would lead to better things and they had been noble gentlemen braving the corrupt waters of cultures outside their native Yahal.

Now the count knew himself corrupt; he saw it every time he looked in the eyes of his wife or his son. Until this accident, he'd tried to control his desires, tried to abide by his wife's edicts, but what was the point? Even the staunch Berrick was turning from custom and there was nothing left to maintain. Darith was ruined and with him any hope of a future.

"There are spiders in my mouth…" Marim muttered, the comment almost lost in the breathy terror of her voice.

"Get out," he said, rubbing his shoulder, pressing his fingers against the old bullet wound there. Scarred over, he found the bump of uneven skin through his shirt. He glanced to his liquor cabinet, but the shelves were bare. The countess would answer for that absence. "Get out."

The door closed behind her. The count stood there with his hands clenched at his sides. Then slowly, he leaned onto the desk. A tear splattered on the neatly displayed bills and sheets of figures. Another followed.

CHAPTER 9

LADIES OF THE NIGHT

T he car passed under the shadow of the Yahal Brothel, and Dr. Trarsius looked up at the towering mass. He diverted his eyes quickly. His face was a little pale. The traffic around The Brothel was always atrocious. Out of towners and off-worlders made their way to see it. The crowding in that sector was one bad side effect of the bustling tourist activity that invigorated the town.

Dr. Trarsius parked two blocks away and let his engine idle. A thought of turning the key again and fleeing occurred to him. It wasn't to be. A smart person didn't flee a summons from The Brothel. Not if you wanted to keep working even in the vicinity of town.

Never having been inside, he didn't know what to expect. He had never wanted to go inside. He saw one of the girls, once, on her rare visit into town. She was the second-most beautiful woman he'd ever seen. He'd never thought to see a more beautiful one. He still remembered the whore walking in the streets, and he'd tried to look away. She a little yellow-skinned woman with eyes bluer than a mountain stream. Her eyes had been so empty and so cold.

Now he was called to The Brothel and not by choice. Officially, The Brothel did not command but best keep the powers that be placated. For that reason, he turned off his car and got out.

Smoothing the lapel of his jacket, he stared down the block. Dr. Trarsius began to walk. The sidewalk was crowded with well-dressed men and a few stray women. Street vendors pushed at him, and wonderful smells wafted out of open doors along the street front. He shoved past the people. Hover cars sped overhead, carrying rich off-worlders to and from The Brothel.

Finally, he came to the large, gold-plated doors. The doorman looked down at him from a grand height.

"What do you want?" the doorman asked in a voice that was minuscule for one of his immense size.

"I was asked here by Mr. Ymel," Dr. Trarsius said. His hands fumbled in front of him until they finally withdrew a note from his pocket. He handed it to the doorman.

The doorman looked at it, then down at the man. "Go inside."

Dr. Trarsius stepped inside and found himself flanked with men almost as big as the one outside. The sweat on his forehead was gleaming in the bright light. The men looked down at him, and he shoved the note in front of him. A talisman.

One of the men stepped up and read it. He nodded. "Sondro will see you there."

Another man stepped forward and smiled in a very disconcerting way. Dr. Trarsius had no choice but to follow him.

No vulgar pictures or ornaments lined the hall that would imply what the place was. Everything within the passage sang elegance. Doorways were solid wood with silver handles and intricate carvings. They stepped into a side hallway. The same graceful design reigned here as well. The carpet was rich and dark, and the ceiling was high and hung with lights that dripped crystals. They stopped at a wooden door, and Sondro knocked and announced himself and the visitor.

The door opened. A man of normal size and a reassuring businesslike appearance stood there. He had an old-world Asiatic quality, with a narrow eyes and rod-straight black hair. A wide, white smile caused the creases around his eyes to deepen.

"Thank you for bringing Dr. Trarsius to me."

Dr. Trarsius gulped and shook the man's hand. "You must be Mr. Ymel."

"Yes, I'm afraid that is me." His smile continued, and Dr. Trarsius shifted nervously under it. "Why don't the two of you come inside?"

Dr. Trarsius stepped into the room as Mr. Ymel stepped aside. Sondro followed him. One other man reclined in a stiff metal-backed chair inside the room. He was fat with long hair pulled back into a ponytail. There was a one-way window in the back of the room, through which the doctor could see numerous shapely women and a few musclebound men walking around.

"Take a seat, doctor," said the fat man. He made no effort to introduce himself.

"This is Mr. Henton," said Mr. Ymel, still smiling.

The wide, leering expression reminded Dr. Trarsius of someone, but he was too disconcerted to think of whom.

The doctor sat down across from the man at the table. Mr. Ymel sat down next to him.

The women began to disrobe out in the other room. Dr. Trarsius tried his best not to look; instead, he reached into his pocket, toying with his wallet. Even if he was comfortable with the idea of buying a woman, those cost more than he could afford. His fingers passed over the crisp bill given to him by Silvia the day before.

"You like our view, doctor?" Mr. Henton asked.

"Your girls are lovely," Dr. Trarsius replied, his mouth dry.

"Indeed, and we're almost open for business," Mr. Ymel said. "Perhaps when our business is concluded here you would like to sample one of our girls. No charge, of course. We never charge our friends."

"What *is* our business? Is someone sick?" Dr. Trarsius asked, with little hope that was the case.

"No, doctor," Mr. Henton said. "We have plenty of physicians here to deal with illness."

"Our business, Dr. Trarsius, is the matter of a woman we have reason to believe you met with," Ymel said. "One Silvia Black and her partner, Halis Black."

Dr. Trarsius stared across the table. He looked to Mr. Ymel and recognized Halis' smile there. He remembered the yellow-skinned hooker who had Silvia's expression. Then he also re-called Silvia's face, her eyes blacker than asphalt and her full mouth poised between one action and another. The bills under his fingers crumpled.

"Silvia Black," he said. For the first time, it occurred to him that she must be one of their girls. Silvia belonged to The Brothel.

"Yes. She has disappeared, you see. We didn't worry be-cause she only has her show once every two weeks," Mr. Ymel said, winking at Dr. Trarsius. "A very specialized show. She's a very special girl, and we became concerned when she missed her show the night before last. So we looked into the matter, and it came to our attention that your secretary remembered a call from a Silvia, and she said that Silvia gave no last name and insisted against a hospital despite your requests. Is all this true, doctor?"

"Yes," Dr. Trarsius said. There was no reason to deny his acquaintance. They already knew. And he feared what had been done to his secretary, what they still might do.

His fear of Silvia melted away as he looked at these men. He believed he understood her. She had to get away from them, away from this place. If there was coldness in her, it was a cold-ness that came from The Brothel. Her darkness belonged to The Brothel and not to herself. He saw her perfect face, and the flaw-less curve of her waist and love replaced what had hitherto been distaste in him.

"Tell us, why has she not returned to us?" Henton asked, but it was not a question, not with a guard like Sondro standing by the door glowering.

"Her brother's injury," Dr. Trarsius said. His hands were shaking, so he clenched them together in his lap.

The women in the window were moving about. They were like wraiths, every one, beautiful faces and bodies that seemed disconnected from anything except the internal rhythm of the other women. They moved as one, even as they moved separately. One girl began to dance. It was the dance of a snake. Her breasts thrust out against the air, and her arms writhed above her head.

"Halis is unwell? What, pray tell, happened?" Mr. Ymel asked, his smile wider than ever. Dr. Trarsius saw Halis grinning up at him from the bed. Halis' smile had terrified the doctor, but now the fear emptied.

The doctor didn't know what to say. He wanted to protect Silvia and her brother from these men. What could he do against the juggernaut of The Brothel? "He was shot twice. Once in the side and once in the arm."

The doctor didn't know if he imagined it, but he thought Mr. Henton went a bit pale.

"He must be brought back to us. We can treat him," Mr. Henton said.

"And Silvia? Is she hurt?" Mr. Ymel asked. His smile was forced, frozen and stiff.

"No."

"You must bring us to them. We must treat Halis. You aren't equipped to do so," Mr. Henton said.

"If she'd wanted you to treat her, surely, she would have come to you," Dr. Trarsius said.

"What did you say, doctor?" Ymel asked.

The doctor swallowed past a lump in his throat but said nothing else. He thought about his neat little office and his chubby secretary. He thought about the house he'd just bought with the backyard filled with trees. He thought of the dinner parties he went to on weekends with other doctors and lawyers and their wives. And Silvia's scent enveloped him.

"Who shot Halis?" Mr. Ymel asked after a moment of silence.

"I don't know," Dr. Trarsius said. He wanted to see his

house again and live his life, but Silvia's face swam before him. He could see her lips forming the word *please.*

"You don't know?" Mr. Ymel said. His eyes were dark behind his smile.

"I'm afraid not. She didn't tell me anything."

"And you did not insist on knowing before you treated him?" Mr. Ymel asked.

"She claimed she did it. He claimed she did not," the doctor said.

"And there was no one else there? No...bodies?" Ymel asked.

"Not that I saw." He thought about the blue-faced man who had lain carelessly outside the door of a bedroom upstairs. He thought of the big burly man with a horrible puncture wound to his thigh.

Mr. Ymel was silent, but his eyes stared coldly at the doctor.

"Where are they, Dr. Trarsius?" Mr. Henton asked.

Outside the window, men were beginning to pour inside. More of the women were dancing. They wore or didn't wear anything the mind could conjure. One woman was covered with what could easily have been black tar; it slanted over her body in a neat strip all the way up her neck and covered one eye. Long, black silk scarves encircled her wrists, tethering them together, though not inhibiting her movements. She danced wildly.

"I'm afraid I can't tell you." The doctor slid his sweating palms on his legs.

"You *should* be afraid, doctor," Mr. Henton said.

"We thought you were our friend, Dr. Trarsius," Mr. Ymel said. His eyes narrowed so only a twinkle shone between the lids. "I shouldn't like to find out that we thought wrongly."

"If Silvia wished for you, she would have sent for you. I gave my word I wouldn't go for help. I gave her my word that I would treat her privately."

"And it was our money that she paid you," Henton said.

"She hasn't paid me yet," Dr. Trarsius said.

"Are you our friend, doctor?" Mr. Ymel asked.

"Yes," Dr. Trarsius said. His voice sounded thin and high. He doubted he would ever see his house or his friends again. Silvia's face haunted his mind, her eyes were scared, and he knew what she wanted.

"Silvia and Halis Black are dangerous people. You aren't doing society a favor by helping to keep them on the loose." Ymel leaned forward. "They could do unspeakable damage."

"And who made them that way?" Dr. Trarsius asked. He stood up. If they were going to kill him, they could very well just do it. He was sick of their game of cat and mouse.

Sondro was at his side in a second and pushed him back into his chair. The thug's hands were huge and powerful.

"Think about what you are doing, Dr. Trarsius. We will find them with or without your help. Do you really want to be our enemy?" Henton asked.

"I will not help you find her!"

"She will not appreciate your efforts. She has no heart and will not value your love or your loyalty," Mr. Ymel said.

"I will not help you."

"I'm tired of this business," Henton said.

Dr. Trarsius stared at him. The women outside danced.

"Kill him," Henton said.

Sondro hauled the doctor to his feet. Dr. Trarsius stared up at him. He said nothing. Sondro grabbed the doctor's head and twisted it. Dr. Trarsius heard his neck snap. He felt himself fall to the ground. He saw Silvia laughing and didn't know whether to be happy or sad. Then he saw nothing; he felt nothing.

△△△

"We should have tortured him," Mr. Ymel said.

"It wasn't worth it. He was scum, and we can find what he didn't tell us," Henton said. "We know why they're still missing. Halis' injuries are the reason. Whatever she went out to accomplish is likely completed. Halis got away from the encounter, and I cannot imagine he left any man standing."

"What now?" Mr. Ymel asked.

"We search through the doctor's things. Find addresses, directions, anything to lead us to her. We trace everyone who was at Silvia's last show. She left after that damn show. Whatever inspired her to leave happened then. We try the locator spells again. We keep our eyes and ears open. Anything else?" Henton asked.

"Check the local papers and rumors for anything about unusual infestations of spiders. They are said to be drawn to Halis' kind," Mr. Ymel said.

"Monitor the doctors. Especially ones who work in Dr. Trarsius' sector. She may call another when he doesn't show up," Mr. Henton added.

"And then we wait," Ymel said.

"As long as Halis doesn't die before we find her. There isn't another to replace him," Mr. Henton said. He lowered his head into his hands.

"And if we don't find them soon? What then?" Mr. Ymel asked. "They must be found. She can't be running loose. With or without Halis, she's a major threat, and it's possible that she could be traced back to us. And him..."

"If we don't find them soon, we call in outside help. We call in trackers," Henton said. He looked toward the window out at the girls. They danced in the crowded room. One girl was walking to one of the side doors. A man followed her through the curtain.

"I can think of few girls I'd dislike losing as much as Silvia. But if we must, we'll call in assassins. She mustn't be allowed to roam free."

CHAPTER 10

ESCAPE

All day, Berrick rested, staring out the window, wondering at life's cruel humor. When the last glimmer disappeared from the sky, and only the lamps kept the darkness at bay, Silvia burst through the door. Her hair was tousled, as if she'd been slowly worrying it free from its braided confines, and her breathing was audible. Halis looked up from his chair, and when he saw her, he stood.

"Silvia," Halis said as he crossed the carpeted floor toward her.

"He didn't make his appointment, Halis!"

Berrick smiled and rested his head against the wall. It was possible that the disappearance of the doctor implied he'd contacted a hospital or other reasonable authorities. *Poor crazy bitch, her evil game is going awry.*

"The doctor?"

"He didn't come. They got him. We aren't safe here!" Silvia flushed, and her hands flew to her hair.

"There was always the chance they'd find us. When was the doctor supposed to be here?" Halis asked. He took her in his arms, but she broke free and moved across the room. Her hands shook visibly. In contrast, Halis didn't seem upset in the least.

"At dusk," she said.

Berrick estimated that meant the doctor was an hour and a half late.

"He's late then," Halis said. "If he did meet with them, we have no way of identifying when. Whatever the case, they'll already know where we are *or* if the doctor kept his peace, they don't."

"No, you put too much faith in my beauty, Halis. That man hated me."

"What a surprise," Berrick said.

Silvia turned to him and barred her teeth. Halis grabbed her again. Berrick grinned. Now they were being hunted—a pleasant turn of events. If he could just sit pretty, everything might yet come out the right way.

"There's no action we can take now to prevent the doctor from speaking," Halis said. "If they know where we are, they'll bring us in. Panicking has no effect on the outcome."

"I won't go back." Silvia screamed now. "I won't stay here. I want off this damn planet. Out of Ymel's reach. I won't go back. I'll kill them first!"

"And die in the process?" Halis asked with his usual smile.

Is she going to hit him? Berrick leaned forward, ignoring the pain in his thigh as he moved.

"Yes, goddamn you! I'll rip my heart from my chest before I'll step foot in that place!" Her hand had flown to her stomach and settled there.

"Calm yourself. This is our warning. We flee this city tonight. If the doctor didn't tell them, we still have time to get away," Halis said.

"Where will we go?" Silvia asked.

"Where it's safe. We'll go home with Berrick." Halis turned with his smile to Berrick.

The expression sent slivers of ice through Berrick's veins; his own smile died under the cruel glint of Halis'.

"And you really shouldn't find this amusing, Berrick. If they locate us, they'll kill you, title or no."

"They—the Yahal Brothel," Berrick said. He should have known it before; they were sitting in the shadow of one of the most evil places in the galaxy—a place that bred women like

Silvia. Her beauty was unmatched by any he'd seen and her evil unquestionable. She was exactly the sort of shadowy creature he'd always thought haunted those wicked halls.

The only reason the link hadn't occurred to him was the whores were not allowed out of The Brothel without an escort. All of The Brothel's shows were kept secret. Even from his side of the planet, Berrick had heard of some of the horrid fates associated with speaking about what you'd seen at The Brothel.

"What do we do now?" Silvia stumbled back against the wall, her face white.

"We take all traces of ourselves and join Berrick in his homecoming. We take Henri with us. He has gone on a business trip or something. His house will be pristine and utterly empty. Then, my queen, we'll pray."

Berrick watched the two of them. A whisper of pity filtered its way into his thoughts and then a remembrance of Marim's smile crushed it. They were scum.

"Gather your things, Silvia. Go tidy your room and then bring the car around back. You'll need to bring Henri down and put him in the trunk. I'll clean out this mess and escort Berrick down to the car," Halis said. After the list of instructions, he took a few steps to her side and touched her cheek. "Whatever happens, we're together. Now go."

Silvia fled the room. Berrick looked away. Dying wouldn't be so bad if his death served to protect Marim.

△△△

Only one task remained until they could flee. Silvia looked fondly at the wolf spider crawling over her knuckle. After a moment, she flicked it to the floor. "Goodbye, little friend."

The song was ancient, and she took a moment to gather its pieces together inside her before parting her lips. Barely a sound came from her throat, and yet her voice carried. Deep inside her, the strands of the web vibrated. She reached into the inky abyss, feeling the lives of the spiders that had come before her, and pulled in a breath.

The presence at the center of the pulsing web added its voice to her notes, and millions of voices churned together in a sad, keening dance from her lips.

The song spun its way into the cracks of the house and down into the basement and the attic. Throughout the house, each eight-legged lurker heard and obeyed. Time to move on. Even after her voice itself had faded into nothing, the song traveled, echoing on the invisible web, flowing from Silvia and Halis, reaching across Yahal and linking her to Marim and Darith. The cracks in the house emptied. Where there had been little glittering eyes, there was only emptiness.

She stood in the night with her breath white against the blackness. The wildness in her faded, but her essence remained stretched over the intricate woven strands. It was then that she felt The Brothel's sorcerers in her mind—searching. She smiled. If Ymel had them searching, The Brothel hadn't located them. The Brothel's sorcerers used puny Yahal magic. It ran off her. She said a word softly, and it darted to Halis and hovered around him. Ymel would not find them that way.

"Try harder," she whispered into the wind, "You won't find me. But someday, I'll find you…"

When Halis and Berrick arrived at the car, both limping along, but Halis holding a gun pressed to Berrick's side, she leaned on the hood, tapping her toe.

"They don't know where we are yet," she said.

"I thought I felt you hovering about me, like the scent of blood and incense."

"Yes, they 'searched' and they failed. Before they even finished their efforts to conjure the spell, I stopped them." She touched Halis' shoulder. Halis gave her a kiss. Her hands slid over his cheeks. Everything was finally going right. She opened the back door of the car.

"You might look into speeding our papers along," Halis

said, shoving Berrick into the cool interior. "For your own safety and that of your daughter, we must be gone without a trace before they come for us. If they suspect that you aided us, there's no telling what they'll do."

CHAPTER 11

INNOCENT GIRLS

D arith rested against a sea of silk pillows in the unlit room and watched the wind ruffle the petals of the daisies Marim brought him earlier. The night was cloudy, so his open window provided nearly no light. The estate was off in the country, and no streetlights intruded on the dark. In the dim moonlight, the web of energy spread out. Silvia tugged at the strands, her fear stroking at him. The connection was more intimate than their night among the flowers. He tasted the spiders floating in the air. Their red intruded on the black, and he waited. Tonight, fear danced in the air. Darith smiled in his blanket of darkness.

Driven to understand, Darith had no choice but to search for answers. What were they? Not monsters from some fairy book to frighten children. They were something real, and real things could be defeated.

A frustrated cry tore from his lips and deep within the spider's web the sound danced. His power glittered in there, tangled with the strands. His fingertips sizzled as he reached into the web. His mind stretched, and he moved along the glittering strands.

"*This way,*" the voice whispered.

The hand he stretched out in his mind was as black as the nighttime void, but it gripped the ripples of magic beneath the web and a strange vitality surged through him. His fingers drank, guzzling the power until Darith closed his fist.

The surrounding room was lit brighter than day by the glow around his hands, traveling up to his elbows. *I don't even know how to command this much.*

"*Destroy the walls, the cage. Walk free, all you must do is accept us.*" the voice hissed in his mind. "*This human cage cannot hold us.*"

Darith lifted his arms, letting the light wash over him. His resentment burned, demanding release, agreeing with the whispers from the web. He thrust his arms forward, the motion like swinging a gavel. The glass of his window shattered and the trees out past the cobblestones bent and snapped. He pulled back as the first of the flowers ripped from the earth.

An image of Marim outside picking flowers to bring to him, smiling as she looked up from her task, defeated the rush of destruction. *Not those. I will not destroy her joy. Not even for my own. Not when she has so little left.*

He moved his fingers. In control of the seething inside, he swept his fingers to the side, brushing the glass out of sight. Marim would come soon and he was not ready to discuss this with her. The darkness hid the mangled mess of trees now that his hands contained his fire.

Darith smiled. His spells that had once been so weak and so limited were fed by the night now. All his study and practice suddenly had meaning. He could kill with the strength in him if he chose. Someday, he would.

With her red hair down, Marim came as she did every night. The wind from the window blew her nightdress against her legs, defining something painfully akin to a woman's form. Darith watched as she crossed the room.

"Darith? Your window is gone."

"I broke it."

"Oh," Marim said as she crawled into the bed beside him. Her hands closed around his.

He tucked the magic back, afraid it would burn her.

"The spiders are crawling in." Marim's voice shook.

"There are no spiders here, Marim."

"Who else broke your window?"

Her warmth caressed him, but Darith paid it no attention. He was listening to the voice of the night. He struggled to hear past the spiders into the true voice behind. He'd touched something there in the darkness that was more powerful than they would ever be. Something he could destroy them with. When he concentrated, he saw the web inside him unwinding and reaching out.

What had they meant that he could walk if he accepted them? And how many deaths would such an acceptance entail?

"You think of death. That shouldn't bring you joy," Marim whispered.

He didn't look at her. She might bring him back with her. She might call him back to where she was, and he wasn't ready to go.

"Please, Darith. I need you."

Shut up, he wanted to say, *shut up!* Instead, he turned to her, and her eyes clawed their way into his mind. "It's not the night that makes me want to see them dead."

"The night makes you dream of murder and see the whole world bathed in red," Marim said. "I see it too, hear the voice, but I don't smile. It terrifies me. It wants to eat me and if you go to it, there will be nothing to stop the web from trapping and draining me."

She still didn't understand. In her eyes, the same child lived, faltering and afraid, who had clung to him at her mother's death. He laughed, and she flinched back.

"Why do you come here, Marim? Why me? You could still escape it. You are not pinned down as I am."

"Because you would have done the same for me." Marim lowered her eyes. "I come because I think you need someone who doesn't see you as a cripple, someone who doesn't see a legacy ending."

"Shut up."

"You asked, Darith." She looked up at him again. "That's not what you are, you know. You aren't the end of a family line. You aren't that any more than before you were the bringer of heirs. No one saw you as just that then, and soon they won't see you as they do now."

"You're a child," he said.

"Yes. But I'll never doubt you."

"I'm cruel to you," he said.

"Yes. But I'll be here with you no matter. You can be cruel to me if you please. I'd rather you not." She shrugged and laid her head against his shoulder.

They lay there, and Darith no longer heard the night. Exhaustion weighted his eyelids, and Marim's warmth and softness beside him drove away the rage. She kissed his chin, and he closed his eyes. The wind flew in through the open window and spoke into their ears, but they weren't listening anymore. It tapped against the hidden shards of glass in the garden. They drew closer together even as they slept, her body fitting itself against his. The rain drenched the carpet by the window as it jetted inside. They huddled together against the storm.

△△△

Empty windows mocked Mr. Ymel as he walked around the ostentatious mansion. The garden had gone to seed, and remnants of spiderwebs trailed from bushes. A solitary spider scuttled across the cobbled path and Ymel squashed it with the shiny toe of his shoe.

Agents of The Brothel had found the house. There had indeed been reports of spiders. The extermination teams had a time of it. Right in the center of the affected zone was the house of one Mr. Trehar, who had been at Silvia's next-to-last show. On finding the house unoccupied, Mr. Ymel was disappointed but not surprised.

When he rounded to the front of the house again, the muscle accompanying him had the front doors open. Ymel slipped his gloves on and entered. Silvia's musk hung in the air.

He walked through the house, occasionally glancing rather disparagingly around him. "What are you doing, my Silvia? What in the world do you think you are doing?"

Ymel scanned the walls and ceiling with his arms folded in front of him. This was the house. He didn't need to search. The small team he had assembled looked around. If something lingered to be found, they would find it. He could feel Silvia and Halis whispering in the surrounding air. He couldn't have been more certain if he had found he was walking through spiderwebs every other step.

They can't get off-world. Containment is key. Mr. Ymel struck a vase, sending it crashing to the ground. How had no one seen the possibility of their escape coming?

"I don't want to destroy you," he whispered. He was one of The Brothel members who had made the decision to keep the pair of children and raise them for a show. Against galactic orders. Exterminate. That was the only proper response, and he hadn't.

Ymel stared at his reflection in a mirror. Gazing into his own dark eyes, he recalled the moment this mess began.

The two women careened to the floor in front of him. The blonde lay, semi-conscious, stones and glass embedded in her cheek. The other woman, however, even kneeling stared up at him with the unmistakable pride and arrogance of her people. The billowing black smoke of her hair and snow-white skin seemed to shake off the muck covering her.

"We came to you," she said. Her voice was like the music of the night.

"Kill her," Ymel said.

A shot rang out, and the woman slumped to the ground. As her body fell, a window opened to the two children behind her, clinging to each other. The two most beautiful children who had ever crossed his path. The girl couldn't be more than five, soft peach-colored skin, huge eyes. Her hair was a golden blonde barely tinged with the Dram-bish red. It would darken in time. The boy was a delicious black all over but for a shock of red hair. They were why the women hadn't been killed the instant they'd entered the camp.

Ymel's mission on Revia was to retrieve a few objects of great value for The Brothel and The Council of Five had signed off on his visit for that purpose. But if something worth more came along, he was open to smuggling some illicit cargo off the doomed world.

The blonde woman on the ground stirred, struggling to prop herself up on her hands. A pair of sapphire blue eyes looked imploringly at him. Her bone structure was amazing. "Please. They are babies."

"It's your lucky day," Ymel said, picking a piece of glass from her cheek. "What are their names?"

"Silvia, Silvia and Halis, please—"

Now they were free, and it would all lead back to him.

ΔΔΔ

The leaves yellowed in the trees, and a few danced downward to the ground. Risa ran out from a farmhouse into the yellowing orchard with all the determination of her six years. Her hair was in long braids that trailed down her back like little rivulets. Her new black boots sank into the moist earth, leaving a trail her father would later find and follow, and she ran. She darted over the mud with the determination of childhood, completely bent on finding something for her rock collection, but if she happened to find something else that caught her eye, that might suffice.

Once inside the trees, the little girl slowed. She picked her way around the tree trunks until she came to a shining stream. Sitting down on a rock, she stuck the toe of her boot into the flow, disrupting the water and making white eruptions churn around her foot. She picked up a handful of rocks and began to toss them one by one into the water.

"Hello." The man hadn't been there a moment before, but now he was. Risa looked up into his night-dark face and smiled. She looked around but didn't see a car parked along the road.

"Where'd you come from, mister?" she said, peering up at him. She held tight to her handful of rocks.

"Oh, my car is parked a ways down the road. I thought I'd walk over to the stream. And you must belong to that farm just up the road."

Risa nodded. The man was quite fascinating, she decided. He wasn't dressed at all like the people she knew—too fancy, too clean. He looked like a movie star. She wanted to ask him if he was but didn't quite dare.

The man picked up a rock and tossed it up and down in his palm.

"I'm Halis," he said.

The little girl wondered if she was supposed to know that name. Maybe he was famous. He didn't look famous, though, on second thought. Famous people didn't just wander around in the countryside. They drove around in cities in nice big car-riages and swam in pools.

Probably they didn't live on Yahal at all. She'd heard Mother say it was a backwater planet. That was before Mother ran off, Risa guessed to find a planet that "embraced modern technology and values." Hogwash, according to her father.

"I'm Risa," she said, pushing a braid back over her shoul-der.

Halis' eyes met hers. They were dark and deep as the lake in winter. Fear tugged at Risa, like a dead weight from her braids that she couldn't shake. She took a step back, and the water sluiced up against the back of her boot. A woman came into view behind Halis, no more than a silhouette against the sun.

"Halis, no," the woman said.

Risa looked over at the woman, whose black eyes were wide and frightened in her ice-white face.

"No? Silvia, no what?" Halis grinned. His teeth were

sharp.

He took Risa's arm and tugged her closer. She tried to pull away, but his hand tightened.

"She's just a little girl," Silvia said, but she didn't step any closer. "You don't have to."

"I'm hungry," Halis said, pulling Risa closer to him.

Risa pulled away again. She meant to call for help, but she didn't make any noise. All she could do was look at Silvia. But when she met Silvia's eyes, she flinched away; they were the same black voids as Halis'. Then she discovered that her arm wasn't being held anymore. She took a few stumbling steps backward into the stream and looked up.

Then she did scream. The creature was hideous; she fell back into the stream, and the cold water penetrated her lungs after one struggling breath. Then the spider was on her. She shrieked and tried to push herself away. All that existed was water and the creature. A mouth like a gaping hole into wrinkled black descended on her, the two fangs dripping. A crippling pain bit into her side, and she struck out. The water around her was tinged with blood, and it poured into her mouth as the creature pushed her under with its razor-sharp leg.

She was free, and she kicked her leg out at the ground and surfaced. The spider stared at her. She turned and tried to run, but the water pressed against her waist and then there was something sticking through her. She couldn't understand. The sky was red, and blackness swooped down on her.

Was she out of the water now? Risa's eyes registered nothing.

"You didn't have to do that," Silvia said into the darkness. "There was no reason. You didn't accomplish anything."

"I was hungry." His words were softer, fading into the void.

I'm scared, Risa tried to say, but she couldn't feel her mouth.

"She was just a child," Silvia repeated.

"She was a human. She was food."

"You're a monster," Silvia said.

"We're one and the same."

And then all was silent.

CHAPTER 12
ENDINGS & BEGINNINGS

The day was golden. The Cortanis' pool glittered, reflecting hundreds of tiny blue skies and brilliant suns in its ripples. Sparks of light bounced around the grassy area and made a playground of the sandy space skirting the pool. The chill of early fall hung in the air and the water, though inviting, swirled in the wind, creating menacing patterns in the ripples.

Having strolled through the gardens, Marim knelt at the edge, trying to see the lapping water as innocuous, but shadows lurked everywhere now. At the corner of her eye, a devilish form with eight long, spindly legs scurried toward her, only to dissipate as she turned. Tiny flashes of light reflected from the water dashed across her skin. The joyous dancing light only brought out the dark circles beneath her nervous eyes.

Time at the Cortanis' had previously been a vacation. She escaped the tedium of doing her needlework and practicing music and hid from the dark corners that ruled her home. Now, the dark corners had followed her and no matter where she went, the sunshine had edges. And off of those edges lurked a terror waiting to claim her.

"Daddy, come home," she whispered. Perhaps he could chase the shadows away during the day as Darith helped to do in the night.

"*He won't. The spiders are gorging on his entrails now,*" a shadow between the roses whispered.

Marim glanced up, only to find the leafy outline of the rose bush outlined on the ground.

I can't do this. Oh gods, how long until they get me?

Farther down the rose path, the countess walked, her arm linked with a well-dressed man. A detective who worked for Marim's father. Marim frowned, chewing at her lip. Why couldn't the countess stop this nonsense about locating an heir? Couldn't she see it was destroying Darith? Didn't she care?

I can't stay here.

"*The countess is the least of your worries, little girl. The count's flushed with scotch and his eyes follow you. Don't you feel it? I think you like it, like the attention… You're nothing but a dirty whore.*"

"Shut up!" Marim slammed her hand into the surface of the pool, creating an arc of water that caught the light, momentarily erasing the shadows from her sight.

"*Darith can't protect you anymore. He can't sleep outside your room when his father drinks. What happens when they force you back to your own room? You can't just keep lying on top of the cripple.*"

Marim turned her eyes to the blue sky. Anything to hide from the dark web clinging to her mind. The monsters that had stalked her for so long finally had their hold.

Her body reflected the pain and anguish around her and wound itself into knots. Even her monthly woman's cycle was thrown off. The monsters whispered horrible meanings for her father's absence and the weight of the Cortanis' cares weighed her down, threatening to drown her in darkness.

She cast a stone into the glimmering waters and listened, contented to witness its splash. The water rippled out in a pretty pattern, and Marim smiled. Only sunlight danced in the water and the troublesome voice seemed to have silenced. As the disturbance died out on the water's surface, she felt another current cut through the air. Magic. She recognized the pull, though she'd never been sensitive enough to feel it before.

Without a thought to its meaning, Marim jumped to her

feet. The writing force in the air tugged at her.

"*Come*," it said in a voice that wasn't a voice. "*Follow.*"

She ran back to the house, her skirts above her knees, and her skinny legs revealed past the point of decorum. *Magic means that the town's witch is visiting.* Marim came to the courtyard. The witch's old nag was absent from the hitching post out front, but Marim didn't stop to wonder. The tug led her, and she dashed through the house. When the trail brought her to Darith's door, she braced her body against the pull. Could they have called in the old witch for him? There was nothing her meagre powers could do for their heir, and her coming would only infuriate Darith.

Marim opened the door without bothering to signal her intent. Only Darith looked at her. There was no one else there. His skin had a smoky, dark tone she'd never seen in it before, but that concern her less than the way he looked at her. He had been waiting for someone, that was clear by the way his cold eyes latched on the entrance. Marim dropped her skirts and stood in the doorway as a blush etched its way up her cheeks.

"Well?" Darith said. "Either come in or get out."

Marim stepped inside and closed the door. What was going on? She looked around the room, searching for something, not knowing what. Her hand moved up to hover in the air in front of her as if she beckoned her lost words forth. Darith turned his eyes away from her, and she followed his gaze, hoping for an answer.

Slowly, it occurred to Marim that the magic had come from Darith. Her gaze found no answers in his handsome profile.

"I called you," Darith said. "I wondered if you would come."

"But"—Marim gasped—"you're not even tired!"

Darith laughed and Marim bristled.

"Don't mock me, Darith. Everyone knows you couldn't do a spell like that without being tired. Even the old witch breaks a sweat, and she's—"

"Inept. Nothing," Darith said, interrupting. "You believe

too easily, Marim. What they taught us was a crock. It always has been. They're afraid of real magic, and so they deny it. No one with any real power dares to use it publicly. This whole planet is afraid of power. Technology. Magic. Anything that doesn't fall into the tradition we cling to so staunchly."

"But," Marim said.

"If you've nothing to say, then shut up," Darith said. Then in a softer voice, he added, "I thought you'd understand. That's why I called you."

Marim walked toward him and took his newly-dark hand. Her heart sang at the tenderness in his voice. "I don't understand, but I'd like to. How is it you can do that?"

"I was taught. I showed a spark for it early, and Father sent me to a teacher. Who knows what Father expected, a son who could light torches or make a light show on holidays? He was disappointed when my teacher told him I'd never go farther than lighting a candle. My teacher told *me* something entirely different. He explained to me that *everything* we're taught was a lie. I studied everything he sent me long after Father took me out of his school. But I was never this good. It was never as easy as it is now." Darith spoke a word composed of something other than sound and lifted his hand. A pen flew slowly across the room into his outstretched hand. "Useful for a cripple, don't you think?"

"Oh, don't say that." Marim clasped her hands in front of her face.

"What? That *is* what you were thinking, was it not? I tell you all this, and you're distressed at the word 'cripple'?" Darith gave a short, barking laugh. His skin darkened more and his eyes seemed darker. His leg seemed to move under the blanket. "I didn't know you were so stupid."

Marim paused as she oscillated between two reactions. Anger at his cruelty and curiosity at the changes in him. Anger served no purpose, so she went with curiosity. "Why did you tell me all this? Something has changed in you."

"Because we're connected. And we are connected to

something else, like a web… when I touch it, everything is different."

Marim inclined her head. "Your magic is strong?"

"Not as strong as I mean it to be."

Marim considered this and Darith lay back against the headboard, his eyes shining as brightly as the pool. The two sat together in silence. There were so many questions she wanted to ask him, but she dared not. He was upset so easily, and he was cruel when he was upset.

At last, she stood. "I'll bring you flowers from the garden. It's so dreary in here."

For once, Darith held his tongue, and Marim departed in peace. She held the joy in his eyes close to her, used it as a shield against the evil that scuttled in the shadows.

△△△

Berrick watched the spider siblings board the craft. His eyes didn't waver off them for a moment. The picture of innocence, Silvia clung to Halis' hand. Clothed in an old gown of Berrick's wife's, she looked respectable. Not a bit like a succubus. Halis wore his own clothes and managed to look a bit less like a dandy with a respectable-looking woman by his side. Just another couple boarding the sky-train. Another hopeful pair, looking for answers that Yahal had denied them on other worlds.

Silvia and Halis were among the first passengers to board. Even after they were out of sight, Berrick watched the craft. Free to go at last, he couldn't move. He examined the windows, waiting for a splash of blood or a spider to scurry across the glass.

He wouldn't feel right until they departed. The other passengers filed on, talking and milling. A family followed after Halis, and Berrick stared at the twinkling eyes of the little girl as she twisted to look back at the crowd. But Berrick's daughter wasn't on that ship; Marim was safe away from the spider and his mistress. The little girl disappeared into the bowels of the ship, tucked out of sight. Next was a group of well-dressed gentlemen, some with hats and capes. They probably had wives and children at home.

Berrick wanted desperately to turn his eyes away from the steady stream of passengers. To look away from the gleaming mouth of the ship. He shifted uncomfortably on his healing leg. The more weight he put on his cane, the less his thigh ached. Still, he couldn't make himself do it, standing here in front of all these people.

His fingers fumbled in his pocket but came up empty. He'd given up all right to hold his badge. When had he stopped believing in the law? His life since Polly's death had carved a hollow inside him and somewhere in there, his faith had slowly bled away. Polly's crime had been so small—artificial insemination. Only for Marim's sake had he resisted fighting the whole system when Petyr and Polly were taken. What little faith he had in law and order shook every time he considered what had almost happened to Marim. He'd spent his life making the world safer, given up everything, deprived his family of luxuries and comfort because he'd believed in the law. Believed in its safety.

But he wouldn't sacrifice Marim to preserve the sanctity of his badge.

Finally, the door swung shut, and the entryway sealed. Hundreds of people locked in the shining monster. Berrick glowered at the sides. How many women and children were shut away in there sipping innocently at tea?

The crowd for the next train already pushed, filling the gaps between the well-wishers waving goodbye. The bustle of people around him pressed in, forcing him to lean on his cane.

Slowly, the ship lifted up into the air, a shining shield flickering up to encase it. Safe inside, that was what that shield meant. Those people were safe inside. Then it was gone.

Would Polly ever have forgiven him for this? Even if she had looked down and judged, she had no right to feel superior. *I'd kill those people myself to protect Marim.*

Whether for ill or good, they were gone, and he could go safely home.

△△△

Inside the ship, Silvia and Halis stared out the screens. The landmass fell away until the world was only a dainty toy of green and blue. Silvia's heart pounded, one hand resting on her chest. Then the planet was just a ball of color surrounded by the deep black of space. Halis smirked, watching the planet recede.

"We're free," Silvia said, her smooth, alto voice steady. Her hand sought Halis' and missed. She tried again, and Halis aided in her clumsy attempt.

"What now?" Halis asked.

Silvia didn't answer for a moment, and then she turned her inky eyes to him. "Oh, can't you just let things be?"

Halis squeezed her hand. "There are so many worlds, Silvia. So many options."

"We're off Yahal, Halis. Right now, that is all that matters to me. Ymel can't touch us now." She turned her face back to the screen. Annoyance thinned Silvia's mouth. "We're *free*. Please, give me a moment just to enjoy that."

Halis stood silently. No matter. He couldn't kill the elation that filled her soul.

"I was four years old... a child, when they took us." Silvia smoothed her hands over the front of the demure gown. "I thought we were saved. Death was everywhere and as far as I knew, that was the last ship off Revia before..."

"More than three billion dead," Halis said. "You are too soft, Silvia. They destroyed our world and our people. Say it. Remember. We're better than they are."

"Yes, I know the story. They feared us. They tried to eradicate us. We remain. They are food." Her singsong voice repeated the mantra they often whispered in the dark nights. The hate, which was so often with her, was absent. She didn't hate them. Nothing mattered except that she was finally free.

"No, they're nothing but nourishment," said Halis. "They are unevolved animals waiting to be culled. You forget Revia. I remember every moment, every scream, and every curse. I remember our mothers' brains and skulls splattered on my face. They knew I was one of the monsters that 'needed to be eliminated' and they saved me, anyway. Gods. They thought they were gods."

"And we'd make a beautiful sideshow."

"They were right. We did, but they're not gods." Halis grinned and kissed Silvia's forehead.

"Do you hate them?"

"No. I understand. If anything, we're gods, Silvia. Free of shackles and hungry." Halis paused. "Ymel will chase us. We need to be prepared."

Silvia nibbled her lip. "Tell me about Revia. Not the mantra, the truth. What are we?"

"You know what you need. Revia's past holds nothing for us."

"If you won't tell me, then take me to Revia."

"It's gone."

"The wreckage remains. Take me. You have memories. I've nothing of my past."

"One place is as good as another." Halis shrugged.

Click. Silvia looked over her shoulder at the young couple who'd entered the compartment behind them. They clung to each other, hardly even seeing the two occupants already in the small chamber. Such innocence and simplicity. There was a strange rough beauty in their embrace, unlike the expensive trappings and companions that had filled her life thus far.

"You have eaten, Halis. Let's make friends."

"With… that?"

"Hmm, perhaps not. Something more refined. Walk with me?"

Taking Halis' arm, Silvia left the compartment to the other couple. They tainted the air with perspiration and their clothes stank of chemicals straight from the store. New outfits and new lives. How dare such inferior creatures believe in their own fresh start? This was not their moment. It was hers.

CHAPTER 13

LOVE

T he sun shone over the Cortanis estate, dispelling all traces of shadows. Berrick approached this vision slowly, afraid his presence would cause the peace to crumble. He wanted to believe in the tranquil picture before his eyes, but he could still feel the spiders' touch on him. Even though they were gone, he feared the webs they left behind.

For this reason, he approached the house of his old friend with both trepidation and joy. Marim, his precious child, was safe inside the mansion. That alone was worth the sharp ache in his leg and the knowledge that somewhere out there, he had unleashed horror on someone else.

I protected my family. Let others worry about their families. I'm done with that life. Never got me anywhere.

Encased in this world of sunshine where no shadow lurked, she was safe from monsters. He wouldn't watch her lowered into worm-ridden soil. She was all that mattered now, not law, not tradition... nothing.

Across the grass, Marim dashed. As if to drive even the murky doubts Berrick tried to hold at bay, her smile blazed. Even from a great distance, she was marked by her hair, which caught the sunshine and cradled the glow close. She ran with the freedom and carelessness of childhood, but a new grace flowed in her movements.

The vision of her in the sunlight, so like and so unalike her mother, stopped Berrick entirely. He simply watched her move. He could almost see Polly and Petyr carved in the beams encasing her.

His joy was short-lived. As soon as Marim stopped in front of him, her face glowing and coated in sunshine, he realized. Perhaps it was something to do with the flickering shadows that played over her, but on nothing else. Or her hand, which hovered unconsciously, where it never had before.

Berrick knew without a doubt and with no proof that Marim was with child.

"Hello, Father," Marim said. Her voice was liquid sunshine, and it rolled off of him.

Questions formed on his lips, alongside accusations of hate for the cursed spiders. It took all his strength not to ask her. Not to demand if the suspected pregnancy was, in fact, true. Not to ask if the father was the spider. She didn't know. Could not have been so happy if she had known. She would be ashamed as any girl of good family would be found in her condition out of wedlock. She would doubt her reception even with him. He did not want to shatter what little peace she had left. For there could be no hurried marriage, no covering this up.

The father had left the world already, and even had he been present and willingly asked for her, Berrick would not have let Marim wed Halis.

I could take care of it. The herbs aren't hard to come by. Marim never even has to know. The weight of infanticide was one she wouldn't have to bear; he would carry it for her. This he was certain was an act Polly would never forgive him for, the killing of an infant. He would take her blame. She'd made her choices in spite of him.

"Father?" Marim cocked her head. "Are you all right?"

"Yes." He reached out and brushed her cheek.

"You were gone so long."

"It's over now."

"They're free then," Marim said. "Come inside."

Berrick followed her with leaden footsteps. How much

did she remember of that night?

"Please, speak to the count. Darith"—she looked back over her shoulder at the word, her face suffused with love —"should see you as well. He'll want to know how your travels went."

"Will he know already?"

"As I do? Bits and pieces only." She turned and brushed her lips over his cheek. "It is all right, Father. Memories fade and grow soft with time. Soon they'll be far away, and we can all forget them."

Marim's hand trembled, and she clutched at her dress to hide her fear. Despite her words, she knew as well as he that not all memories faded. She clung to his arm, glancing at an empty corner, terror making her grip too tightly.

Inside the house, the halls had livened up since the last time Berrick had arrived. The servants bustled about. The only banners that hung were of the family crest. Waiting there near the door, alerted by Marim, stood the count and the countess. They had improved, just as their house had. Even so, there was a vague medicated look about their eyes.

Berrick clenched his fist. Something, anything to strike would have been appreciated.

Marim set her soft hand over his fist. Would the spider baby hold on even if he offered a remedy? Would it cling like a parasite to her insides?

He barely heard the halfhearted greetings of his old friends. He certainly did not hear his own answers until they said something that mattered.

"Did you find your revenge?" the count said.

"Darith's revenge," the countess said. Her lips were a hard line even as she spoke. "Our revenge."

"Father sent the culprits far away," said Marim. "We need never worry about them."

How strange that somewhere during this whole process Marim had learned to dissemble. Her half-lie was meant to placate and protect. Only Berrick didn't want her fragile protection. He wanted to suffer because he had failed her. He had failed them all.

"They live," he said.

The countess glared. Without a further word, she ascended the stairs. She turned to the left. Darith's new quarters were to the right. Marim's shoulders stiffened and Berrick wondered if she noted the direction as well. The countess' anger was over a son she no longer had, not for a son harmed.

"Darith will want to know," the count said. There was no anger in him, at least not for his friend. Count Cortanis had never wanted revenge. He wanted to forget.

The count motioned with his hand. Marim and Berrick ascended the stairs alone.

"The countess will warm to Darith soon," Marim said. "It's hard for him being alone. They'll see that soon."

The countess warm? Berrick doubted that. He recalled the first time he'd met the woman. He'd invited the couple over to Polly's and his home just outside the college grounds. They'd shown, the count as jovial as ever, and settled right into a conversation with Polly about which of the off-Yahal conveniences they would miss when they returned home. The countess, however, had sat stiffly in her chair. She was a lovely woman, but the air had seemed chillier near her and her voice had been a cold snap.

Still, it was she who had found a way for Polly and Berrick to return to Yahal. He'd despaired of it when job offers had come in. Nothing had been available on Yahal. But with the pull of a few strings, the countess had made room for her husband's college friend. And he and Polly had happily said goodbye to the off-world conveniences.

It wasn't until later that Polly began to resent the restrictions.

Berrick clenched his jaw as well as his fist. These were things Marim should never need to know. How could any mother care more for a line of descent than her child? Only, had he been any better? He'd run off for revenge rather than staying with Marim. It hurt to see your child in pain. He understood better than he'd like why Darith's parents wouldn't visit their son, and Berrick doubted if they would change.

Marim opened Darith's door and slid inside. Berrick followed with a sinking heart. He didn't want to meet with the sullen teen. Another pair of eyes that knew what they should not was hardly what his guilty conscience desired.

Darith sat up in his bed. Somehow despite being bedbound, he was the same prideful, angry youth he'd always been. Where Berrick expected wreckage, he saw strength. Good. Here, at least, was something that had survived the spiders.

"Marim, will you be good enough to leave your father to me?" Darith asked.

Berrick almost smiled, a warmth pervading the concrete sinking inside him since seeing Marim. In all the years of watching Darith grow, Berrick had never heard Darith speak so softly or respectfully to a woman. He had finally found something he cared about as much as himself. Berrick was happy for them for a moment. Then he remembered what their lives were to be. Darith was a cripple and would never properly take a wife. Marim was cursed by the spiders' touch, and unless Berrick could find the strength to do a dreadful, unforgivable thing, she would never be anyone's wife.

His unformed smile left his lips by the time Marim left the room. The two men regarded each other across the lavishly furnished room. Slightly wilted flowers swayed in the breeze from the open window and the tissuey drapes billowed, making soft, flapping sounds. Berrick did not know how to judge the man-child in this nest. Whatever Darith saw, he must have found satisfactory because he nodded and then said the last thing Berrick had expected.

"Don't worry about her. I'll take care of her."

"Marim."

"Who else? We are, neither of us, fools, so let's not play games."

"How can you take care of Marim?"

The words were cruel, but Darith did not flinch. Instead, he smiled, the smile one would award a slow child.

"You know that already."

And Berrick did know. Darith saw the same thing growing inside Marim that Berrick did. In a way, Berrick had been blind too. The solution to both Darith's and Marim's problems rested with each other. All he needed to do was guard them and see them safely through it.

"Yes. You have my blessing."

Not exactly the way a father dreams of betrothing his daughter, but better than the alternatives.

△△△

The direct sunlight, even coupled with a chill wind, lifted Darith's spirits. Other than the whistling air and Gretta's crunching footfall behind his wheelchair on the path, nothing disturbed his thoughts. This was the first time he'd dared to leave his room and the fact that the world remained as he'd known it reassured him.

Gretta swept up beside him, her parasol shading both of them as she twirled it.

Darith glanced back at the house. What was Berrick saying to Marim? How was she taking it? Doubts clouded his mind. Was he doing the right thing? Maybe even pregnant, she could find a better husband than a cripple... and he might have convinced himself if he hadn't seen how she glanced at the shadows and the tendrils of black that sometimes flooded her eyes.

Will I even get to see her before Berrick takes her home?

How will I sleep with her gone?

The garden had thinned with autumn, but the line of shrubs they passed was still plush and green. Gretta swung her curls over one shoulder and ran her free hand over the foliage.

"Didn't expect to hear from you," Gretta said.

The cover of green grew taller, obscuring the mansion so that Darith could almost believe himself in private with her.

"I've had time to think and my situation has altered." He halted next to a garden bench and waited for Gretta to sit.

"Your situation seems the same to me." She closed her parasol and leaned it against the bench before selecting a spot on the bench to sink onto. "You mean ye changed yer mind about it."

"No." Darith glared at her.

Gretta pursed her lips and motioned for him to continue.

"I mean it has changed. Does your offer to help me stand? My request is not a small one."

CHAPTER 14

AFTERMATH

"Course my offer stands, Darith," Gretta said. Her back stiffened where it pressed into the garden bench. "I want to help ye where I can. Else why'd I have come? Get on with it. Some of us have to work fer a living. I should be back at the shop with Papa."

"I've agreed to wed Marim."

Gretta arched a brow and fingered the end of her parasol. "And she consented?"

"Her father did."

"Are ye really going to tell me ye didn't ask her yourself?"

"Her father will broach the subject with her, as custom dictates." Could Gretta never stay on topic? The woman was a ball of emotions. This was not the point at all. Darith opened his mouth to tell her so.

Gretta spoke up first. "Stupid noble tradition. Ask her—"

"I didn't ask you here to argue the point. In two months, we will be wed and by then her pregnancy will show."

"Oh." Gretta clapped her hands over her mouth. "The poor thing. I didn't know…" Then Gretta's eyes got colder, and her lips tightened. Her gaze bore into him.

"I didn't impregnate her, Gretta." Darith rubbed at his temples. "But you're the only one who needs to know that."

"Why would ye tell me? Certainly not to spare my feelings."

"Because I need you to take care of her. The baby... well, it's affecting her mind. She talks to creatures that aren't there, and at night, nightmares hound her. She's leaving here tonight. Her father will never let me stay with her before the wedding, but she needs someone to care for her, to sleep at her side, and hold her when the demons inside her won't rest. The endpoint is, she'll be in no shape to be countess unless she gets better. I need someone to oversee my household. She doesn't have the strength. You do."

"What are ye saying?"

"Physically, I'm limited, and I need someone to do what I can't. The first of those things is to look after Marim until she has the baby—maybe even longer. The second is..." Darith drew out an envelope and extended his arm to her. "Do you know what a Timmy is?"

Gretta's nose scrunched, demonstrating she did and though her hand lifted, she didn't take the envelope. She eyed it, suspicious of both the paper and him.

"Every month, I need this amount to go to Timmy."

Gretta leaned away from him, condemnation in her brown eyes.

"No," Darith said. "Don't worry. I never need to visit the boy. I've never used a Timmy's services, but events in my life have led to me feeling indebted. I need to help him. An account in your name is established already. It will provide money for you and him on a monthly basis—for you, an equivalent amount as would be provided to keep a mistress. There's also a hunting cabin just outside of town that I will sign over to you. This should allow you to have independence."

"Independence as long as I watch yer household matters."

"This is a trust set up for life. Just take care of Marim as long as she needs it. See that the current Timmy has a shot at a future outside of The Brothels, and your life is your own. You could choose a pauper to wed if you wished."

"That's a lot just fer watching a girl and dropping an envelope."

"And for your silence. You'll see things with Marim that cannot be explained."

"I'll do it fer you, though I don't understand. You've gotta do something fer me."

"The money is sufficient."

"I can get up and walk away." Gretta grinned.

"Fine." Darith's finger's pressed into his legs. No sensation traveled into the dead appendages. But at night when he touched the web inside, he could feel again.

"Ask that poor girl to marry you. Do it yourself. Sounds like she's getting a raw deal from life. You're good at doing the right thing, but not so good at doing the kind thing."

Darith nodded and dropped the envelope in her lap. She was right. He had no expertise in keeping a woman happy.

Gretta folded the paper and tucked it in the pocket of her full skirt. She then smoothed out the wrinkles and stood, retrieving her parasol.

"I suppose," she said, "I ought to learn where to find Timmy."

"There is a map in the envelope. You have no need to search the net."

"Good." Gretta nodded and then took a step away, pausing once more to speak. "Looks like I'm yer mistress, after all, Darith Cortanis. Next, ye'll be having me run yer estate."

"Father's still alive." *Regrettably.*

She chuckled, and with that, she bustled off down the dirt path.

Darith remained by the bench as long as he could bear being out under the cold sky. The spider's call inside him was quieter in the sun and the truth was he missed its song. When his fingers numbed from the cold he wheeled around and headed to the garden entrance of his room.

Lost in thoughts of the future, he didn't notice Marim until he was reaching for the handle of the sliding glass door to his room. She sat on the edge of his bed, her fingers picking one petal at a time from daisies in a vase.

Darith heaved a sigh and entered, leaving the door ajar behind him. The wind whistled its cursed secrets through the gap.

"Marim," Darith said. How did you ask a woman to marry you? She had no real choice in the matter, and they both knew it.

"Father says…" Her huge eyes lifted to him. How sweet she looked, with freckles fanning out over her nose. "He says I'm pregnant. That he knows I am. I think he's right. I feel like I knew, deep down."

"You are. I can see it inside you… the darkness curves into you. There is no doubt, not with this web that connects us to them." Darith crossed the room and took her small hands. "I want to marry you, Marim—to give you some of the life you deserve."

"Father said you would, but why would you? I ruined myself, Darith. I let Halis do things… I let him—"

"That doesn't matter. Not to me. Many women are not virgins. No matter what the old biddies say. You are no less valuable now than you were before."

"This"—Marim sobbed into her hands—"isn't what I wanted—for you to take me because you had no other choice. You feel you must protect me."

"I *do* have a choice. Stop crying. You're acting like a child. I'm giving nothing up. If anything, you are. Perhaps you could not find a noble husband, but I can be no real husband to any girl. You realize I'll be like this forever." He waved to his legs.

"I don't care!" She flared, her shoulders straightening and fire returning to her gaze.

"You should." *She should be some man's wife. A real man. A man who could take care of her.* "I've asked an old school friend of mine to go with you back to your father's house. You'll need her. Don't argue."

"Why? I have servants."

"Your nightmares are getting worse, and the web tugs at you. She's trustworthy. I can't protect you from here."

Marim leaned closer to him, a ghost of a smile on her lips.

126

"I love you, Darith."

"I know. Now go. Your father will be looking for you."

$$\triangle\triangle\triangle$$

Berrick took in a deep breath of the city air before stepping into the single modern building in the entire downtown area. His office, due to the regularity of visiting dignitaries and communication from other worlds, was a fantastic creation of metal, glass, and circuitry running over the walls where in other offices artwork might hang.

The marble-floored lobby narrowed at the far end, making it look deceptively large—an intentional ploy of the architects. Most of the halls that led off of the lobby led to offices of bureaucrats and the crystal-doored elevators led to the meeting rooms and farther up to the governmental lodging. But at the far end sat Sue-Ellen's desk and behind it, Berrick's office.

Berrick started down the corridor, avoiding eye contact with the detectives and officials who littered the chairs like landmines waiting to destroy what remained of his composure.

I can't continue to do this. Marim is out of danger. I need to know what it was I unleashed on the universe.

So far Sue-Ellen had been unable to obtain any information on Silvia and Halis. It was as if they didn't exist. But everyone had a record, somewhere, somehow.

Few glanced up at him as he stalked by, most absorbed in their own worlds, but Steven, an older fellow who worked directly under Berrick, stood and crossed to meet his boss.

"How was the sabbatical?" Steven asked. He shoved his glasses up higher on his nose. Berrick doubted he needed the corrective lenses—they were an affectation. He'd lived on other worlds. He would have gotten any issue with his eyes fixed.

"I'd prefer not to discuss it." Berrick gazed at the glass door of his office. The longer he stood, the more likely his contemporaries in the government would spy him. He needed time before meeting with them.

"Ah. I suppose that's why you're back so soon." Steven nodded repeatedly and, noting Berrick's gaze, he shot out a quick, "So sorry. You must be in a hurry to get back to work."

"Yes. If you'll excuse me." Berrick didn't wait a moment longer and hurried toward Sue-Ellen. He had no intention of cutting his sabbatical short, but even on extended leave, he had enough clearance to do what he needed to do. Berrick intended to take the entire year available to him if that was what it took.

At his approach, Sue-Ellen stood and unlocked the door to his office, went inside, and turned on the light. Berrick entered behind her and closed the door. Sue-Ellen set the privacy screens on the glass office, dimming the glass so from the outside it would look like a marble wall.

"Thanks, Sue. Talking isn't something I want to do today. Any news on Silvia and Halis?"

"No, sir. Still nothing. We've been asked to stop looking. The Brothel discovered our inquiries and while denying that such people existed, it also requested we desist."

"Blasted corporations. With their backing of High Councilor Trilda, they get away with murder and worse... This whole government is beyond redemption."

"Might do to keep that opinion between us." Sue-Ellen tugged at the high white collar of her blouse.

"I will." Berrick went to his desk and sat down, eyeing the pile of paperwork with disdain.

"There *is* something else, sir." Sue Ellen stood stiff and her fingers continued to fidget.

She's nervous. He watched her well-manicured hands fondle the lace edges. *She's incredibly nervous.*

"Go ahead, Sue."

"A missive came in from *The Council of Five's* messengers." She stressed that name, not the Galactic Council but specifically the highest branch of that council. "They're interested in your daughter's case and are offering to send officers to continue the investigation."

Berrick dug his fingers into his thighs. The High Council? No. They wouldn't be coming around—over his dead body.

"It seems something in Darith's witness statement interested them."

"The ravings of a teen?" *What did Darith say? Why would The Council care? It doesn't matter. No way are they coming out here and taking up that investigation. It will take them no time at all to find my involvement… and to ruin any chance I have at getting back at Silvia and Halis.*

"As far as I can tell, it was the mention of an eight-legged monster."

"Message them back. Let them know it was just a boy's ravings. Tell them we found a syringe and after testing the contents we found a hallucinogenic—"

"Lie?" Sue-Ellen raised both eyebrows. "Lie to a High Councilor?"

"Yes." A High Councilor, not The Council of Five. Interesting, so only one of them was involving themselves. "This is my family, Sue. Do you remember when they sent their agents for Polly's death? I won't let them do that again—erase the whole thing, not with Marim in the middle."

"Berrick, we can't lie to a High Councilor."

"So don't. But be convincing—there was no fucking spider. Just a young boy who'd been drinking. That's true. We can get Darith under oath if need be. Which councilor?"

"Councilor Trilda."

Berrick sighed. Too bad. Trilda was a cold bitch; no use appealing to the family element with her.

Sue-Ellen shuffled her feet and Berrick waited for her to finish her internal debate.

"We found a corpse floating downriver from The Brothel. No name, no family. According to the papers, he fits the description for the male assailant. Though from the picture I don't see the link. Still it might help if we had a dead culprit to show the councilor… but then you'll need to close the case. Am I right in assuming you intend to handle this off the books?"

Berrick nodded.

"Well, we have someone who fits the bill. Someone we can send to Councilor Trilda if need be."

"Do it."

"I still don't like this. I think you need more time away. You aren't ready to be back here."

Berrick pulled a stack of paperwork to him. "Ready has nothing to do with it. Just get The Council of Five away from my daughter's case."

Sue-Ellen nodded and silently exited the office. Berrick slumped against his desk, burying his head in his hands.

CHAPTER 15

WEDDINGS & HOUSES

T he church was a solid structure—squat and remote. On all sides spread rocky fields with grass and flowers sprouting from the cracks. Beyond the rocks, the horizon sported trees and mountains. A distant city rippled in the waves of heat. Dual roads, one for cars and one for carriages, spread out both North and South from the church. Darith stood outside, watching the grass ripple.

The new suit clung hot and heavy to his shoulders. Darith struggled to recall the last time he'd ventured to this place.

Belief in the gods was almost nonexistent, so the church only opened for weddings and funerals. Several weddings had passed since Petyr's funeral, but those memories were hazy and distant, irrelevant to his life. Only the funerals stood out, and as he watched the grass dance, he pictured the ashes being scattered, gray flecks coating the yellow flowers.

"I didn't understand back then what the crown of flowers you helped me make really meant," Marim said. Her hand draped over his shoulder. "Those flowers grow from the dead. I imagine now they watch with the eyes of those passed."

"Go inside. You need to be getting ready," Darith said, moving his eyes to her. The intricate white lace of her wedding gown rippled in time with the flowers. She touched him with one hand and the slight protrusion of her belly with the other. He wanted to hold her, kiss those soft cherub lips. "Mother must be livid at your hair being down."

"Please, Darith, don't tell me to put it up. My mother wore hers down with a chain of pearls. I want a flower chain. I need it. My heart says that is the only way to have Petyr and Mom with me."

His throat pinched closed, and he took a deep breath to clear it.

"We should leave this planet, Marim. Leave the past." Darith placed his hand over hers on her belly. The child inside, as if sensing him, moved, the vibrations traveling through her fingers to his palm.

"I'm afraid that's impossible," Marim said. "In the day-light, I can pretend, but I feel it. The day this child comes, the cocoon of their web will be complete. I don't know if I'll be able to find the light again. It's too late to escape."

"All those years ago, I swore to protect you. Here, in this field, I gave my word. I may not be much in the way of a gentle-man, but I keep my word. Your father allowed himself, then and now, to be hindered by the law. I have no boundaries, Marim. I won't let them win."

"Mom was pregnant when she died. Odd thing was, doc-tors said she was infertile. They didn't know how I'd even been conceived. Mom and Dad never talked about it, but she changed after Petyr's birth. She was afraid. I saw it. She'd welcomed the bad in when she took those drugs, and once you do that, it's only a matter of time."

"That's nonsense."

"No. I let Halis' poison in, and the rest must run its course."

Darith forced his eyes from her. He wanted to hold her until her voice lost the wandering listless quality. That the world would harm her, his one pure thing, was like a rat gnawing at his breast. For now, all he could do to shield her was wed her, but it wouldn't always be so.

He focused the drive inside him, dwelling on her smile, and stretched his hand in front of him. Slowly the skin darkened as he reached to the web, loosening the thing that sat so firmly against his spine. One at a time, the yellow flowers snapped free and bound themselves into a triple-rowed crown above his knees.

"Darith," Marim breathed.

When he looked up a soft smile changed her expression to one fit for an angel and tears shone in her eyes, one racing down her cheek to her chin.

"If I could stay with you, I would," she said.

"I wish I could be a real husband to you. I try to believe as my parents do, despite all logic, that the child is mine. That we will have a life. But if all I can give you is a few months, I'll give you the universe for a few months." *And I'll get you back. If I must destroy this world and all on it, I'll get you back. And Gods, I'll find a way to harness this power and be whole.*

"I trust you." She took the completed crown and settled the flowers onto her head. Her fingertips brushed over the petals.

Making the flower chain had left a tingle in his fingers, as if the magic remaining awaited expression. He set his hand on her stomach and freed the residue. Inside Marim, the fetus' joy, instinctual and fresh, traveled to him.

She is mine.

"Marim!" The sharp cry came from the church. Darith didn't have to turn to know his mother strode out toward them. "What are you doing, child? You must get inside. Your father is waiting for you."

"Of course, countess," Marim said. Before departing, she leaned down and kissed Darith. Compared to the kisses of village girls, the touch was chaste. Yet the soft brush, the slight parting, of her lips warmed and chilled him at once. She was present over every inch of him for the moment the kiss lasted. His breath hitched as she pulled back a mere few inches.

"Nothing could ever make you less to me. Whatever you are, that is all I shall ever want in a husband. And if chance gives us more one day, it will not make these moments less."

Darith wanted her lips back, not the sweet meaningless words. He almost told her how foolish she sounded. A marriage that did not include coupling was not a marriage that could satisfy anyone. But on this one day, he would give her the gift of delusion and perhaps one other thing.

"I"—the words stuck, his nature fighting the utterance—"love you."

Her brilliant smile was worth the effort.

△△△

Berrick paced in the small room, his badge burning against his leg. When Marim dashed in, sunshine clothed her, and his heart seized. For an instant, she seemed Polly's ghost. He flinched as she moved, becoming Marim again.

She surged, a force of nature, to his side.

"Marim, there're things a father says on his daughter's wedding day."

"Don't, Father, please," Marim said. She kissed his cheek.

"Do you have questions?"

"Only one, but you won't like it. I don't need to ask, but…" She paused and clutched his hands. "I'm afraid of so many things, Father, but there is one wound that festers. One that will bleed at an answer, perhaps, but an answer is what I need, lest doubt be an infection in my soul."

"Ask," he said. *This will be about her mother. How will I answer? How can I?*

"Could you have saved her? I recall them coming around, the planet's elite, the day she went missing. You screamed at them and I ran and hid. But I never knew… was she already dead and your anger aimed at their betrayal and your own acceptance? Or was she alive and… you couldn't or wouldn't sacrifice what was needed to save her? Please, please. I know what the question means."

Marim's eyes burned and Berrick closed his own to block the stare. *Could I have saved her? Yes, but not in the way she means. I could have fled Yahal years earlier… The moment I knew she was pregnant with Petyr and that she must have used illegal means.*

"Father? Please. No answer could make me hate you. Nothing can change my love."

"She was already gone when they came. The only one I could save that day was you and that was with a promise that I would not investigate, not call The Galactic Council's attention."

Marim's arms wrapped around him and her head snuggled against his chest. A flash of Polly's gray face flashed through his mind. Her death never avenged, her husband working for those who'd taken her. He shoved her back and turned away.

"I failed her, Marim. Darith is a good man. He'll take care of you."

"You aren't handing me over, Father. I'm still yours. I always will be. Love doesn't need limits. Wherever Mother is, she'd forgive you. She loves you."

Berrick said nothing as her footsteps drifted away. After safely tucking away his memories, burying them beneath mental walls built and rebuilt over the years, he walked to the door of the sanctuary. He paused there, resting his forehead against the doors.

"How lucky they are," murmured a woman from inside. Berrick couldn't see who.

"Indeed, to have a youthful indiscretion give his house an heir. To think the night before his accident!"

Berrick huffed. He hadn't started that rumor and though it served Marim's interest, he didn't like it. Speaking out would shatter her peace, so he held his.

"And her… What a match!"

"Too bad he—"

Berrick pushed past the door, cutting off whatever comment came next. These nobles grated on him now, leaving him raw. Work friends were scattered in the pews, but they were almost as bad. Most didn't know the secrets of his wife's death and those who did never spoke of it. But he saw his failure in them.

Polly had asked to leave Yahal once when she'd learned she couldn't conceive a second child. She'd begged him, showing him leaflets of procedures done on other worlds. She'd even found job listings on those planets. But Yahal had been safe, had shared his values. They'd never find an equal station on another world, and he'd doubted she really wanted to start scrimping and saving. No, it had seemed wrong to leave for access to drugs they'd agreed together were immoral. He'd been a fool to think she'd accepted his decision. Blind and stubborn, he'd even excused Petyr's inexplicable birth.

He walked directly to the front, not speaking to anyone or making eye contact. After settling in the front pew, he waited. It wouldn't be long. Enduring the chatter around him was torment. A few minutes later, Darith entered with the priest at the front of the room and the groom positioned himself on the platform. The priest spoke opening words Berrick didn't hear and then the door at the back opened and Marim entered.

Auburn hair burned like a fire of blood against Marim's pale cheek and her white gown. Her face, which had never been exceptionally beautiful, had altered in the past three months. She was as lovely as an angel now. That she was carrying a child was hidden from the naked eye in the loose, white dress she wore.

Still, everyone knew she was pregnant.

Berrick watched her with the same sinking feeling that accompanied everything. If he could have for even an instant shaken the doomed feeling in the pit of his stomach, he would have been happy for her. He should have been happy.

Why do I feel nothing but hopelessness as my daughter walks down the aisle? He watched Marim. The color of fresh blood crowned her hair as it toppled over her shoulders adorned with little white flowers. Her eyes had faded to the night.

Marim reached the flower-strewn arbor and set her hand on Darith's shoulder. They should have seemed ridiculous, or at least pitiful. She was so young, though Polly had not been much older, still his views had changed since then. And Darith could not even stand for their nuptials. They looked dignified. Pride covered them. Pride in each other and pride in themselves. She did not kneel to come even with him. He did not crane up at her or look overly doleful. There was no performance for watching eyes, just a doting smile passed from one to the other.

Berrick stared at her stomach and wished the laws on abortion were not so stern. Had the punishment not condemned Marim even without her having knowledge of the act, he would have destroyed the thing inside her. He'd considered it still. The proper herbs would be in lockup somewhere and it would be a matter of minutes for him to access them. Perhaps he should have.

The thing inside her was not a baby. It was a spider. He would kill it when it emerged, when it crawled from her womb. Then its death would only be on his head. Marim would never need to suffer again. He could give her back her life, her freedom, and this man she loved, who loved her in return.

She would feel Berrick's absence. She loved him too. He was not oblivious to her devotion. Adoration for a father was a loss that could be overcome. A father comes second to a lover.

Berrick had long ago condemned himself to this. He had grown accustomed to drawing ever closer to his incarceration. What he would never become accustomed to was how much Darith and Marim looked like Halis and Silvia.

Would Darith's paralysis someday be no more than a slight shuffle in his step? Perhaps his skin would darken like a shadow had passed over it. Then from a yard or two away he would be almost Darith's double. Day by day, Marim became more like Silvia. Her hair darkened, along with her eyes. Even her body bloomed to look more like Silvia's. *Is her chin changing?* He knew her steps had become more graceful.

She should be growing to resemble her mother. If I had cut the child from her, would she have grown as she was meant to? Would it have made a difference? He never thought of anything else.

Marim lifted the cup of wine to her lips and then passed it down to Darith. He drank. Then he lifted her hand and touched his mouth to her pale skin. She gazed down at him with a soft smile suffusing her eyes. Had he seen that smile on Silvia's face when she'd looked down at Halis? No, surely, Marim's smile was still her own.

Then Marim's head turned slightly, and her dark eyes met Berrick's. The soft smile continued. It stung his heart. Her love took his breath away like a painful blow to the gut. She was in there, his little girl, behind the eyes. She was in there, and he plotted to hurt her.

As she turned back, he saw her hand lift to rest on her protruding stomach. Not for the first time, Berrick wondered if she knew what he planned. *Perhaps she forgives me?* The hope was more painful than despair.

Darith kissed her hand before they turned and traveled down the aisle together. She shone, as a bride ought to.

CHAPTER 16

WHAT WALKS THE NIGHT

W ith hair made pitch-black by the night, Silvia stood, her face turned to a house above them on a rise. Its wide windows faced out to the sea, on the edge of which Silvia stood with Halis. Her black hair was pulled back in a plain braid. Her dress too was plain. She shone from amid the night's shadows like a star.

Halis did not. His dark skin faded with the dusk and left him nearly invisible in the night. Where she shone, he moved like the shadows children see lurking at their bedsides. He was the boogeyman. If the face he wore was wonderful, it was clearly only a guise for evil. He stood behind her, the demon at her back.

"I want that one," Silvia said, lifting one moon-white hand to point at the house. The house itself was not the largest on the cliff overhanging the moon's cratered surface. Its gardens were its real beauty. They spread out on every side, even up to the drop-off to the moon's barren surface outside the protective air-shell of the colony. They were a rich man's gardens and a rich man's house.

The grounds appealed to her. She could relax and listen to the moon-sand pounding against the air shield amid the moonlight and watch dewdrops glisten on spiderwebs spun over unending months across branches and paths. She could bathe naked under the stars in the splashing fountain. Most importantly, the life growing inside her would be able to learn magic, as she had from her own mother, by bending nature to its will.

Halis smiled. His teeth glowed as Silvia did. "The house shall be yours, my queen."

Silvia touched her stomach. It was not as flat as it had once been but it was just as hard. "It'll be ours."

She'd spoken to herself, as Halis was already climbing up the cliff. His human form discarded easily. Now a different form of blackness slunk among the true shadows. Silvia smiled brightly and tilted her head up to stare at the house she had chosen. The current owner was the only impediment. Soon he would not be.

Two birds with one stone, as the humans said. Halis would feed, and the house would be for sale.

Wealth was a simple matter. For years, Silvia had ferreted money aside. If Yahal had not been so backward, had used electronic currency, it would not have been possible. But paper was easy to hide to store and to exchange.

What she hadn't managed to save, well, that was easy enough. Silvia closed her eyes and thought of the first ship they'd boarded after their vacation to see the remains of Revia drifting in space. A small, sleek black vessel captained by a strange furry fellow. They used pods to put passengers in stasis, so the speed of the flight did not cause them illness. No one had woken up, and when the ship had come to harbor, the officials had labeled the stasis pods as malfunctioning. Inside each was a corpse. But oddly, money had been withdrawn by each deceased passenger after the flight.

Halis said the furry captain tasted foul.

Silvia sank into the cover of trees that lined the drive up to the mansions on the hill. Once there, she wove strands of the surrounding blackness. Energy crackled around her, and her human form faded. Using all eight legs, she pulled herself into a tree and waited for Halis' return.

△△△

Darith reached out across the bed, where Marim tossed and whimpered. The two months they'd spend apart before the wedding had altered her—and not for the better. These nightmares that hounded her gave neither of them peace. As his hand fell on her shoulder to wake her from the visions that haunted her, she turned to him.

Her large eyes swirled with inky black. Like Silvia's eyes. A shiver ran down him.

"Gods, Marim," he said.

He let go of her shoulder. How could he wake her from this?

Why is it doing this to her? The night filled his blood and like a web. Energy pulsed through him—in the distance Silvia lurked. The eyes within the web were Silvia's and even now the shadows danced with her form. The voice in the web was not Silvia's, but a hiss of thousands of voices.

In the night, he saw the web as it linked to him. But Marim was not attached as he was. She was trapped, stuck to the strands.

Darith set his hand on the still slight swell of her stomach.

Marim gave a screech and her hands flew up to her face, her nails scoring her pale flesh.

Darith grabbed at her thrashing hands and pulled her close against him.

"*Give her back,*" he said into the web. "*You cannot have her.*"

The voices hissed their wordless hunger.

"Come back to me, Marim. Come back."

"The eyes!" she screamed, struggling against him. "They watch me."

"I'm here. Come back to me." The words were a mantra. Gretta said they worked better than anything else, she'd found. Darith faced Marim, still leaning his weight on her and holding down her writhing arms.

Black eyes stared back at him.

I can't help her. She can't hear me.

But the strands inside him tugged with her struggles. Disturbingly thrilling jolts of her fear coursed through him, but something else too. In the darkness, he tasted Marim's adrenaline, her tears like an aphrodisiac.

That's not me. Those are not my emotions, not my desires. Yet the hunger flowed in him. A metallic tang hung in the air and it jolted through him.

"Marim. Marim, I'm here," he said.

As if responding to his wants, a strand of darkness deepened, widening like a road. He threw himself forward into the dark, tasting her, seeing her. He played the strand and moved closer to Marim. He found the baby there with her, half-formed, just a mess of legs and eyes.

He kneeled by them in this place that wasn't a place.

"*You're hurting her. Let her go.*" Darith reached into the web and stroked the infant's head. Then with a sweep, he tore the strands that held Marim.

"Marim." He fell from the web back onto his bed, back into his body. For the moment, his legs responded, pulling up so he crouched over her. "It's me. Come back to me."

Beneath him, Marim's slight form relaxed, and she lifted her face. The self-inflicted scratches on her face were beaded with blood, as previous lines marked her neck and arms. But the eyes that stared out at him were no longer black. Nor were they Marim's eyes.

Her eyes glowed a bright yellow and the tears that flowed from them were starlight, filling the dark. For the first time since the party, Darith lost the pull of the web. Feeling in his legs departed. Everything was gone but Marim and those luminescent eyes.

"Darith, the dark tugs me." Marim touched her stomach. "She doesn't know any better. It isn't her fault, Darith."

"I won't let any harm come to your child. You must rest."

"You can't save me. I—"

"Hush." Darith lay back on his pillow, tugging her against him. *I can't remain like this. I can't help her—useless.* A man with a wife he couldn't touch, couldn't protect. *I'll find a way.*

PART TWO

Spider's Heart

CHAPTER 1

SIX MONTHS LATER

T he Agency, as it was called, being too powerful to need any other moniker, was stationed primarily on an exquisite spacecraft. Anchored in the galaxy, it orbited a moon and waited, shields always up. Invisible to any who entered the quadrant.

Allison wondered as she stared at words in a book how long the blue metal edifice had served her as home. Hundreds of years? Thousands? Like most of The Agency's operatives, she'd spent a great deal of time in stasis. *To avoid time-madness as the owners claimed? Or do they just not want us to form bonds with each other?*

It was a useless train of thought. She belonged as completely to The Agency as any slave. She'd signed over her life to be their agent and in return, they'd given her a surgery that ensured she would never age. Her body and mind would never degrade.

The cost of such a thing was staggering. When she'd been new to The Agency, she could not have repaid the debt. Now, perhaps she could, but where in the seventeen worlds could she go? Everyone she'd known and loved was either dead or also a member of The Agency. And as long as she performed well and obeyed their rules, she could have anything she wanted.

There was no point at all in thinking about freedom.

But she did.

Lifting her eyes from the unread text on the screen, she gazed at her chamber. Scarlet, crimson, and burgundy covered everything from walls to floor. From the ceiling hung a red crystal chandelier that sent claret beams darting about. Only Allison was a splash of white against the fiery madness.

Uncurling her long limbs, pale as cream, she pressed one red-tipped toenail to the floor. As if called by her disquiet, the door opened and Mr. Red entered.

Mr. Red was a handsome man. He appeared to be in his late thirties, though since he'd been with The Agency longer than she, he must have seen countless years. Only in his amber eyes did his true age make any appearance; there was no youth there. He was hard and emotionless. His blond hair slicked back away his face and lent his aquiline features a stern, meticulous cast.

The one asset the company valued above its agents. Their trainer. And the one reason she couldn't forget the call of freedom. To be able to speak to him, to put into words the aching longing inside her when she saw his hand resting on a table and was unable to reach out.

"Red," she said. Her voice was soft and breathy like the fluttering of a butterfly's wing. Could she use an utterance against him as she did in the field and bend him to her will? No. That was why he was their trainer—because the agents couldn't manipulate him with beauty and wiles. Still, at some moments, she was tempted to try. That was strictly forbidden.

Instead, she stood and extended her arms to him.

"Agent," Mr. Red walked over to her and took her small hands. Mr. Red looked at her fingers curled over his. "I heard the other owners revoked the decision to put you back in stasis. No word yet on an assignment. Did you request this?"

Allison moved a step closer to him. She did not lower her pale lilac eyes but stared fearlessly into his face. "I appreciate you thinking of me, Red."

He jerked his eyes away from hers and looked around the room. A sneer came to his lips. "What have you done to your chamber?"

"Don't laugh at me." She took her hands from his and turned her back to him. Her silk dress fell against her tiny waist and the slight swell of her hips. The flawless white skin of her back burned brightly against the red of her gown. It was her job to be constantly aware of these things, of her own beauty.

"What is this, Allison? Your way of sleeping with me?" A trace of mockery threaded his tone. From the corner of her eye, she caught his glance to her red bed as she moved away from him. She flinched at his voice.

Was his detachment an act, like the skills he teaches us?

"Don't be cruel." She glanced over her shoulder at him and he lowered his eyes away from her.

"The others wouldn't approve."

His voice had softened. If he hadn't been so well-trained, she might even have heard fear in it. At least she supposed so.

"No," Allison said.

There were words she couldn't say, sighs she couldn't sigh. Restrictions would be tighter for him. If he ever felt anything behind those robotic eyes, he never showed any sign. One of The Agency's few rules for its agents was that the operatives never engage socially with other staff members. Agents were too dangerous and any attempt to fraternize was taken as a betrayal of the company, punishable by death.

He walked over to the bed and touched the velvet hangings. Did she imagine his eyes stayed longer than they ought? "You looked prettier amid all the blue."

"I didn't request a stay. What about the new girl, Glory?" Allison went back to her chair and sat down.

"Yes, I recommended Glory to ease her into the life."

"Perhaps they decided I would be better." Allison shrugged. "I'm the best, Red. The best you've got."

"Don't get cocky."

"Did you come here to lecture me?"

"No. Get rid of this display. You look like a petulant child."

Mr. Red had her best interests at heart. He always did.

There was a constant tug-of-war between him and the other board members, and if she watched closely enough, she could sometimes catch the steps. What she gathered was that he genuinely cared about all of the agents under his care. He was their advocate.

"It's a color, not a display," she said.

"You think you and I are the only ones capable of reading between these not-so-subtle lines? Get rid of your little outburst. Immediately."

"As you say." Allison pursed her lips, not bothering to hide her discontent.

"Allison." Mr. Red looked at her, and for all the power in the universe, she wished she could read his eyes.

"I'll do as you say."

"Thank you."

The door let out a little puff of air as it closed and re-sealed.

CHAPTER 2
BIRTH & DEATH

T he world split in two. In the back of her mind, Marim knew that giving birth was not supposed to feel like this. There were supposed to be boundaries to the pain. Agony as brilliant as a lightning strike drove through her and when it receded its absence left only a blind black. Her mind tore in two. One half knew that she was giving her child to the world. The other half charred amid a river of magma.

She screamed that she was dying. Tumbling into the churning nothing, she could not hear her voice. Then she sunk beneath the waves once more. Beneath the waters, her mother smiled and danced with a figure covered in thorns that pierced her. Her mother's blood spread slowly out, staining her browned skin. With every movement, her flesh was torn, leaving more of her oozing wet. Yet she kept smiling. As she turned, Marim could see into her mother's eyes. They were black as night, and they were leaking a tar-like substance.

Light flashed against her closed lids. It blinded her mind until she stumbled inside it. She crouched and held still, hoping to stay within the slender circle of light. The darkness at the periphery scared her. She held her thoughts close, not daring to reach out. The pain of her body rippled dimly through this mist of beautiful light.

When the light ripped in pieces, she cried. "No! Oh no, no!"

A brief vision of the room around her trickled into the crack. Darith sat at her bedside. He was crying. He knew how the web reached to claim her, clung to her, left her no more than a fly beating useless wings after its legs are entangled in the spider's web. Words rose in her, but her voice couldn't find purchase in her throat. She wanted to touch him, to tell him she loved him. Tell him to survive and to forget revenge. But she couldn't move her arms. Her wrists were bound with cords to the bed. Darkness enveloped the room.

Millions of tiny little eyes stared at her. They didn't blink. They all watched her, and their harsh, quick tongue struck her ears. At first, they seemed to be rising, and then Marim knew that she was sinking. She could feel the cold slime rising around her ankles.

Leave me be! she screamed at them. There was clacking around her, thousands and sharp little clicks.

Wrenched back to her body by pain, she screamed. Her voice reached her ears. Her eyes caught on her father, who stood at the foot of the bed. His features were distant, almost unrecognizable. They all seemed like figures on a screen. There but not real. The torment held them at bay.

This is not how it should be! She screamed, but her voice made no sound. Her lips did not even part. Then for a long moment, the pain in her body, the fatigue, and the ache was enough to blind her to all else.

She heard a child's cry. *My baby.* Her vision went black, and she choked on a scream. There was nothing in this blackness, but she could hear their legs shuffling her way. The sweat on her lip was cold.

"The baby, Annabelle, is the key. Keep her safe for me; keep the world safe from her. I know... I know..." She heard her voice echoing in a place far away. The sound separated from her, and she lost interest. What could such a voice accomplish? Nothing. She would sing. So she lifted that faraway voice into a wordless song.

The spiders were close now. They would take Marim

away with them. She reached out her hand and felt a single prickly limb. She did not recall that her arms were held down. That was not real. The world back there had no meaning.

"Where are we going?" she asked the shadow spiders around her. Her voice now rang in both places. The baby no longer cried, but she heard distant whimpers.

The creatures all around her did not respond. She heard their answer. She laughed, as light as a child. "Will I die?"

Then the terror reached her, and she whimpered. They were close. She felt their breath on her. She could almost taste the poison of their fangs. It would hurt, this death. They held only inches from her. "No, no, no."

"Come with us. You will be safe, but you must come now," a harsh voice said. *"We are so few in body now, but you will have good company here."*

"But my child. My Annabelle."

"She is out of your hands. Follow if you like or stay here with them. They are hungry, and we do not begrudge them a meal."

"I'm tied. I cannot come," Marim said. Her arms pulled against the ties.

"Bodies are irrelevant."

Marim pondered this. The creature was only a voice in her head. She wasn't certain about the other ones.

"Goodbye, goodbye," she said once again in a singsong voice. Her decision was made. Maybe somehow, she could find her way back to Annabelle and Darith, but not if she died.

$$\triangle\triangle\triangle$$

Ymel slammed a fist into the desk and then with a glance about the room, he straightened his jacket. He disconnected his net-glasses and threw them in disgust onto the ground. No news on Silvia and Halis. Or, he should say not *good* news. He'd really had hoped for this lead to pan out.

He even had a video feed of Silvia on the planet. But his agents told him they were gone.

No more waiting. They've been out there too long. If The Council of Five gets wind of their existence…. No. It was time to start hiring assassins.

△△△

Umbu slipped into the house. The door was ajar, as if to welcome him. He spurned it, wary of such easy entry. He chose instead to pry open a window on the third floor. There he crept inside. He trusted his skin to shield him from view.

Darker than many of his people were, Umbu blended with the unlit interior. His skin was as dark as coal, only paler at his palms and the soles of his feet, both of which he smudged with coal when he worked. Even the whites of his eyes he hid with a dye made from a rare plant.

Tonight, Umbu had taken extra care. Not often did he get a call to take out a murderer who could well have been in the ranks of his guild. Not often, either, did he get to take on a near-mythical creature.

Umbu always researched his hits. His was a gentleman's guild, not one of those plebeian criminal undertakings. This job demanded more research than any before. Every scrap of information was classified, much of what he suspected had been destroyed. He found the information as much with luck as with skill and perseverance. But he found enough to tell him this kill would be one of legend for whomever took down the beast. The last of the spiders of Revia. Buried in one of the largest and most comprehensive libraries was a reference to a species of creatures that could go effortlessly between the form of man and the form of a giant spider.

The notes were adamant that this race was extinct. *Irradicated to the last one* was the wording used. No samples taken, no genetic preservation or study. This species, called the Drambish, were said to have a taste for human flesh. They could prey on anything but preferred sentient beings. The humans on their homeworld had fared badly.

When the Drambish had branched out, looking for new worlds to prey upon, the neighboring worlds had wiped them out, not wishing to suffer the same fate. It appeared to Umbu that they had missed one or two.

He was curious to see them, this scholar admitted. Fear also pulsed in his blood. The drumming of his heart approaching either a kill or death was the entire reason for his chosen profession. The notes were incomplete. With such a minuscule amount of information, it was impossible to know who would be the victor in a struggle. Umbu slipped out the door of the room he'd entered. The hallway, like the room, was dark. He crept forward.

Were they asleep? His readings had implied they were mostly nocturnal, requiring less than four hours of sleep.

His hand caught on something sticky that hung in the air. A shiver traveled from his shoulders down his back. His eyes were abnormally adjusted to the dark. Now that he searched, he saw small forms moving along the floor and the banister. A few dark spots hung in the air. Were they watching him?

He slipped silently into the next room and stood, letting his eyes adjust to the forms. Before he could fully identify the dark shape in the corner, a light turned on. He'd accustomed himself to sudden change. It didn't do to be blinded by a light coming on.

The woman who sat in the chair was a far cry from the picture he'd built in his mind. Her black hair was stained with blood. Her full breasts thrust up against the lace gown she wore, which was no less sensual because her stomach was ripe with child. She stood with the grace of a snake. Were spiders so graceful? He had never noticed. They certainly were not this beautiful.

Her white dress fell to the floor, covered in pearls and

delicate lace. He had never liked the look of pregnant women, not even his wife, though his memories of that time overflowed with fondness. Women with child were swollen and awkward. She was neither. She dressed like a bride in glaring white. Her arms were almost as pale as the dress. Only her hair falling in unconstrained waves was as shadowed as he imagined her soul.

"Will you have a drink?" this vision said. The hand she lifted was studded with glittering rings. She moved over to a cabinet before he could find a voice.

"You cannot seduce me," he said. "I know what you are."

"And I know what you are." She poured two drinks. Hair obscured her face. "You want me dead because they've told you I must die."

"Your beauty might have stopped me, Silvia, but that you're a Drambish, a killer of humankind."

"Am I? Drambish, hmm." Silvia lifted her face to him and took both drinks up in her hands. "I've never heard that word before. Nor am I a killer."

Umbu said nothing, but he took the drink. He did not sip the clear liquid. She sipped at hers. Her mouth parted beautifully. Her insides glittered like one of the jewels on her fingers. He wanted to protect her, not harm her. The feeling that overcame him made no logical sense, but it was as solid as the floor beneath his feet.

"Drink," she said.

He took a sip.

"Now let me tell you your options," Silvia said. "I am telling the truth when I say I'm not a killer. I respect you and your profession. I acknowledge that there are people who should die. Perhaps I am one of them. My partner is a killer, and he does deserve to die. You'll not kill him. I wouldn't let you, and in any event, you wouldn't prevail. So you have two options. You can leave here as you arrived, that is alive and secretly, or you cannot leave here at all. We'll kill you. Make no mistake, there's no third option. I don't die, and neither does Halis."

A large, but not unnatural, spider crawled up the skirt of

her dress and stayed there.

"What if I leave and return, and that time I take you by surprise?"

"You could try. You would fail."

Umbu believed her. He did not want her to die. He also knew if he returned without taking out his mark, he would have no life. They would kill him if she did not. One did not take a mark and fail without forfeiting honor or life. Slowly, he lifted the laser pistol at his side. His hand did not shake. He knew he would never get to fire it. The single *clack* behind him told him that Halis had been there all along.

One long, hairy leg thrust through his spine and emerged in his stomach. He dropped the gun. His eyes never left her. She sipped her drink as the other's teeth sank into his throat. When he slumped to the floor, Silvia set down the glass. As his life fled with his blood, he heard her speak.

"No challenge at all. I don't even think he intended to shoot me."

Black as the night and pale as a star, she curled against the spider's hairy hide. They lay together, and her hand of starlight stroked his abdomen.

"*You smell of lust, and no man wishes to kill that which he desires,*" the night whispered to her in a hiss of his voice.

Umbu tried to drag himself to the side, perhaps stanch the blood. His limbs didn't work. Had there been a poison in the drink she'd given him? Or something from the spider itself? It didn't matter. He had no choice but to sit there and hear her nonchalant voice and the spider's voice that moved through the blackness of the mind. Unspoken yet heard.

"They have found us, my love. We must flee. Where will we go?"

"*Nowhere. We'll wait here and catch them all in our web. We'll consume every morsel.*"

She moved her hand to her stomach. "And this one? He is too small to defend himself. For his sake, we cannot let them come at us."

"We can forge more. We will forge more."

Silvia jerked up. Her hands formed into claws, but she struck at nothing. Umbu felt nothing, not hate and not pity. Lethargy had crept into his thoughts. What did he care what became of them or the universe? He was going to die. After a moment, that didn't bother him either.

"The other one remains behind. You do not worry about her. For Annabelle."

Silvia laughed then. In her laugh crawled millions of hairy, eight-legged creatures. "Marim will keep it safe—that's a mother's desire."

"And I'll protect you and your child. Nothing will come at you here. I'm not ready to move on."

"I do not fear for us, you and me. But he'll be defenseless."

"No child of ours will ever be defenseless."

CHAPTER 3

MADNESS

T he sides of the meeting room curved, turning the room into a bullet-shaped oblong of blue steel. Nothing broke the sleek, metallic curve except for a table with three chairs on one side and a lone seat on the other. The furniture was across the room in front of the single flat wall. The legs of the chairs and table had been built at a slant, so they sat evenly on the curved floor. Two of the three chairs at the far side of the table were filled with two elderly gentlemen.

The Agency's owners. One a gray-haired scientist with thick spectacles and large sausage-like fingers. The other a tawny-skinned gentleman, his head shaved and shined till it formed a reflective surface. The third chair, Mr. Red's chair, was empty.

Allison walked down the center of the floor, her metal-tipped heels singing as they brushed the floor. She strode directly behind the lonely chair facing the men and set her hands on its back. She leaned a slight portion of her weight against the chair back, nothing more than an indication she'd stopped.

Do the other girls ever sit down? Or is the seat simply to demonstrate the inequality between the seated men and the agents who faced them across the table?

"Have a seat," said the gray-haired man, Johnny, as he liked to be called. Though Allison had done a little research and found his birth name, she'd never say it aloud.

"If you command, I'll kneel," Allison replied, making no move toward the chair.

"As it has ever been," Johnny said.

The shiny-headed bald man, Lord Wassem, rarely spoke, and he didn't now. His steel-nailed hands rose and a cascade of clicks rang into the room as his fingers drummed on the table-top.

"Tradition is both a garland and a chain. In either event, it demonstrates our role." Allison could ask why she was there but assumed they wanted to retain the reins of the conversation. Her silence demonstrated her docility. See, the unspoken words said, I expect nothing from you, demand nothing. I only obey.

There were two things they could want from her—either to hand her another role, an assignment of some sort, or they wanted a report on the new girl.

"You are getting on well with Glory?" Lord Wassem asked.

Not even a question. Then they did want to feel powerful, to know she would answer without being asked. This was usually a game they played with inexperienced operatives. *They already know they own me.*

"Glory is strong. She has a streak for empathy that Red will stamp out, but she is settling in admirably."

"Yes, Red can handle her now," Lord Wassem said.

An assignment then, since the comment implied an end to her brief mentorship. Too bad. Talking to Glory made her feel almost human, gave her something she was allowed to care about.

"Red is a magician. A sorcerer of sorts," Johnny said.

They were dwelling on Red, and he was absent. *I'm being tested.* Allison's heart thudded, and she forced it to slow, lest the slight movement of her chest give her away. Red would have noticed. These two might not have the skill, but wisdom dictated not testing their abilities.

"If you are the art, he's the craftsman." Johnny leaned forward, his thick glasses making his eyes huge and bug-like.

"But I'm not art, merely the paintbrush. The work my hands do on your behalf, that is the art," Allison replied.

"Which places us as wealthy patrons of the arts," Johnny said.

Lord Wassem's fingernails pounded on the table.

"Or the talent, the inspiration of the artist," Allison said.

"We have a minor masterpiece that craves your brush-strokes." Johnny released a file from his net implant to hers.

Lord Wassem shoved a file across to her.

Allison opened the physical folder. A face stared out at her. Allison stared back as she read through the file in her implant. Skin a color she'd never seen in nature, a color like smoke, a deep velvety gray. Despite the man being attractive, something lurked in the gaze that made her hope the assignment wouldn't involve sex.

"Halis Black," she read aloud after a onceover of the entire file. A kill job? She read the information again, but nothing new appeared. No second page. No secondary assignment. "Track his movements. Report back with an emphasis on whom he sleeps with and what happens to them. After reporting back, kill him."

She didn't phrase it as a question, but everyone knew it was. She waited for the interjection, the complication. They hadn't wasted her skills on a simple kill job for decades.

"The body must not be found," Lord Wassem said.

I can read the file. Allison smiled. "Disposed of discretely. Destroyed."

"Go. Pack. You leave tomorrow," Johnny said.

Allison picked up the picture and, holding it between two fingers, she walked back across the room.

△△△

A scream ripped across the daisy-strewn night. Marim's red hair splashed like blood across the pillow, shredded petals from Darith's daily gift of daisies dotted the bed. Her eyes stared, filled with a vague, blind terror. Her nostrils flared. She smelled them on the night air. She felt his fingers, but even more than that, Silvia's distant pain ravaged her. It was so like another pain she dimly remembered. Her fingers clenched on the sheets of her slender, hard pallet.

After the first single shout of fear, she was silent amidst the voices that crowded in around her. They held her snug away from the pain and darkness. She clenched her legs closed as if she could trap it inside her. The being that came belonged to another, housed in another's womb.

Another born, good. We will fill the earth again, the voice in her head said. It was like a chain against her, binding her to Silvia's torment and weighing her down in the blackness. *Not just a child, a god. He will teach humanity to kneel.*

Silvia's hair splashed out like a nighthawk's talons, and it struck a pillow somewhere worlds away. There was sweat between her breasts and it trickled down along the line of a rib. The beast moved. Marim let out a laugh that was more like tears than laughter.

He comes, the destroyer, the redeemer, the voice chanted.

Silvia swore. Her hand struck out and, somehow over lightyears of space, Marim recoiled from the sharp tear of a nail on her cheek.

"It's nothing," Silvia said between barred teeth.

Marim's thighs hurt from cramping them together.

Silvia cried out now. Marim was silent, her mouth drawn together.

Black and red mingled together. Breathing crescendoed harsh and fast. A whimper. Marim's head fell back against the pillow, sending out a puff of daisy petals. Silvia strained her head upward, her eyes wide and conscious—hateful. A tear slipped from Marim's eye and rolled unnoted down to the pillow, settling near a lock of sweat-tinged hair.

A laugh like a sigh, tired and joyful, emerged from Silvia.

"A boy," Marim whispered.

"Havoc," they said together. And the voice that belonged

to neither echoed the name with a million other voices in one.

ΔΔΔ

Berrick forced his eyes to the staircase at the sound of approaching footsteps. They led Marim by the arms. The two men were as stiff as their uniforms. As if they too had undergone the starching process. They were not men at all but hands and bodies that led Marim away.

Her hair, loose and untended around her shoulders, was blood-red. Somewhere deep inside she was bleeding, and it manifested itself in her hair. Everywhere else, she was blank and corpse-pale. Her eyes, a flat brown once more, glazed over. Her face, despite the scratches she had deposited on it in the night, was slack in the daylight. She wore her nightdress, now torn from one shoulder. The lace hung free where she had shredded it with her nails. It no longer looked the part of a wedding gown. What was left of her pregnancy weight was covered in the dress, leaving her resembling the slip of a girl she'd been not too long ago.

"She's stranded, halfway between here and there," Darith commented.

As usual, Berrick could not tell what lurked behind the boy's dark tones. Nor could he see his face. Neither man looked away from the girl being led across the entrance hall toward the door. One look, one word from her and Berrick would rip her from the hands of those neat, pompous men.

Just look up, baby. Give us some sign you're in there.

"How can they take her?" Count Cortanis asked. He did not understand.

"Two months is not enough to condemn her to that place," the countess added. "She has a chance yet to recover. She is so young and well-bred women do have troubles with childbirth. You must give her more time."

"Call this to a halt, Darith," the count said.

"I granted them the right," Darith said. "Why would I call anything to a halt?"

"She's your wife. How could you?" the countess asked. "Have you no concern for the family name?"

"She'll be safer there. We can do nothing for her here," Berrick said.

"I'll never understand..." the count began.

Darith cut him off. "You don't need to. I'm aware of your limits, Father. Aware of how delicately you treated your own wife. Your opinions mean nothing."

Berrick tuned the rest out as the men led Marim past him.

Marim stared passively straight ahead as she passed them. She smelled of daisies. Darith brought them to her room. Every day, Marim sat by them and every night, before ripping at her flesh, she tore the flowers to shreds. Berrick cleaned the mess in the light of morning. The first time Berrick had mentioned the mental facility the words had tasted like acid.

From the start, Darith maintained that Marim was never coming back. The traumatized boy talked about not being able to feel her inside his mind. Berrick tried very hard early on to disbelieve Darith's stark predictions on Marim's account, but nothing looked out of her eyes, and she would do herself real harm eventually. After the initial month of her raving, Berrick bode his time with Darith until they could legally send Marim away.

The starched men led her from the house. Count Cortanis and his bitter-faced wife followed to see the girl loaded in the car. The countess gave the healthcare workers instruction on how to leave the property without being noticed.

"Look at them," Darith said. "One might assume that genuine feelings motivated them. But it's just the shame of their daughter-in-law being institutionalized. Never admit weakness. Anything but that."

"They aren't perfect, Darith. No parent is."

"You don't know them at all, do you? You've known my

father for twenty years and you don't know a damn thing that makes him tick."

Darith held the spider-child in his arms. The baby was as pink-faced and plump as any human infant.

The baby squalled. Berrick saw the creature and knew the spider by its already black eyes. For two months, he had awaited a moment alone with the evil beast. But even if he had it, would he have the bravery to do what needed to be done? Monster or not, it was his grandchild. How could he judge the Cortanis?

"You meant to murder her. You still do," Darith said. His hold tightened on the child, and he pulled back.

"Yes." Berrick hadn't realized till then that he was reaching to take Annabelle. He lowered his arms. Today was not the day. The more time passed, the more his attempts felt like a shallow fraud. One night, he had stood over her crib when Darith and the wet nurse had been absent, a pillow clutched in his hands. And what had he done? Nothing.

"I would've stopped you."

Berrick looked at the wheeled chair that Darith sat in. "It doesn't matter now."

"So now you will go after Silvia and Halis and *try* to slay them."

"Yes."

"And you think *you* will succeed?" Darith smirked.

"No." But what other choice was there? He had less than a month left in sabbatical left. After that, he either had to return to work or risk having his status revoked, and with it his clearance. "Do you think you would have succeeded in stopping me?"

"I know I would have," Darith said. Then his arms extricated themselves from the baby's body. He spoke a word that filled the air with silent noise. His long fingers moved on the air as if he scooped sand. Annabelle lifted from his lap and hung suspended. Then Darith's hands moved to the side of his chair.

A whisper of gray tinged his skin and his eyes darkened. Darith levered himself up. Another word exploded from his lips. Had the sound blown in another direction, perhaps the house would have fallen around their ears. Instead, Darith stood.

Though his muscles must have been weak, the boy remained standing and moved his arms to take the spider. "And when you fail with the spiders who hurt Marim, I'll follow you and see that they meet a messy end."

Darith sat back in the chair. His face was pale and drawn, and his hands shook.

Berrick had seen magic like this before. Because he knew Silvia, he did not question Darith's abilities. "Why not go now?"

"I'm not impatient. And I have Annabelle to look after." Darith glanced at the baby. "She'll probably be one of them. But just think, perhaps instead she'll be something more. Forged like a sword, there'll be no weapon of greater power."

"She isn't your child."

"She is." Darith looked up into Berrick's eyes. His gaze was hard, not starched, but genuine inflexible strength. "There will be another child out there, and that child will be mine in the way you mean. But it'll also be Marim's in the way that Annabelle's mine. There are two children and four parents, and each belongs to each. We are all caught in the web together. You cannot remove anyone without tearing the web into pieces."

"Makes no sense," Berrick snarled.

"Go chase them. That's your part in this—a bloodhound bound for failure." Darith waved a hand, a smirk plastered to his face.

Berrick turned and strode out the door, Darith's laughter on his back. The car that held his daughter headed down the long driveway.

The countess wept, though she had never liked Marim. Berrick hated siding with the sullen boy, but the only worry that woman had was for her image. The count placed his hand on Berrick's shoulder and said nothing. There was nothing to say. Words were dry and empty. Vengeance did not dry up and melt away on Berrick's tongue. He'd locate the spiders, and he would destroy them. If he was not irradicated in the process, he would return and kill the one spider he'd left behind.

"I'm going off-world."

"Must you talk of this now?" the countess cried.

Berrick clenched his fists. Her child was safe and sane inside her home. He'd ignored her judgments once before, pretending he hadn't known she'd told Marim that Polly had asked for her fate. How had no one killed this nasty woman by now?

"You'll have to resign," the count said.

"Eventually," Berrick replied. "I should have resigned four years ago. But my clearance will be of help where I'm going."

"Do you recall how happy you were when the position vacated and we got you an interview? Odd, looking back. So much hope back then, so much belief and faith."

"I need to believe in something again. Can't live this way. I have to fight, or I'll wake up one day and be just like the rigid bastards who took my family."

"I try to be a good man, Berrick, but you were always better at it than me. I won't ever break free, but I do wish you luck in it."

"Thank you."

"I hope you find what you're looking for."

"I will." There was no other option.

CHAPTER 4

A PATH

T he station was sterile despite the hordes of people who traipsed through each day. A slight stink of bleach hovered in the air. The last time Berrick had entered an interplanetary hub like this was when he'd taken his family to DelRion to see the dinosaurs. Petyr had been about five then. The station hadn't changed an iota. But Berrick liked the locale better this round.

He felt lost in the crush of people. In the steady stream of humanity, he almost shook free the thoughts that stalked him.

The windows that looked out to the shipyards had no animations. After crossing traffic, he sat down in front of a window panel to stare at the starry sky. Great ships occasionally blotted out his view of the vast expanse of glittering stars and endless black. His mind wandered from star to star and escaped, sometimes for a minute at a time, the lingering memory of Marim birthing a monster.

Memories arose instead from years before of his wife laughing as Marim and Petyr stood against these same windows, their flushed faces plastered to the glass. *I failed them.* The old mantra took over, but now it boasted a new line. *I failed her.*

Twice before, he'd been in the station and those moments echoed. The first with Polly, her belly big with Marim. Berrick thought then that he had landed the job of a lifetime and Polly had beamed with pride. Both had been filled with dreams of the wonders in store for them. Moving back to Yahal had been a dream for them, a promise of a bright future. That was before the real world had come crashing in. Before Polly's dreams of a big family had been squashed by complications in Marim's birth and she'd learned that the technology that had stood any chance of helping her conceive again was illegal on Yahal.

The second visit had been only months before Polly's choices had caught up to her. Looking back, Berrick should have seen the signs. Weight loss, dark circles under her eyes, hands constantly fidgeting. Why hadn't she told him? Had she thought he'd condemn her, choose the letter of the law over his family? If he'd seen, could he have saved them? Would he have even believed that the world he loved, the values, could condone the thing that had been done? The punishment for violating the laws exceeded anything he could believe was necessary.

This time, he was alone, leaving Yahal. The land of opportunity and peace hadn't worked out for him. Why not give violence and self-destruction a go?

He'd spent all morning thumbing through news headlines for the nearby planets, looking for something to lead him to Halis. Even having given up his job, his security clearance still gave him access to a great deal. But so far, the glittering sky told him about as much about where to proceed as the news.

"Mind if I sit?" The voice was young and girlish. A timbre that reminded him of Marim before the spider mess. When Berrick looked over, he expected a girl his daughter's age, maybe younger.

What he got was something else entirely, something that elicited a burst of terror. She was delicate as a piece of handmade lace and so pale, she might have been translucent. Her eyes were an awe-inspiring pinkish purple. The oddity was not what scared him, though her coloring did remind him of an ill-fated albino rat Petyr had once owned. The disquiet that rose in him came from her beauty, which if anything, exceeded Silvia's.

It was no coincidence, a woman like that was standing there.

When no reply was forthcoming, she sat. A woman of her physical caliber didn't expect *no* as an answer. Probably hadn't heard the word her entire life.

She smiled with her colorless lashes fanning her cheeks. "I know you, sir. You're Yahal's police chief. Trehar? Correct?"

"Not anymore." Berrick's hands trembled, longing to reach out and comfort her. His mind held back. She was dangerous and too beautiful to trust. The ticket stub in her frail little hand was a white splash across her black leggings. The plastic stub was displayed perfectly for him to view. He doubted that was an accident, even though there was no proof to back his opinion. "You're not coming from Yahal. How'd you know me?"

"My employers have dealings in many places. Mr. Trehar, if I may, trust me when I say your suspicions of me are unfounded."

Her effortless assessment of the inner workings of his mind did nothing to reassure him. "And who're you?"

"I've been known by thousands of names. Given our current entanglement, you may have the name my mother gave me: Allison. It's no conceit to say if I wanted you on your knees, you would be licking the floor." No bravado blared in her words. If anything, there was a trace of a plea in the silence of her breath.

"Say what you came to say."

"You're looking for Halis. So am I. My job's to see him in the dirt and I'm unmatched at my job."

"Hired killings are illegal."

"So are vendetta kills."

"I won't help you find them."

"Of course. You don't know where he is." Allison set an unpunched ticket down on her leg and spun it so the destination faced him. There was no mistaking this gesture. "I do."

Why does she keep referring to him as if he's alone. Why hire someone to kill Halis and not Silvia? "You know where Halis is?"

Allison nodded.

And why would a hired killer help me get to Halis?

Once again, Allison either read him like a book or had

some ability to access his mind. "Despite rumors, I have a heart. It doesn't matter to my agency if your hand or mine starts the decomposition process, as long as Halis dies."

"And Silvia?"

Allison's shoulders tensed almost imperceptibly, and her breath hitched. If he hadn't spent a better portion of his life looking for tells, he never would have noticed his words had upset her. Certainly, when she spoke, there was no hint.

"My employers sent me for one person."

"Turn around, Allison. Regardless of any crimes you've committed, you don't stand a chance against Halis. Not if information is being withheld from you. They aren't human; they are something else. They are monsters."

"All the more reason for you to go there. Mr. Trehar, what I'm about to say will sound crazy."

"Spit it out. I'm accustomed to crazy."

"If I get there before you and Halis doesn't wind up in the ground, find Mr. Red. Tell him I know it's a trap. Tell him I don't regret anything and none of this is on his shoulders."

Before Berrick could answer, she was on her feet and gliding away. He jotted down her odd words in his evidence journal. A death request deserved to be honored, even if he didn't understand the meaning. Once he committed the words, he started to weigh the pros and cons of following her to the Veesp moon colony.

△△△

Marim? Marim? Darith prodded outward with his mind. The maze of dark strands inside him spoke to him. He felt all of them pulling at him. Silvia's eyes sought him. They often did, but this time he, too, traversed the web. At first, his movements had been random, just scurrying away from the dark-eyed witch. But once the fear left him, it no longer felt entirely like a web to trap him.

A road ran in the web. And somewhere along the twists and turns, Marim waited.

Darith ignored the grating voice of the web as he moved. He wanted only one thing.

He walked toward the dark light of his wife. Her physical body lay in front of his knees, her dark, vacant eyes like a vortex into the underworld. He held on to the memory of her running to him, warm from the sunlit gardens, and falling into his arms. The sun in his dark life. She'd believed in him. Loved him regardless of his merit. He wouldn't give up on her.

"*We need her. We'll not give her back. She is ours.*"

The Marim who sat at the heart of the darkness looked up. Her body never twitched. Stuck in the web, her image was eyeless. She smiled at him. Tiny black legs wiggled between her teeth. One minuscule spider escaped her mouth to crawl over her lip.

He clung to the sunlight she'd once brought him, hoping somehow the remembered rays could warm her. More spiders squirmed loose from her smile.

"I hate them, Marim. Our daughter is the only reason I stay now. I'm strong, not meant to play nursemaid to you or her. Your father seeks Silvia and Halis, but *I* can find them. I'll kill them. Wake up. I can't leave Annabelle or you. Wake up. Just wake up."

The Marim in the web wept blood tears, and he moved to hold her.

"I love you," he whispered.

Her body moved. Her bony physical hand tightened on his and something stared out at him. It wasn't Marim. A vile gurgling poured from her throat, setting free a puff of smoke. After taking his hand back, Darith understood.

"I'd kill you if your demise wouldn't kill Marim."

Why not kill her? Slice her open and watch the dark blood pour out? Darith would be free and so would she. But that was letting go of the only unsullied thing that had ever come into his life. If he abandoned her, would that piece of himself that he'd fought so hard to maintain, that crucial piece his mother called a soul, go with her?

"You're a contagion, not a person." Darith stood and took a step back from the bed.

"*One mind. We are remnants—the soul of our people,*" the voice said. "*You are one of us.*"

His mouth opened to say something else when he realized that he was *standing*, without even having tried. He felt his legs under him and the dark, deep song of his blood. No magic to hold him aloft, but true sensation and feeling. *I walked the darkness. I used it.*

Then he toppled down, legs a useless accessory beneath him. Marim laughed, a cruel maniacal sound that wasn't composed of her voice. Darith smiled. If he did it once, he could do it again, and he would learn why it only seemed to work when he used the web's power.

If I can be cured... He let the thought dangle, not wanting to risk the precious hope to the darkness threaded inside him. He looked at Marim and then hauled himself back into his chair.

CHAPTER 5
NIGHTCLUBS & ANGELS

H alis prowled the flashing club from the dimly lit edges. Most of the others lining the wall either shot glowing junk into their veins or copulated with an urgency foreign to Halis. He assumed such base animal mounting was linked to their pure mammalian genes. But he gave credence to the possibility that they were simply an inordinately flawed species. Other mammals might be more appealing.

The interior of the dancefloor pulsed with those who had already polluted their veins and those looking to do so. The most appealing of the lot were the lost souls seeking genuine connections through gyrating hips. All of this in air filled with cheap plastic glitter and flickering near-pornographic images projected over the crowd.

As hunting grounds, it was abysmally easy. Might as well be a buffet.

Depressingly dull, but after the first wealthy neighbor had gone missing, Silvia had insisted he couldn't kill near home. For her sake, because she enjoyed living in this place and walking in daylight, he preyed like a rat confined to the cellars. She deserved a home, and so did the beautiful little boy. For a short while, he would placate her and avoid notice.

Eventually, oh, eventually, we won't need to hide. We will crawl from the shadows in renewed numbers and eat their hearts.

The dim flashy lighting of the place fooled human eyes

into glossing over the flaws in both environment and clientele. Halis' sharp eyes saw every revolting detail: broken needles imbedded in the plaster walls, a pool of piss near a garbage can smeared with white sticky goo, a residue of vomit and booze that had sunk into the cracks of the floor. The combinations made his stomach churn. At least The Brothel had been clean, and the food unspoiled.

Life was a tradeoff.

Hunting, truly hunting for his prey, was glorious, and Silvia's smile as she looked out at the craters and whipping flurries of sand merited braving the acrid taste of drug-ridden blood.

"*Yes, the hunt is good,*" the hive voice threaded his mind. It was stronger now, attached to Marim's life. It thrilled inside him to hear the vigor there and he would feed them.

The game of the night, a dark-haired thing, painfully naïve in this crowd of wolves and lepers, struggled away from her intoxicated partner. Halis watched her, patiently waiting for the correct moment. All night he'd made sure to meet her gaze, always looking away. Best a girl like that approach him.

As he offered her a tentative smile, something else caught his eye. A shining white in the filth.

Like a beam of moonlight, a female entered. White and pure to her core. He wanted to move closer, to smell her and be sure. She decorated the arm of some middling drug dealer and soon disappeared into the crowd. But not before her eyes, a vivid violet, briefly met his.

She would make a worthwhile hunt. Perhaps even be worth seeding with child.

"*Yes. She's the one. Born on her, your children will be strong,*" the voice said.

She'd taste like honey and wine. But not tonight. That would spoil the rarity. Best wait.

Halis grinned at the romantic fool again. This time he didn't look away. Having extricated herself from her lecherous partner, she was nearly at the bar. The sustained gaze was enough to alter the dark-haired girl's destination to his side. *Yes,*

I'm harmless.

Her mouth moved, shouting something over the din. Halis couldn't understand and shrugged to emphasize his helplessness. Her smell—too much perfume mingled with a tinge of hope—intensified as she leaned closer. No desperation clung to her, and her eyes were unclouded.

Come, he motioned to her.

She smiled in return, her hand settled into his, and he led her toward a back door. Out in the night, the stench receded, and the deafening pulse of recorded music quieted. Only a dozen people littered the patch of cement, most blowing puffs of thick, noxious green smoke.

Halis led the girl off to the side. She was a score. Out in the clearer light, she was still attractive. Dark skin and dark eyes went with her long hair. If it hadn't been for the pale angel who'd crossed his vision, he would have considered this one to seed with child.

"*Seed them all,*" the voice said. "*Our numbers are depleted. You can make us strong.*"

No. This time, he didn't care what the hive thought. Having seen the angel, what did he want with the creature of earth?

"I'm Talva," she said in a husky voice.

"Halis," he said. He already tasted her.

ΔΔΔ

The night sky above her spread in every direction, broken by no manmade structure. Sullied by no constraints, just an endless expanse of freedom. Silvia allowed her eyes to drop closed for a moment and let her lips part to permit the grainy wind to coat her tongue.

Her son's warmth against her chest brought a feeling with it that didn't agree with the perfect night. Fear rode her, nibbled at her, and whispered in Darith's voice, "*I'm coming.*" Her precious Havoc was so small and blameless.

The voice of Halis' people that threaded the web and sang its poison melodies in her mind was silent now. But it was there, waiting, knowing, and finally it would judge who was the strongest of its children.

A crackle like a vehicle approaching made her look back over her shoulder, but no one approached. Halis was gone. Again. Always gone.

Her arms tightened around the bundle until Havoc squirmed.

Halis had been a sullen child, and she'd delighted that his smiles had been reserved for her. Then, at thirteen, he'd transformed for the first time. Silvia shivered, feeling an echo of her terror, hearing her screams reverberating in her ears.

"Ymel," she whispered. He knew. He'd always known. She'd seen him that day watching, smiling. Pleased with, not afraid of, the giant spider lumbering toward Silvia.

Silvia's eyes closed, and she indulged in remembering.

The creature that moments before had been Halis clicked slowly across the room toward her. Numerous black eyes all riveted on her and in none of them shone even a trace of her only friend. Its jaws dripped. Silvia's scream died out as her lungs exhausted their air supply. She stumbled back. The beast advanced, making a clicking sound with its jaws.

She screamed again. This time, her voice formed the solitary word that meant safety. "HALIS!"

Only it was Halis. She turned and ran toward the window that divided their room from the viewing chamber on the other side. She slammed her fists against the glass, trying to divert Mr. Ymel's attention from the spider to her.

When he did look at her, his smile offered no relief.

"Dearest Silvia," he said, "You must calm down, you know. The spider's a carnivore and partial to human blood for nourishment. Your fear's exciting him."

"Help," she pleaded, flattened against the glass. She spared a glance behind her. The spider wobbled, seeming to have trouble with

its new legs, but it continued toward her. Somewhere at the back of her mind, she felt Halis' voice, but her fear drowned out even this thread of comfort.

"I cannot aid you. That creature would consume me in moments. You, dear girl, if you calm down, he may view as one of his own. But I'm afraid the screams are riling the beast."

Ymel smiled, and Silvia ascertained from the toothy grin and the emotionless voice that Ymel didn't care one way or the other if she was consumed. The hatred and disgust that welled up in response overtook her. She spat on the glass and spun to face the monster.

Her shoulders squared, and her black hair cascaded down her back. She met the spider's eyes. Words slipped past her anger into her mind. Halis spoke in a voice made of congealed blood and the remnants of a thousand screams.

"Silvia, never, never, Silvia."

As she calmed, she stepped forward and offered the spider her trembling white hand. The words in her mind became solid and clear.

"I'd never hurt you, Silvia. I've always been this and always loved you. Please smile, Silvia. This is good. I'm strong. They're weak. We're strong."

Silvia threw her arms around the spider and sobbed against its side. A bony leg curled up to hold her close. Her fingers dug into the rough hide, trying to find evidence of the boy she loved. There was nothing of the slender youth except the tenderness with which it held her.

"You were a caterpillar, my love," she whispered. *"And now you're my butterfly. What of me? I want to be like you."*

Not like him, *she thought, casting a glance at the grinning man behind the glass.* He's a monster.

"Do you not know what you are, my Silvia? You're not what I am, but you are a butterfly. No, you're better—a queen to rule the hive."

The next week Silvia transformed, but it wasn't the same —she chose the form and used her power to achieve it. The form was part of Halis.

After that first transformation, he smiled for everyone.

To Silvia, he confided that he'd never felt at home as a boy, and more and more, he'd chosen to live as a spider. Ymel tainted all her memories of youth. Halis smiled with the other man's cruelty. She would never be free of him.

But Ymel would not have her son. They would never have Havoc. Never do to him what they'd done to her, to Halis. She didn't care if Havoc changed or didn't change when puberty hit. Except that he was defenseless until then.

For Havoc's sake, she did not engage in the game Darith played on the dark web connecting them. Until she knew he wouldn't lead Ymel to them, she didn't dare risk Darith locating them. She didn't press the remnants, which Halis called "the hive," to test Darith.

Silvia walked to the edge of the garden so she could look out at the vast vacant moonscape. Havoc's mind moved, and she smiled at the simplicity of his infantile needs. Warmth, food, and love.

"Love I have, little one. I love you more than life and will feed you to the void before they'll have you." Somehow, in the darkness of the night, Silvia's black eyes glowed outward. Her human form slipped from her, and she curled on the ground, eight legs wound around the child as she sang a spider's song.

She waited another hour in the howling cold before retreating into the house. Halis was still absent. He would come home stinking of blood, content and distant.

How can he be so careless? We could be a family, but instead, he's out there drinking skanks. Could it just be hunger? No. He had never been the animal they'd wanted to make of him. She felt it every time she touched his mind. This was revenge. This was the hive's will and even she couldn't alter its course for renewal and revenge.

The humans had burned their world, their people. He wanted to destroy the perpetrators. Just as it had been the first day he'd worn his arachnid form, her safety was the only other thing that mattered. His Spider Queen, now the mother of a new god.

CHAPTER 6

MARIM'S BOYS

The space-train was only a few minutes from its destination, and Berrick shuffled the last of his notes and clippings into order. The veiled woman who'd shared his compartment gave him one last suspicious glance before standing. The blue skin of her forehead creased in a frown as she passed Berrick. Since leaving Yahal, he'd gotten those looks every time he'd handled paper—as if him departing from the net-glasses as a means of viewing information was an appalling sign of psychotic behavior.

It made sense out here. Probably most people only used things like paper or any physical research to hide their actions. After all, anything done on net-glasses could be tracked back to you.

The upside was no one he traveled with had a clue what he was researching. No one would be able to direct any trackers his way, to this little, mechanized colony at the edge of civilization.

Just when he'd almost decided to follow Allison, he happened across a news article mentioning a rash of murders—murders that had begun right around the time Silvia and Halis had left and had ended three months ago. They wouldn't still be on the dinky asteroid colony. Probably, Allison was correct about their current location. But they had detoured to this distant outpost for a reason. He wasn't going to be caught unprepared a second time. No more surprises. No more rushing in. They had to have a weakness. He'd find it here.

He was the last passenger off the train onto the slick metal platform. Worse even than the space station, everything here was metal or plastic. The air had a stale recycled quality like someone had opened a freshly minted plastic container. The fumes burned in his lungs. "Contaminant free," the air processors bragged in giant lettering. *I'd take contaminants any day if it meant air that tasted like something other than burned cellophane.*

He couldn't imagine the elegant Silvia in her gowns and jewels walking these efficient streets. The people were clothed in what appeared to be badly fitted plastic bags. Logical attire that they programmed to heat and cool but lacking the romantic horror of the spiders. No. They hadn't come here with the hopes of residence. There was another reason.

"Hotel?" Berrick said to the driverless hover-car that zipped to stop in front of him. Relief flooded him when the door slid open. The vehicle responded to speech commands. He still felt like a crazy person talking to a car, but at least he didn't garner any more attention from the surrounding people by rambling to an unresponsive machine.

"Rank." A mechanical voice addressed him when he sat down.

My rank or the hotel's? "Law enforcement global level, on sabbatical. Cheap and central lodging."

The vehicle lurched into motion and the metal patchwork city whizzed by. The only variations in color were in gaudy plastic and flashing lights. Berrick closed his eyes and twisted his wedding ring.

They'd lived in a place like this, him and Polly, before Marim had been conceived. How Polly had wept coming to the neon city. The shock of the college had been extreme for her Yahal-bred sensibilities, but he'd feared the space colony would shred her. She didn't leave their apartment for two weeks, but after that had squared her shoulders and endured.

How had things gone so wrong? How happy they'd both

been to escape the rampant crime and drug use. Pregnant with Marim, Polly had been prone to nightmares of raising her children in what she'd called a "den of thieves." She'd clapped her hands for joy when she'd heard they would have a chance to raise their children on Yahal. Peaceful, moral, and safe, it was all they'd wanted. So why had his family fallen so far?

The vehicle stopped on a crowded downtown block, and Berrick clattered out of the vehicle, unsure how he was supposed to pay, but the car immediately departed. The silver oval faded, becoming just another moving part in the giant machine.

Colonies like this made him queasy. No real ground beneath him, just layers of metal atop an asteroid, forced into a false orbit by engines. Just space trash hanging in the void waiting to break and career off into space until it devolved into no more than a meteor.

Berrick stepped inside the nearest building and heaved a sigh. Free ride. Worth every penny. This was not a hotel. This was a police station. Berrick rummaged for his badge, his fingers expecting to find it gone. The chunk of metal and leather was a symbol of him as a lawman and now that was a façade. He was a criminal and criminals don't have badges.

He'd intended to visit the station; he just thought showering and getting a night's sleep first was wise. Clearly, the universe had had other plans. He glanced around the room, which appeared to be four solid metal walls with three large input machines. Likely, the wall behind the machines had low-level officers sitting behind it.

Berrick strode over to the center display and punched in his request for information and his authorization. Then he eyed the wall for lack of anything better to occupy his time. His badge burned in his pocket, but he refused to turn to its comforting familiarity. Five minutes later, a circle cleared in the dark surface.

A face, not immediately identifiable as male or female, stared out. The person's bored eyes flicked over Berrick and a plastic gloved hand reached up to touch a plastic helmet.

"Where you from?" an androgynous voice asked.

"Yahal. Do you have my authorization code?"

"Honorary level four clearance for crime reaching from ten months ago to three months ago."

"Not just crimes. I need access to records."

"It goes hand in hand, *sir*."

Berrick leaned forward. Kids. Bloody kids. No one ever taught them respect out here. "Before you take that tone, consider, you have what? A level one, maybe two clearance? I'm on sabbatical which lowers my clearance, and I still get a level four. Maybe your 'sir' should sound a little more respectful."

The kid's face reddened. Berrick felt a twinge of pity for the little punk. But the youth's discomfort gave Berrick a wonderful opportunity. Before the young official could stumble out a response, Berrick continued.

"Two things I need from you. Where's the library and where's your physical-record room?"

He could see the thoughts traipsing over the kid's face. But as Berrick hoped, the youth held their tongue. Berrick was aware that the library was no respectable place for anyone, let alone law enforcement. A den of perversity frequented by all manner of scum who didn't want their actions and proclivities seen. But that was precisely what Berrick needed, a place to research that wouldn't easily be tracked.

More importantly, so would Silvia and Halis. They hadn't come here to live, so presumably there was some sort of information here and if nothing else, they would need to research where to go next. The library and its security footage were the best place to start. The spiders were too paranoid of being followed to be caught with net-glasses.

For the first time, he had a leg up on them.

△△△

"What do you mean, *gone*?" Darith asked, sitting in his chair. He set one hand on the spotless reception desk and glared at the skinny girl in her crisp, white uniform.

"The paperwork says she was checked out, sir." The woman leaned as far back in her chair as it would allow without tipping backward. Her eyes darted about, presumably searching for support, and she picked up a pen, wielding it like a magical object capable of making him see reason.

"Impossible," Darith said, bending toward her. He smiled as he imagined prying her eyeballs from her skull with the pen she clutched. "My wife has no one to check her out but her father and me. Her father is off-world. So either this place is incompetent in keeping records and Marim is in her room or it is even *more* incompetent and you let a stranger take my wife. And my family will have this whole place shut down."

"Sir..."

Darith growled and clenched his fist. The woman's hands lifted to her throat and pawed as her jaw silently moved.

"Woman, I am not interested in what your paperwork says," Darith continued. He stood, leaning over the counter slightly and tightened his fist. He hardly noticed the darkening of his skin anymore. "Tell me the facts. Is my wife in her room?"

The woman shook her head, the whites of her eyes large. Her nails made little scratches on her throat.

"You know this? You've seen?"

She nodded.

"Were you here when she was removed from the facility?"

She shook her head.

Darith opened his fist. The woman gasped and sputtered behind the desk. Darith waited a beat for her to still before continuing. "What name was she taken under? She *did not* get up and walk out."

"Your name, sir."

Darith tasted the metallic glory of her blood and held his smile frozen on his face. If she stayed there, looking helpless, useless and defenseless, he doubted he could retain control. Little spider voices screamed to drink her death. *"Kill her, eat her, show her our strength."*

"Find me someone who saw her leave, or I swear I'll burn this place down. Do you believe me?"

"Yes," she said in a tiny voice.

"Go."

Marim's absence didn't make sense. Halis and Silvia had not returned. He would have felt that in the dark remnants they left behind. Nor were they dead, so Berrick would not have come back. Who else had any interest in Marim? The count and countess disapproved of Marim being held in a *public* institution. But it would cause a scandal to remove her like this. They would never invite scandal.

So who? And why?

Darith struck the desk with his fist.

Access to police records would be great, but without Berrick, Darith had no power to investigate. He didn't even know how.

The first woman returned with another in the same crisp uniform. It was not a nurse he recognized. That was worthy of note, as visiting almost daily, Darith knew all the nurses in the little ward.

"You're new," he accused before she said anything.

"Just transferred, sir."

How long had this been in the works? How long had they been waiting to steal Marim? Who were they?

"The person whom you allowed to steal my wife, what did they look like?"

"There were three men there," the new nurse said. "The one who cleared our system as you looked, well, like you only in a wheelchair. Our records say you can't—"

"I couldn't. Now I am perfectly able. Looked like me how?"

"Dark hair, dark skin, young. He had that look, sir, the way all nobles look, as if…"

Darith glanced down at his hand, only to note the assessment was valid. His pale aristocratic skin had darkened not just slightly but as if a thick shadow lay over him.

"Yes, how do nobles look? Do continue."

"Like they're just daring you to question them so they can crush you."

"Honesty is good. Anything else?"

"One thing, sir," the woman said. "A rumor, but they say he came in a hover-car. All the girls twittered about it."

That made even less sense than anything else. Hovercars were illegal to buy or sell on Yahal. He knew few people who could afford to import one, considering the astronomical import tax. His parents possessed the wealth, but it couldn't be them. Why would two people so image-conscious risk the social censure that would come with such a flagrant transgression of propriety? No. Whoever this person was, they had not been sent by the count and countess. But who else would come here with an air of nobility and wealth, interested in Marim?

CHAPTER 7

WINDOWS & NIGHT WALKS

E ven dead and leafless, the tree stood tall, barely stirring in the Veesp colonies' heavy winds. Allison stared out at the witch-finger branches, yearning evident on her face. She ached to throw open her bedroom window and leap to the branches, to see if she could reach. She'd had a similar tree outside her parents' mansion growing up, and she'd dreamed of climbing it, of having the strength in her limbs to swing from branch to branch like a monkey.

The Agency had given her strength, but the dream had disappeared, and now her employers wanted her dead or they wouldn't be withholding information. She'd looked into Berrick's comment about Halis being a monster but found nothing. Perhaps it was metaphorical, perhaps not. Either way, it didn't change her goals. Something clawed in her chest, demanding she leap from the fourth-story window and trust to the fates.

She threw the window wide, letting the wind whip into her face. Her fingers stretched out, but her fingertips brushed only brittle twigs. The distance to the stronger branches was too far to leap, and she doubted shimmying up the trunk would fit the image she needed to build.

No, no one could travel from her window to the tree. And the only beings who seemed capable of bridging the gap from the tree to her room were a plethora of spiders. Even a hover-car could not have accessed the window—they could not hover that high in the air. The room was ideally situated for her purposes, even allowing her to leave her window open and not fear intrusion.

The spiders were a drawback. She'd considered calling maintenance, but in a dive like this, she didn't want to deal with obtaining adequate help. And she'd take the spiders in exchange for a fresh breeze and birdsong—both luxuries even the wealth of The Agency couldn't buy.

With another deep inhale of air, Allison retreated into the dim apartment. Everything was set in place. Objects seemingly carelessly thrown were placed with meticulous care. Should anyone enter in her absence, she'd know it. As she exited, she angled the door until it was at the precise degree she desired.

She strode to the kitchen counter and swiped up a set of secondhand net-glasses. The type she imagined a girl like 'Lilly' would own. She absently wiped at her right temple. No physical sign showed of her net-implant, but putting on the glasses she missed the instant access.

Her net-implant was turned off, as it had to be on all missions. She could only store bits for upload. She added a note regarding the location of Halis' home and the best prospective hiding places.

Then she picked up a small notebook and pen. Here she jotted by hand, her handwriting easy and fluid. These words were not for The Agency and she needed to get them down before she forgot. She'd already written up her Agency report on the incident. She'd written it five nights before on the night that it happened and set it in the queue for upload.

Followed Halis from the nightclub. Took me a while to get free, but in the end, he was easy to locate. Where, after all, would someone go in the slums to engage their prey? I still hoped at that point that perhaps the girl had survived...

Allison remembered as she wrote, and goosebumps lifted on her arm.

Outside the club was mostly empty industrial district, but in the distance, she saw a line of trees. Pulling her black cloak around her whiteness, she darted into the darkness. In and out of pools cast by the streetlamps, she trod carefully, keeping to the shadows as much as she could.

It was not until the deep shadows of the woods embraced her that she relaxed. She threaded through the trees slowly. Then the scream shattered the night air around her, and she flattened against the nearest trunk.

Already? She hadn't anticipated he'd go directly for a kill. The trunk she clung to was ambivalent to her and to the screams. Allison calmed her breathing and waited. The agonized sounds tapered off. She stared at the sky and counted stars until her instinct told her it was safe to approach.

When she did, each step was placed so as to not stir so much as a leaf. When she came to the place, following her recollection of the origin of the sound, the girl's body was ripped open, an arm thrown against a tree, separated by a good foot from the body. Eyes stared at Allison, glazed with death but still retaining terror and betrayal.

Allison touched her net-glasses and dialed the local law. It was a relief to let her voice tremble, as was its natural inclination. The arm had not been cut free… It was something else. Something she didn't understand. Allison crept forward, all her weight on her toes so her stiletto heels didn't catch in the soft dirt.

At the woman's side, she kneeled. Her eyes narrowed as she looked at the numerous stab wounds punctuating the corpse. This was not a clean kill. From the blood around the wounds, most of these had been made while the woman had still been alive. But how? What weapon made those marks?

"Sick bastard," she whispered.

After a deep breath of woodsy air, Allison reached out and lifted the sequined skirt. Underneath, the lacy undergarments were relatively blood free and in place. He didn't rape her, *Allison thought.*

The pen dropped to the countertop. Allison turned it and pushed it back an inch before picking up the book and tucking it into her purse for safe keeping. Her fingers trembled, and she wiped them down the cheap fabric of her dress.

That is the fate The Agency wants for me. To date, the fact Halis didn't sexually violate his victims was the only consolation she had. If she failed, the death that awaited her was not pleasant and the weapon used in the murders still eluded her.

It wouldn't matter so much if she had been hired to simply kill Halis. But her instructions were to gather information then get close and gather more. She couldn't do this task at a distance.

The glowing numbers on her kitchen clock startled her from her thoughts. Writing had taken longer than anticipated and she had to dash to catch the public transport hover bus.

It wasn't far to her stop, but she needed to show up by bus. She couldn't let the diner know she'd already put a contract down on an apartment. It was better they thought her desperate rather than that she *expected* them to hire her.

The interior stank of cheap grease and instantly Allison could feel it clogging her pores, seeping into her hair. A chubby, older woman frowned at her from behind the counter. She gripped a stained counter cloth in her calloused hands. Allison smiled, lowering her eyes and looking up timidly from beneath her lashes.

"Yer Lilly, ain't ye? The girl from the city, called 'bout our help ad?"

"Yes," Allison said. "Is the position still available?"

It didn't matter. She could convince this woman easily to create a position, but she didn't want to do more than she had to. She had to play the part perfectly for Halis. City girl who fell in with the wrong crowd flees to country for a new start. If she played her part, he'd play his. Wealthy handsome man sweeps in to the rescue. Of course, she knew he would only be playing a role.

"You ever waited tables before? Dun seem the type."

"My daddy owned a restaurant."

CHAPTER 8
MR. N & MR. Q

T he hover-car was parked in his parents' looped driveway next to the hitching-post the old witch sometimes tied her nag to. If he hadn't already been warned about the hover-car, Darith would have mistaken it for a normal high-end vehicle. The sort all the rich paraded around in. But the wheels were a dead giveaway when he bothered to look.

Darith sat in the Town Car, glaring at the metal wheels. He was wrong? Were his parents involved? Would he find Marim safe inside? The thoughts racing in his mind brought back the familiar, spiteful anger he had lived with since the "incident." One more betrayal to add to the list of how his parents had failed him.

His display at the asylum had left him empty. The secret strength drained from him quickly, and he settled into the chair his driver brought out for him. With that hover-car sitting there, he itched to stride into the house on his own two feet and confront his parents. He couldn't.

The driver returned to the car once Darith wheeled up the drive. What little strength remained, he wanted to keep as a reserve.

I'll kill them before I'll let them touch her. Meddle with my family. Darith smiled at a mental picture of his father lying in a puddle of blood. *I'll open their jugulars if they've so much as touched Marim.*

The front door was ajar. His parents' guests were careless. Darith reached out on the threads of darkness but felt only his daughter within. Marim wasn't here. Where else would they have brought her?

A loud crash from the direction of his father's study startled Darith. For the first time since discovering the car, Darith noticed his surroundings.

Door ajar.

And along the hall, things were off. No servants had come to greet him and ahead, at the juncture of the hall, a table was overturned, its contents scattered. A cracked Avartia vase rolled across the floor.

Darith stopped. *Not my parents. Then who? And why come here? Why would someone want Marim and my parents?*

The air felt twenty degrees colder. *No, no one wants my parents. This revolves around Annabelle and me.* Darith held his breath, torn between two actions. He recalled the crash from his father's office. *Whoever did this, would they hurt the count?* A habit from childhood overtook him, and he crossed his chest in prayer, but it was not toward the office he turned.

The count would have to fend for himself.

But my mother... I can't just leave her to them. Darith clenched his jaw and forced the thought of his mother from his mind. Her heir was in danger—she of all people would want him to protect Annabelle. The only time he'd ever seen an outward display of pride from her was when she'd found him curled in front of Marim's guestroom door. He had slept there that week when she'd first came to stay with them to form a barrier between the grieving girl and his father.

"This is what you are, boy. Don't ever forget. Outward softness counts for nothing. It's the heart, the soul that differentiates the monster from the angel. Let the world worship men like your father. I know a hero when I see one," she had said. Then, *"I've all the alcohol locked away. I promise you, to get to her he will need to tear through me before he ever reaches you."*

"I'm sorry, Mother," he said.

Whoever was here hadn't come for his parents. No, anyone who wanted Marim wanted her because of the darkness, which meant that they had come for him and for Annabelle. If he paid for his daughter's safety in his parents' blood, he would experience not a moment's regret.

Annabelle had a beautiful nursery set up for her, painted in purple with unicorns etched in silver on the walls. She wouldn't be there. From moment one, Darith had trusted his daughter with no one but himself for any extended time. The nanny would not have dared take Annabelle out of Darith's room.

Darith stretched his fingers, recalling the sharp sound of his hand striking the last nanny's face. Hearing her tears as she pleaded to keep her job, claimed she needed it, would not disobey again. But some things weren't to be forgiven. The woman had taken Annabelle to sleep in her nursery. Where anyone could get at her. The count could get at her. No, it was bad enough he required a nanny, but no one else should have access to his daughter without his express consent. Only the dreary rooms the count and countess provided to their crippled shame of a son would do to isolate Annabelle from harm. Or harming others.

Darith arrived at his rooms without meeting anyone. When he came inside, the nanny gave a little scream. When she recognized Darith, she relaxed. Slightly.

"Someone's here, sir. In the house."

"Yes. They'll be here soon." In their shame, his parents had moved him to the guest wing, but that act might just have saved Annabelle's life. His old quarters would have been among the first searched. "Who are they?"

The woman shrugged, and a panicked sob escaped her lips. Darith wheeled himself across the room and took Annabelle from her carrier. The babe's black eyes met his. How long until she changed? How long and who could he trust? Not this sniveling girl. It was impossible Annabelle was human. Darith held no illusions about his daughter. He could touch the blackness inside her human shell. He could feel her need and her hunger. The voice in both of them cried for blood and vengeance.

But that gulf of darkness might work in their favor today.

"Leave," Darith commanded the woman. She would only be caught in the crosshairs. Her energy flickered at the edge of his mind. If it came to her life or his, Darith wouldn't hesitate to drain her and leave her empty shell discarded. She was a kind woman and deserved better than to be used for fuel. To someone, she was probably as real and important as Annabelle and Marim were to him. Power coupled with selfishness could do more damage than pure evil.

The nanny got no more than three steps before the door burst open, and two men thrust themselves inside. They wore black suits and had slicked-back hair. One was chubby and fair-skinned and the other was built like a giant rock with dark skin.

"Ah, Darith Cortanis and little Annabelle," the chubby one said.

"I'm at a disadvantage. Who are you?"

"Mr. N and Mr. Q. Agents of Mr. Ymel," the dark-skinned one said, pointing first to his companion, then himself.

"You have our property, Mr. Cortanis. Annabelle is Halis' and as such, she belongs to us," Mr. N said, his pasty white finger pointed at the baby.

"And Marim?" Darith asked.

"All will be explained if you come with us," Mr. N said. His arm lifted, and in his hand, he held a gun. He leveled the weapon at Darith's head.

Darith laughed. Annabelle's darkness pulsed in his arms. Her rage rushed through him, merging with his own. He stood, the air drawing in around him. At the base of his spine, the darkness lifted and settled into his fingers.

His muscles, mildly atrophied, shivered at holding his weight, but his magic focused outward. His arm lifted, and the gun melted. The dark-skinned man screamed in agony until Darith tightened his fist, closing off the man's airway.

"The mistake you made was thinking you had me outmatched," Darith said. "Now that is cleared up: Where is Marim?"

The chubby man was white-faced, and he stuttered a moment before forming words. "Halis and Silvia contaminated her. Even if you kill me, they'll keep coming. You're contaminated, too, boy."

His fist still clenched as Mr. N writhed, struggling for air, Darith walked forward. His brain was clouded with the clot of rotted power Silvia had left in his spine. He snapped his wrist to the side and Mr. N flew to the side, his neck at a crooked angle.

"One less agent." Darith grinned. He stepped down and barely managed to keep to his feet. He was empty. He stumbled. His arm tightened around Annabelle. The rage remained, hers mingled with his, but he was dry inside, his power spent along with the spider's residue.

The wide-eyed agent lifted his gun.

The air was dry, no currents to feed from. The nanny huddled in a corner, her energy a smooth silk song to his senses. She bore his mark in his service. That alone allowed him access to that great deep pool of strength. *Mine. Her force is mine.*

The gun leveled at his head.

I won't be that. He clung to the memory of Marim's eyes as she ran across the room, filled with sunlight. It was the only strength he had against the dark, bitter cloud. *If Annabelle is to be better than Silvia, than Halis, I must be better. I must be strong.*

The agent smiled.

Darith closed his eyes. *Annabelle.*

To use her was to bind her, but he wouldn't use anything. The empty dry core of him gripped her strength and rode out until they touched currents—millions of tiny strengths. He drank.

The gun went off.

Angrily, the bullet ripped through the air.

Darith's eyes opened, and from them spilled all the little lives, glowing and screaming for release. The bullet crashed into this wall of light. The air smelled of burned corn and wheat.

The bullet hung there, caught. Darith stretched his free arm out. Warm as honey, the freed power slipped around his fingers in a pool, and then it hurtled away from him in a raw force, screaming and free.

The agent's skin was the first to go, peeling back from his body. Then the soft tissue melted away. The blood showered out. Bones dressed in a drenched black suit fell to the ground.

A screaming nagged at Darith. He turned to the red-faced nanny, whose nails had scoured her cheeks. *Little ingrate.*

Annabelle wanted her silent. Darith's stomach knotted with her hunger. His mouth watered at thoughts of biting into the woman, the nanny's bloody face filtering into his mind.

"Leave!" Darith thundered at her.

When the girl was gone, Darith took a few tentative steps on legs that held him up on pride alone as the unused muscles strained. He collapsed next to the corpses. With the last of his strength, he dipped his finger into the blood and let Annabelle taste her first kill.

CHAPTER 9
A WALK THROUGH THE PAST

Darith slept, even the whites of his eyes eaten by black. Across the void in his mind, Silvia stretched. Solid and aware of his surroundings, Darith looked back at her, his as black as her own. The surrounding web thrummed with his power. Deep inside, lodged in his spine, was the darkness Silvia planted, the ichor of her own mark. He twisted these, using them, drawing them out of him to surround himself.

"*They found you. I can help,*" Silvia said. The nothingness around her roiled like storm clouds ready to crack with thunder.

"I don't need your assistance."

"*But you do. They've come for you, and without us, you can't fight them.*"

"I'm going to cure myself of you."

Silvia laughed and the silver of her mirth shot like lightning from the clouds rolling around her. "*And then cure Marim? Only they have her. Do you think you understand?*"

"Enough. I *will* kill you and your wretch of a brother. I'll save Marim, and I don't need anything from you."

"*You have my pride, boy. Once, I deemed myself a match for The Brothel That's pride, nothing else, and it'll see not just you but your Marim destroyed.*" Silvia reached out and touched him, and as she did, the storm encased him too, locking out the emptiness. "*You're family now. Though you have yet to accept it, you are part of Halis and me. So is Annabelle. I have information you need.*"

"I was clear on my need of you," Darith said. What could she tell him that the voice of the web could not? What could she possibly know that it did not?

"*Darith,*" she said. "*The people who have Marim are evil and you don't have time. You must get her out. Look.*"

With the word, he plunged into a thick convoluted tangle of emotion, light, and sound. Then he looked out from her eyes. Her heart raced. Her palms were sweaty, and as her panic welled up, it nearly overtook him. She flinched back from a line of men strapped into chairs. Their wrists and heads were secured, and greedy eyes stared at her naked body as she tried to cover herself with nothing but her hands and her hair.

"*I was thirteen,*" Silvia's voice informed him. "*Eight days earlier, I'd witnessed Halis turn into a spider for the first time. And then, I was brought to this room, shoved inside. I always knew I was intended to be one of The Brothel girls. What other fate awaits a woman raised in those walls? But I was thirteen. I'd had my first woman's cycle only four months prior.*"

Silvia stumbled and Darith, stuck inside her mind, stumbled with her. The click of a door opening alerted her to a new presence, and she pivoted. A robust man wearing a leer and nothing else entered. At over six feet tall and sturdy muscle hidden under his girth, Silvia endured a wave of panic as it occurred to her that she was powerless.

Silvia backed away. "*Please, don't...*"

The man approached. Silvia froze in the center of the room. His fingers latched around her arm, and a sharp pain shot up her, mingling with an unnamed painful clutching in her gut.

"*Let me go!*"

He laughed, and driven on instinct, Silvia darted forward and bit his arm. Her teeth sank in until the metallic tang of blood filled her mouth.

A hand slammed into her face, spinning her to the side. Her eyes fastened on Halis' form behind the open door. Three men held the spider back; it strained forward. The hand caught her jaw again, twisting her head the other way, to the wall of men. Men who'd paid to be there. Paid to see this.

She slammed into the ground. Blood trickled from her mouth—hers and his mingled. This time when she looked up into the eyes of her tormentor, she did not speak. There was no point in begging. No one would help her. Only...

"*Halis, I'm scared,*" she said.

"*I'll fucking gut him,*" Halis replied.

A great weight pressed down on her. Silvia closed her eyes, but she could still feel the crushing weight of the man's body on top of her. Raised in a brothel, she comprehended what was happening in a distant way. Unprepared for the forced experience, the fight drained from her limbs. To be held immobile, all choice ripped from her, elicited an illogical reaction—Silvia screamed.

"*Stop!*" Darith cried, but he remained pinned with Silvia. He smelled stale booze and sweat, tasted blood, and her panic threatened to sweep him away.

Then the man was ripped off of them, blood spraying from his mouth. And Darith, carried on Silvia's emotions, felt a surge of love and triumph as the spider drained the man.

"By all that is good in the universe, why would you share that?" Darith yelled. He yanked free of her. The clouds surrounding them swept away at his outburst, leaving them in a vacuum of emptiness.

"*Those are the people who have your Marim,*" Silvia said.

Elegant and distant as always, Silvia appeared unaffected by the memory. She glanced down at the nails on the hand that had held him, inspecting each finger as if for damage to a nail. Darith trembled, ashamed to show weakness in front of her but unable shake off the weight of that man lying on top of her, on top of him.

"*You don't have time for your pride,*" Silvia said. "*You don't have time to struggle through these discoveries on your own. Darith, you need me. Like it or not, we're your family, Halis and I. Come to me, Darith.*"

"*Come to us*," the dark voice echoed.

Darith disengaged, pulling away from the web and falling back into the sunlit world around him. The mess in his room seemed less random. The Brothel. It wasn't just Silvia and Halis The Brothel wanted. They wanted Darith, too, because he carried the contamination.

They'd kidnapped Marim.

Holding tightly to the arms of his chair, he dragged himself up into the seat. Only once his daughter rested in his lap did he leave the blood-splattered room and head down the hall. He took the time to ponder whether he should bother checking on his parents.

They were dead. If he hadn't known it before, sharing in Silvia's memory left no doubt. Those people weren't likely to care about who they killed as long as they accomplished their goal. But he owed his parents something for raising him, so he wheeled himself back to his father's study.

The room was in disarray, papers and books scattered everywhere. The butler, or he assumed the corpse belonged to the butler, lay on top of the desk, his face a pulp. Like a scarlet fruit half-eaten by a wild beast. Could a gunshot do that? Or was this something different?

Wheeling carefully through the wreckage, Darith came around the back of the desk.

"Hi, Father." The back of his eyes burned. Annabelle began to cry, the sharp tuneless cry of a human infant. One of them weeping over the old man was enough. "I'll clean you up. You wouldn't want to be found like this."

In the mess of the count's torn clothing, a scar stood out on his shoulder, a small discolored circle. Staring at his father's stripped corpse, a knot of fear in his gut unwound.

He can't hurt me. Tears slipped from Darith's eyes unheeded. The scar demanded his attention and, drained from killing the agents and witnessing Silvia's pain, Darith couldn't fight the images. Distanced from it by ten years, Darith heard the crack of the gun. Saw blood spurt from the wound as the bullet embedded itself in the wall by his bed. His father's drunken eyes cleared, and his hand fell from his belt buckle.

"Next time, I won't miss. I'll live with all manner of indignities, but you won't touch my son. Darith is the only good thing you ever did, and I'll see us both burn before you ruin him." His mother's voice was flat, emotionless. But the pistol in her hands shook and tears streamed from her eyes, coating her cheeks in mascara.

Darith turned angrily from his father. He thought of Timmy in town, for the first time since the accident, he truly thought about it. Remembered the person he wanted to be, the person his mother thought he was.

As he finished cleaning his father to be found, Darith pondered how he could honor that part of his life. He couldn't be that boy anymore. He smiled as he thought of Gretta. The girl who'd promised to help him, the one he'd parted ways with to avoid entanglement.

He only hoped their monetary arrangement didn't put her in danger.

ΔΔΔ

Not possible. Berrick stared at the file as if by doing so, the words would begin to make sense. Everything besides the punctuation was blacked out. Every damn thing. What could be that classified? And why was Silvia interested in an event that the government had tried to scratch out of existence?

For days, he'd pored over videos of Silvia at the library. Every appearance coincided with violent attacks. The same crimes that had led Berrick to believe they'd stopped here in the first place. At first, that troubled him. Silvia delved into her research only when Halis went on a killing binge. In the end, any discord between them could only serve to benefit him. He'd set his mind on finding what Silvia was doing that she didn't want Halis to know about.

Figuring out her goal proved to be no challenge. He tracked her research. He had to give her credit; she managed to hack into files no civilian should have been able to access. But if she'd had his rotten luck with finding answers, that explained why on her last visit she had broken some poor sap's arm, then proceeded to kick him repeatedly in the head and casually walk out.

So far, what had he learned? A planet had existed. The government destroyed the planet twenty-five years ago. Everything else was classified. The basic fact probably would have been classified too if there hadn't been a burned-out hull of a planet visible to all passersby.

Berrick stood up, giving one last disgusted look at the black-lined document. There was one more place to look. A place Silvia never would have thought of. The physical files. If this colony was like most of these tech colonies, physical files stopped being kept about twenty years prior. Most of the old files were supposed to be uploaded. But that was a lot of manual entry, and no one prioritized the project.

Back in his office building on Yahal, they had a basement filled with files just like these. Occasionally, they punished a new officer who stepped over a line by making them input a box.

If this particular incident was uploaded, that would be the end of the line. The physical forms would be destroyed. But they wouldn't be uploaded. Good old bureaucracy and its overwhelming ineffectiveness. The files would be sitting there, forgotten.

On his walk through the town, unrest filled Berrick. *I should have drowned that damn baby. Should be with Marim. Instead, I'm out here tracking ghosts. When things are classified there is a reason.*

He'd checked, a level six clearance would be needed to see the unedited documents. Even on Yahal, he only had a level five. Six. Only members of The Council of Five, the highest members in The Galactic council, had a level six clearance. Whatever those black lines held was deep and nasty.

This whole time, he'd been so convinced they were all playing Silvia's game. But they weren't. She might be the queen on the chessboard, but she wasn't the player. So who was? If this wasn't the spider's game, then whose?

He let himself into the building. Like every other building, it was spotless, cleaned by machines until it stank and looked like the inside of a factory. He went directly to the door at the back. The descent was murky with dim lights that flickered on at his movement. Like plunging down into the underworld.

At the foot of the stairs, a robot jerked to life. "What can I help you find?"

"Files from twenty-five years ago."

With a whir and a few blinking lights, the metal box equipped with a smaller second box with a speaker and a camera moved out of a puff of dust. The robot led him past rows and rows of boxes. It stopped at one and a little puff of dust particles lifted from it, flitting in the light. "Any particular interest, sir?"

Berrick stayed silent a moment. Telling it the truth might mean being denied the files. But lying put him at risk of treason and might mean a fruitless search.

"Intergalactic issues with a focus on the cold months."

"Third row down, sir. Blue coded boxes."

Berrick walked the echoing aisle between the rows, grateful that the robot didn't trail him. He pulled out the first box and leafed through. The papers were old and yellowed, a few with water spots. It only took him thirty seconds to find something. The box fell to the floor as he gripped the neat sheet of paper. The page gleamed white as if the contents of the sheet had burned away all signs of age.

"Gods forgive us... Gods forgive me."

CHAPTER 10

ALLISON

Halis found his human legs awkward. They didn't bend at the correct angles and there were far too few of them. But as a disguise, it was flawless. He walked across the room to the closet, where he picked amongst the clothes Silvia had provided.

The sun glared through the window, penetrating the wooden blinds. His nose curled, and he shielded his eyes. Another thing he despised about human culture—its instance on being awake during daylight hours.

"Silvia?" he called. No answer. She was probably in the gardens.

He opened the door and took the spiral staircase down to the lower floor. The glass doors of the patio provided a perfect view of Silvia. She lay in a hammock swing made of spider silk. Beside her lay Havoc. Halis paused to admire her. Even in her human form, Silvia pleased.

Through all their days, he'd never regretted his mother's choice. The day Silvia came to him as a bond mate was the luckiest day of his life. Halis was two at the time, but he recalled perfectly as Silvia's thin mother, her face lovely even with malnourishment, had set her daughter on the floor in front of him. He'd tried to bite Silvia, unsure of this girl child, who smelled of mammal excrement. She seemed no different from the others and those his mother had fed to him.

Halis opened the door and strode over to Silvia. Long ago, Silvia's mammal smell had burned away, faded into a scent like distant smoke and ripe berries. And the baby smelled as a spider baby should. Havoc looked like a weak human waste, but he was as pure as Halis.

Halis' pride grew watching his family rest there. Soon, this world would be overrun with Drambish, but none would ever be as perfect as these two. Halis had already found a few girls adequate to birth companions for his son. The hive's voice was pleased but called for more. The women who carried them would not be worth keeping, but the children... How lovely his queen would look surrounded in little spiders and the white bones of women picked clean.

No mistakes this time. The Drambish would thrive.

Silvia raised her gleaming, black eyes. "Your latest girl, Lilah, made the papers."

Was she lecturing again? He located no accusation in her eyes.

"Maybe it's time to move on," she said. "With The Brothel capturing Marim... who knows, she may have picked up some clue to our location. Between that and all the clues you have littered around..."

"Soon, my love, a girl worthy of investigation was also there the night I met Lilah."

"I don't think I've ever seen you look that way about a human. Shall I be jealous and tear out her heart?"

"Never." Halis gave her the soft smile he reserved only for her. "But maybe she can bear our son's one true companion."

"No. When it comes to choosing a companion for Havoc, I'll make the selection." Silvia's black nails slid over Havoc's cheek.

"Of course." That was only proper. It was a mother's choice, but Halis would make sure the pale girl's child was among the possibilities. Just in case.

"Halis?"

"My queen?"

"When you go into town, pick up food for Havoc. Human food. I still have a kitten or two."

This was a dismissal and Halis stopped himself from correcting her. There were still three kittens in the cage. The walk to town was a solid fifteen minutes, and those minutes were his favorite part of freedom. Clear air, open sky, a godlike family behind him and a variety of human meat down the hill.

Halis whistled as he left the garden and started on the walk.

At the bottom of the hill was a small café. Calling it anything but a claptrap was ambitious, but the sign read, "Café." The place served caffeine, sugar—in the form of frosted treats —and block-like sandwiches that tasted like something from a cross-universe transit vehicle. Whenever he went to town, Halis stopped in for disappointing pie and informative gossip.

They wouldn't let Silvia back in since she'd broken that kid's arm. It had been the child's fault; the little beast had tried to touch Havoc. Silvia didn't seem to mind the banishment and occasionally, Halis brought her back a caffeinated beverage.

Today differed. He halted in front of the window. Buried inside, beyond metallic seats and a rotating counter, stood the girl from the club. Silvia's caution that it was time to move on rung in his ears.

Halis chuckled and allowed himself to gaze at the pale woman, shining amid her dismal surroundings. The night before it had not occurred to him that this lovely creature had wanted him to notice her. She was subtle. A practiced predator. What she wasn't was a waitress.

The door creaked as he entered. The new girl didn't look up, but over the smells of grease, stale bread, and coffee, her awareness wafted. No doubt about it, she was here for them. Nothing was visually off. She was perfect, but the smell didn't match. Not only was she hyper aware of his presence, but the perfume embedded in her hair had elements worth more than she'd make in this place in a month. The cheap toilet water she wore to mask it was a new purchase.

Halis approached his would-be assassin. Her name tag read Lilly. Which was a lie. Too bad she was here to hurt him and his family. Otherwise, she would be well worth converting. Her body remained completely relaxed, even showing slight signs of weariness. The vein in her neck pulsed. She would taste of honeysuckle and cloves.

Lilly looked up. Her eyes were a color no eyes had the right to be. *I should look into preserving those. So pretty. Maybe I could string them so Silvia could wear them like jewels.*

"What can I do for you?" she asked.

Halis said nothing. "I'd like to eat you" didn't feel like the correct opening line. What would the man she thought he was do? She would think he was smart and dangerous. She must think he was human, or she would be approaching the whole thing differently. Which begged the question—were her employers lying to her or was The Brothel sending everyone out crippled?

"What kind of pies do you have today?" he asked.

Lilly smiled and looked up through her lashes. "Only have sour-cherry today."

"I'll take it, Lilly."

"Aren't you...? I'm sorry, I shouldn't ask."

"Aren't I who, sweetheart?" He grinned.

"Aren't you the guy who lives on the hill with his sister?"

Halis noticed she didn't refer to Silvia as "that crazy woman." She wanted to be on his good side and clearly, she knew nothing about Silvia. Only marks and fools mistook Silvia for his sister. "That's me. Are you new to town?"

"I came to the colony a while back, but I only left the city yesterday."

"Already had the job lined up?"

She chuckled. "Not all of us are so rich we can waltz in, buy a mansion, and then not work."

"How about, I buy you a drink after work and show you around?" Maybe he could learn something about this strange woman. Her sad eyes tugged at him. Was there a way not to kill her? These days Silvia was always seeking ways to leave people alive, but until that moment, Halis had never understood the drive.

"I'd love that."

△△△

Mr. Red closed his eyes, feigning boredom. There wasn't a soul who wouldn't have been fooled, but he was anything but bored. In the time since Allison had gone on her mission, he'd spent painstaking days hiding his research in a plethora of everyday tasks. Nothing bold or the other owners would notice his interest in something they clearly wanted him out of the loop on.

He loathed being out of the loop.

With his eyes closed, he indulged in the luxury of picturing her. Allison. So pale, she seemed always just a step away from death. Even he suffered from the tug on seeing that delicate porcelain to protect her, to shield her. The job never came easier to any girl. She'd brought down nations with a bat of her lashes and a soft word whispered in the correct ear.

That was what had bothered him in the beginning. Why would they ever send Allison on a simple kill mission? And why leave him out of the planning? The others rarely ever selected a girl without consulting him first. No one knew the girls better than their trainer. Something was off.

He opened his eyes. After scrolling through the information, pausing only once at a picture, he stood. A word blazed through his mind, but he didn't know what it meant. Drambish. A thought lingered at the back of his mind, just out of conscious reach. He fumbled to pull the meaning forward and understand the word. When he did, a tightness settled on his chest. One thing was certain; they hadn't sent her out there to kill something.

They'd sent her out to be killed. She was bait. The Brothel

didn't want the marks dead, they wanted them captured and sending people after them was a method to get the couple to flee the moon colony. But Allison was worth more than a sacrifice.

She'd one of my girls. No, my *girl.*

Not an iota of the rage inside him made it to his face. The Agency. His agency had betrayed him. *Did they fool themselves into believing I wouldn't notice? I never touched her; never even looked at her a moment too long. I'm coming, Allison. I don't know how, but I won't let them do this.*

CHAPTER 11
COMPOUND DR567R-4

Dried blood coated Darith's hands as he wheeled his chair from the mansion. Annabelle slept in his lap. With his parents dead and Mr. N and Mr. Q's corpses cooling inside, there remained no reason to look back. There was no one alive in the mansion. They'd dug their own graves. He'd said his last respects and nothing more remained to give to the corpses of his parents. The police could sort the rest out.

"Holy…" Darith said. His eyes swept out along the driveway. Everything was dead. Every blade of grass, every flower. The leaves on the trees were brown and their trunks papery, as if the slightest wind would turn them to dust.

I ravaged my home. No… That's Annabelle's handiwork. I provided a focal point.

As far as the horizon, only death met the eye. A butterfly lay still in front of the wheel of his chair. How far had they drained the land? The destruction traveled to the edge of the Cortanis estate, but the dried husks of trees blocked any farther view. In the graveyard's stillness, accusations whispered. Blind and careless, he'd used the world around him like it belonged to him to plunder. It was not his father's appetite, but the act reminded Darith of dear old dad's actions.

I lost control.

A muttering noise separate from Darith's internal recriminations teased his ears. Darith rolled forward.

His driver prayed to some plebian god inside the car. The driver's folded hands shook as if sensing Darith's attention.

Darith laughed, his head thrown back.

ΔΔΔ

Berrick felt the tap of his case against his leg as he dragged his feet one step after another. Did he look as guilty as he felt? For all the emotional security he had left, he might as well have walked under a neon sign reading, "I stole classified files," but he couldn't leave the sheath of paper.

What to do with the files was hazy. If he sent them anywhere or spoke of the contents, he was putting his confidant in danger of losing their life to a metaphorical firing squad. A few hints to Darith perhaps, to give the boy a fighting chance in his own searches, but nothing more.

I'm an outlaw now. What if I'd given in sooner? Could I have saved Polly? We could have run, fled as outlaws with our children. With Petyr. Berrick cursed himself, cursed every choice he'd ever made. To wind up where he was, even now, even in breaking the law, he was heading off to enforce The Council of Five's orders. How pointless to make his stand now, after everything he loved was gone.

The ticket machine flashed at him as he approached. Hopefully, Silvia and Halis were still on that moon colony. That pale woman, Allison, maybe she'd lived. *If she dies, that's on me too.*

A ticket mark imprinted itself on his palm. From his other hand, he took a deep drink of a liquor that tasted of nothing. He much preferred the warm burn of whiskey, but this starched colony didn't carry anything similar. The weight of the flask calmed him, gave his hand something to grip. Something to ground him in reality. Aware the switch of talismans from his badge to a flask signaled nothing good in the long run, he excused the change as inconsequential.

After all, he wasn't planning on the long run. The weight of deaths was too much for him to survive under. It would crush him.

As he walked across the platform, he took several more swigs, indulging in the respite of fog over his brain. The case tapped against his leg in rhythm with his step. The beat spelled out the name: D.R.A.M.B.I.S.H.

Not even alcohol kept words and phrases from the files from surfacing. Entire passages floated up, taunting him.

Dr. Alroy Drambish's project on Revia must be considered unrecoverable and taken as a loss. With reluctance, the decision of The Council is to dispose of the remaining samples of compound DR567R-4 and to terminate all subjects exposed. Due to Dr. Drambish's state of contamination, all inhabitants of Revia must be considered carriers of compound DR567R-4, whether or not in direct exposure to the compound.

A scuffle in front of Berrick on the platform buried the words, providing a moment's respite.

"You've gotta be joking! I haven't done anything!" a woman shouted.

Berrick transferred the case to his other hand. The process meant putting his flask in his pocket for a moment, robbing him of his only comfort.

"Just a few questions, miss," a deep male voice asserted.

Berrick scanned the platform for the source of the disturbance. The woman's thin body made the swell of her pregnancy evident. Four, possibly five months along, Polly had looked like that with Petyr. When she'd carried Marim she'd still had the plumpness of her teen years clinging to her.

"No. No!" she shouted.

Odd, it was like she was trying to get noticed. The man wore an official law enforcement uniform. Resistance made her appear guilty. None of the other citizens traversing the platform paid her shouts attention, but Berrick's eyes clung as if this everyday criminal provided a lifeline to drag him from the abyss.

Early results were overwhelmingly positive. Subject A's wife bore a child who had a stronger bond to the Drambish gene than Subject A. The child proved that compound DR567R-4 would be obsolete in time. The genetic alteration sustains itself. Prior to exposure, the couple tested infertile.

Further tests showed that a subject carrying the Drambish gene was almost guaranteed to impregnate any partner who did not carry the Drambish gene. The only limitation for procreation up to this point seems to be that two contaminated parties cannot interbreed.

"One more time, miss. If you do not comply, we will sedate you," the officer said.

What? That sounded a bit over the line. Was that how they did things here? Berrick lowered his flask, his eyes narrowed.

"I know what you're doing," said the woman. "I've heard about this. You won't—"

The man's fist hit her jaw, and he produced a needle from his jacket.

"Stop!" Berrick yelled, striding over.

The officer paused and looked over with a sneer. "Mind your own business, sir. This citizen poses a security risk."

Berrick dropped the flask in his pocket and pulled out his identification. The officer's expression changed upon seeing Berrick's rank. But his posture adjustment didn't just denote respect and training; his hand tightened on the struggling woman. This officer hadn't expected help from an unknown superior officer, which begged the question of what his precinct was up to.

Something was off.

"What has she done?" Berrick asked.

"Orders, sir. She fits the description of a suspect in a case of galactic security. If she's guilty of nothing, she'll be let free in the morning."

"After they've killed my baby!" the woman hissed. Her

dark eyes pleaded with Berrick for help.

"Is that true?" He wished he could tell her he was no one's savior, but his mouth fell into old habits and tried to protect her.

"I just round them up, sir."

Them. How many women had he rounded up?

Did it matter? Berrick's limited resources and even more limited time disallowed him from looking into any of this. He had to get to Silvia and Halis. If Allison was still alive, he had to save her before they killed her or broke her. Before the Drambish contamination spread.

"I'll bring this one into the station," Berrick said. "Go."

The officer walked away, glancing over his shoulder periodically—definitely guilty of something. The woman slumped on the floor, blubbering something along the lines of "Don't take me in" over and over again.

Berrick helped her off of the ground, holding her carefully. Now that the officer was gone, the woman let her eyes trail to the ground. In his memory, their color grew darker, blacker, until the gaze was the same cold black stare that Marim had had as she'd stared up from her asylum bed.

"Why're they aborting babies?" Berrick asked. "You're making a serious accusation. Do you have proof?"

"No. I don't even know why!" The woman wept. "But they didn't pick me up off any personal description. They didn't. They're taking all the pregnant women. Six of the ten women I went to clinic with already went in. Each lost their baby the next day. I can't lose this baby; I've been trying for years to conceive."

Even in his fogged brain, the math ticked off. She would have conceived right around the time Halis had visited the colony. That meant all the women in her clinic session would have been close to the same conception date. The remaining alcohol in his mouth suddenly tasted very bitter. If it was true, was he doing anyone any favors by helping this woman?

He looked into her brown eyes and tried to imagine bringing her into the station. The color of her eyes, a warm brown, not black at all, broke him. It was almost like staring into Polly's eyes. This woman could almost have been Polly all those years ago.

What if someone had had the chance to help Polly back then? Pregnant again after Petyr with her second illegal child, knowing she was being hunted, but not daring to confide in her husband. What if someone had stepped in and helped her?

"I'll look into it," Berrick said. "But right now, I have a train to catch. I suggest you do the same."

"Yes, sir. Thank you, thank you." The woman held a hand over her stomach, protecting the baby inside.

△△△

A piercing beep emitted from the intercom. The noise immediately repeated itself.

"Whoever that is, get rid of them," Ymel said, giving a dismissive wave to the bulky security guard in the doorway. The insistent buzzing taken care of, he approached the metal table at the center of the mirrored room. His image hovered on each shiny wall panel, reflected back and forth across the walls. He admired himself as he strode over to the girl.

Pale yellowy skin, a sharp intelligent slant to his eyes, a fitted net-suit—the picture of success and wise breeding.

She was nothing special and Ymel, not for the first time, imagined slitting her pasty throat. But he needed her. Marim. Since his team had failed so abysmally in bringing in the two who actually mattered, Marim was more valuable than he'd intended.

He set one hand over her mouth. The contrast between his warm lively skin and her death white struck him as charming. She might already be dead for all the pigment in her disappointing face. In herself, she was useless. Lacking Sylvia's looks, she would never make it as one of The Brothel's girls. Even if she did regain consciousness, which his knowledge of the Drambish gene told him was unlikely, she was just a useless girl.

Some humans just weren't suitable for the gene. Their minds, unable to bend to the center hive mind, would cave in. The reports were clear on the fate of people like Marim. The hive mind would consume her from within until she was nothing but a puppet or a corpse.

Her worth rested in her meaning to Darith. She was meant to be a safeguard to keep the boy in line. And he... damn that boy. Darith was the one whom Halis and Sylvia would come for. He'd grown powerful from the exposure and that made Darith one of the Drambish clan.

Logic told him that all Halis had wanted since getting free was to recreate the Drambish population. The benefit of this was it slowed the couple down. Where location spells failed, live trackers succeeded. The couple had gone so far as to buy a house, settled in like ducks waiting on a pond to be shot.

Now, he just had to hope Darith wanted Marim enough to come for her. Then, as long as everything else fell into place, he could kill both of the sniveling kids. Maybe have a little fun with Darith first.

Ymel licked his lips. Darith was a lovely young man, far too handsome for the skinny freckled thing on the table. Ymel's own taste in men was far too clean for The Brothel, which specialized in deviations. But Darith fit perfectly.

"Is the visitor gone?" Ymel asked at the sound of footsteps. But even before he got a response, the reflection in the mirrors revealed that it was not his bodyguard entering the room. No, a blond man with a perfectly trimmed beard strode inside. His suit was impeccable. All of him was. Nothing exciting about him, just an average man except that his suit must have cost a small fortune.

"No. I did not come all this way to depart, and I find your reception inordinately rude."

"And you are?" Ymel said.

The blond man ambled across the room. Ymel restrained himself from releasing invectives against the interruption. There was something about this man that was vaguely familiar and until he knew whom he was dealing with, it was best to retain a semblance of respect.

"A forceful attempt to evict me is not the welcome I expect from someone who has hired one of my girls."

Ah! "Mr. Red, I presume."

That was stupid. Ymel cursed himself. There was no hint on the other man's impassive face that he'd noted the slip up. But from what Ymel understood of Mr. Red, nothing escaped Red's notice. And now, Red knew that Ymel and the other owners of The Agency had discussed him in his absence. If Red wasn't already suspicious, he would be now.

"Do you often keep women tied to tables?" Red asked.

"Only the good ones." Ymel winked as he forced a grin. There had to be a way to get the upper hand. From appearances, there was nothing special about this man. He'd expected a man with looks worthy of brothel work from the way The Agency referred to him.

"The Brothel hired one of my agents." No judgment tinged Red's voice. There wasn't a hint of anything in the flat words.

Ymel's heart raced, and he took a step back bumping into the table. "Yes. A simple kill job."

"That's what my partners said."

How much did he know? This wasn't what he'd envisioned when he'd hired The Agency. He'd been thrilled at the discount The Brothel got. No one hired an Agency girl for that price. But he liked the plan as much as the discount. The Agency's asset would go out there, make a good showing, and end up dead. Her death being what they wanted, or he would have had to pay far more for their help. If all went well, his spiders would decide the moon colony was too hot to remain stationed on. Silvia and Halis would flee the planet and this time, several professionals were waiting to catch them in transit and bring them back to Ymel.

Capturing Silvia and Halis on the Veesp colony posed too many risks of exposure. The Brothel couldn't afford to have them using their abilities publicly or to be tied to the dead body of a Drambish. The Drambish mustn't make the news or everything was over. A space train was an environment he could control. Ymel had faced angry senators before. He had no wish to face a Council of Five representative out for his blood. The Agency offered him the perfect plan and all because some little chit had fallen in love with her trainer.

Him? This was the trainer? Again, Ymel wondered at the slim man. He preferred his men either younger or broader in the shoulders. Certainly, Red wasn't unattractive, but there was nothing about him that should drive a sensible girl to throw her life away.

"Do my words bore you, Mr. Ymel? Shall I repeat myself? Perhaps I'll lower the conversational bar for you and resort to direct questions," Red said. His thin mouth showed a slight snarl. "Where did you send my girl?"

Ymel took a deep breath. Well, there went any hope that Mr. Red suspected nothing.

"Your girl?" *If you didn't refer to her that way, she wouldn't be in this mess.*

"They're all my girls. Where did you send Allison? I have limited patience, Mr. Ymel."

"Why not ask your partners? They arranged the whole thing."

Mr. Red was flush now. His eyes were the color of honey. "Because you're the one I find with a child strapped to a table. Even for a man with your reputation... This might not go over well. A noble girl, no less. Imagine if her name and location were to creep out to the media. I'll ask one more time, try and pay attention. Where's Allison?"

Red rocked back on his heels, completely relaxed. He inspected the perfect crescents of his nails. Ymel's cheeks grew hot; if he could have, he would have called security and had this arrogant, pompous, preening punk dragged out. But that would be suicide. His options were limited with one of the owners of The Agency.

"Veesp moon colony."

Mr. Red strolled over to Marim and wiped a tendril of red hair from her cheek. It was a tender gesture, but only clinical detachment showed on his face. Ymel judged that Marim meant no more than a bargaining chip to Red. That played in his favor. He didn't want to face off against The Agency to keep her. Though The Brothel might win the struggle, they'd lose more than they could afford in the battle. They had to keep the existence of the Drambish from The High Council.

He'd stretched the budget already buying off a chunk of the police force on the first asteroid colony the spiders had visited and paying for The Agency girl. Keeping the spider's adventures quiet was paramount.

Red circled Marim's bed. When he finished his round, he strode to the door. Before passing through, he paused.

"I'll be in touch," Red said in the same flat, emotionless voice he'd employed the entire encounter. "My agents are my sole priority at the moment, Ymel, but I harbor no love for men who harm little girls for kicks. That girl will stay in a gleaming state of health from here on. If I hear otherwise, I'll squash you like the bug you are, and understand, I don't have time for threats."

Ymel swore under his breath, and then louder once the door clicked shut on Red's exit. He barreled across the room to Marim. Red clouded his vision, and his fist slammed into the girl's pale cheek. Her head rotated to the side, making a thunk as it struck the hard slab.

Marim's eyes opened, revealing a deep black that seemed to sink down inside her. The once-white cheek turned a vivid red and began to swell.

Marim laughed. The voices coming from her throat made a crackling cacophony and smoke curled from between her lips. Mr. Ymel stumbled back a few steps.

CHAPTER 12

THE WIZARD

T he old wizard's home was in the last place one would expect a follower of the hidden arts to dwell. He resided in
one of the stations that hovered around Yahal. Places of ref-
uge for the technologically inclined tethered to Yahal for one
reason or another. Most inhabitants were college professors,
scientists, or politicians.

The commute to Yahal mainland was under an hour, to
and from the sky-train station. Darith tucked himself and Annabelle in an out-of-the-way seat toward the middle. He knew a
few kids he'd gone to school with who lived out at the sky-sta-
tion and as the train filled, he watched fearfully for them.

He'd kept his name off the books, but if he was recognized
despite the current dark hue of his skin, it would leave a trail
linking him and the old wizard, Parl. That wouldn't do. *Could
I kill them, childhood friends, just on the off chance their deaths
would help protect Annabelle?*

"*Yes*," a voice whispered.

"No," he said, gazing into Annabelle's eyes.

He gave a sigh of relief when a man he didn't know sat
down next to him and settled a pair of net-glasses over his
face. The train jostled into movement, a brief moment without
gravity causing Darith's stomach to lurch up to his throat. Then
gravity reasserted itself.

Darith tugged at the ratty sweatshirt he'd found in one

of the servants' rooms. It was too big, and the hood did a passable job of obscuring some of his face. He leaned back into the shadow for the remainder of the journey, tugging the web tightly around him. The thrum of energy obscured his face.

The whispering voice of the web wound around him. Its words encouraged him on. Darith would have broken free of the cocoon except that the shadows hid him from passing eyes.

Would Parl even remember him? It had been years since they'd had any contact. The last time they'd spoken, Parl had accused him of having an attitude worthy of a spoiled noble brat—had insinuated that soon he would be just like his father. Looking back, Darith regretted taking offense. He should have taken the words to heart.

Now, Parl was the only one he dared to trust. The only person he knew who could keep a secret and the only possible person who wouldn't try to harm Annabelle if he knew what she was. What Darith was.

He glanced again at the smoky gray of his skin. Using the web had been a necessary part of this journey. He was too conspicuous in a wheelchair, but the link seemed to grow roots every time he used it. How long until he couldn't disconnect?

The train pulled into the station, and the three vacuum doors opened onto the eclectic metal suburb. Darith stepped out onto the self-propelling ground. For a block he let the walkway carry him along, but the ground propelling him reminded him too much of a wheelchair. He strode along the walkway, achieving a pace akin to a run with the added movement of the ground.

Above him a screen stretched over the sky, displaying a view of a perpetually sunshine. It would display that image until the clocks indicated sleeping hours and then it would clear, showing the vast expanse of stars and on occasion Yahal below.

Each segment of the station glowed a different color, illumination seeping from the cracks in the walkway. These colors defined the districts. He followed the walkways until he reached the green section. As he approached the clusters of fantastical houses, the revulsion bred in Darith rose.

The displays of tech were excessive and vulgar. He half-expected drug addicts to start tumbling into the street and murdering each other. That was what happened in all the "documentaries" they showed at school. All that actually happened was a continuation of the mechanized bird chirping.

Parl's house, at the very least, didn't float. The small shack stood on long bird legs. He'd mentioned it once, called it an ode to a witch of legend. From all appearances, the house over his head was a wreck of old wooden boards with shutters loose on their hinges, but that was a façade.

Darith clutched Annabelle close to him and resisted the urge to simply fly them up to the door. Connected to the web his access to energy to bend seemed endless. Instead, he searched out the alert panel along the street and buzzed up into the house. Only moments later, the giant bird legs bent, and the house lowered so its stoop touched the ground. The door creaked open and Parl's weathered face appeared.

He hadn't changed in the years. On his head, scraggly gray hairs grew long and sparse over a shiny scalp. Only the beard that covered two-thirds of his face was thick, his long, pencil-thin nose sticking out over the mass of hair.

"Darith Cortanis?" The old man wheezed.

"Invite us in, old man."

"I've heard your name, even up here. Didn't expect you to *walk* to my doorstep."

Darith shoved past Parl into the temperate interior. The décor inside was diametrically opposed to the outside. Everything shone with factory freshness. Lights flashed and a small hunk of plastic shot out to clean any dirt Darith might have tracked inside. Darith strode over to a sofa and seated himself. Once off his feet he cut himself off from the web and watched the darkness drain from his hands.

Parl furrowed his brow; this caused a few long hairs to drag across his eye. But he didn't mention the change in Darith's looks, or how he'd come to be smoke colored to start with.

"Parl, you once schooled me in lost magics, unspoken laws." Darith waved for the old man to sit. "My wife has been taken and I have every reason to believe those who've done this will return for me and my daughter."

With a groan, Parl settled into the chair opposite Darith. "How're your parents?"

Darith shivered at an unbidden image of the blood-soaked parlor and high-heeled feet sticking out from behind a typically white lounge chair. Beneath the countess' glazed eyes was a blue-lipped smirk, the same smile she'd worn when anything bad happened. Her "I told you so" to the world, the perfect knowledge she'd held at her core that nothing would ever go right. *I never proved her wrong.*

"Don't waste my time," said Darith, avoiding the question. "I'm here because you are the only person who might be able to protect her."

"There's more to this tale. The air around you hums and you walk to my door, though everyone knows you are crippled. If you want my aid, do me the honor of being honest and respectful."

Darith lifted a hand to massage his forehead. If anyone deserved respect, it was Parl. He formulated his words before speaking to avoid the harsh edge he otherwise couldn't seem to avoid.

"My life's a mess, Parl. I don't expect you to wade through the sludge with me. I'm stronger now, stronger than I ever was or ever should have been. I found a way to heal myself. The process will take time to perfect and time is something I have little of, so I need help. First, I must find a safe harbor for Annabelle. The things I need to do won't be safe for her. Please, I have no right to ask anything of you, but I am asking."

"I'll protect the baby."

"Touch her."

"Why, young Cortanis?"

"Because she isn't what you think she is and you need to

understand that. I need to see your face when you learn if I am to trust you with her."

Parl reached out and set his hand on Annabelle's chubby cheek. He recoiled and wiped his hand against his leg. His voice shook when he next spoke. "Do you know what she is?"

"My daughter."

"She is not yours, Darith."

Darith glared. "She is no one else's. Trust me when I say she's more than that thing you feel. I intend to see to it. But she needs her mother. Marim is the one who will teach Annabelle love and kindness... Hell, Marim will teach me."

"Are *you* spouting love conquers all? You? That thing in the child... is like thousands of claws trying to pierce my flesh."

"Not claws and not thousands. Legs and—"

"Eight."

"My love won't change her, but with love, protection, and guidance, she'll be more than the creature that poisoned my wife. I'll arm myself, find and heal Marim, but first I'll figure out why The Brothel wants us, and I need Annabelle safe. She cannot come where I'm going or see those I go to see."

"The Brothel? And if they come looking for her here?"

"They won't. I shielded myself coming here. No one saw me and there is no trail. As far as the world knows, I spent one month failing to learn magic from you, so there's no reason to believe I would come to you."

"How?"

"The people who attacked us left bits behind like an infection. The other day I moved the contamination. I'm certain that, given time, I could remove it. But I need to understand it first. I'll be the test subject and then I'll find Marim and I'll cure her. But I'm missing pieces, and it's imperative to find those that infected us to connect the scattered bits."

"You cannot hope to cure the child. If you removed the beast... there is nothing else inside her."

"I know." Darith grinned. Annabelle's excitement made his heart pound. "When I find the black widow, I'll rip the beast from her and see how she fares."

He didn't allow himself to think of Silvia often. Halis was safer, thoughts of Halis brought only hate and anger. Silvia shouldn't have been more complex, but she was. Along with the anger was the memory of her warm, smooth flesh, as if the memory of slipping between her thighs somehow remained separate from the rest. Kill her, yes. That remained the primary urge, but there were others and he didn't appreciate that those desires lingered.

Not when he'd never been able to hold Marim as a husband should. Not when Marim suffered. He shouldn't listen to the words Silvia sent him or pity her for the wrongs she'd suffered as a child.

"Revenge, Cortanis, is the wrong thing to show that child... I can feel it rolling off of her. If you hold to those thoughts, you will lose any chance of making this 'cure her nature' bit work."

"It won't be me who cures her. It'll be Marim."

Parl stood and paced the length of the room several times before meeting Annabelle's eyes. He tapped his finger on his chin through the layers of hair.

"I'll care for the child." He looked up, meeting Darith's eyes. "I'm proud of you."

"Thank you." Darith enunciated the words with care. They were not words he was used to uttering.

CHAPTER 13

A WALK THROUGH THE PARK

T he sun's warmth flickered over Allison's back, stroking her cheek with a softness matched only by a mother she barely recalled. A lull fell over her. Her eyes fluttered closed for a moment and she allowed Halis to guide her down the path.

Moments existed in staccato bursts in her memory. Could she keep this one? Maybe forget whose hand held hers? She played a dangerous game lowering her guard, but she doubted he would try to kill her here. No. He, like her, planned something in private.

A kill was an intimate thing, the culmination of a complex dance.

She'd seen enough of his kills to know the final steps.

Allison turned her face to her companion. Her heart shivered at the sight of him, his dark skin fading into the shadowed trees, leaving his white teeth and the whites of his eyes bright. He stepped closer and her body took over for her heart. Her breath quickened at his closeness, a giddy warmth spreading over her. Her flesh desired him, yearned for him to reach across the infinitesimal distance and touch her.

If she'd required any warning that he was dangerous, her reaction to his nearness would have sufficed. There was no cause for the reaction. Oh, she might have taken it for love, even with all her training, were it not for Red. Every time she thought Red's name or pictured his occasional smile, her heart sang, and the world brightened. No. She didn't love Halis.

"How did someone like you end up here, with me?" Halis asked. His dark hand brushed her white cheek, and she leaned her head into it to prolong the touch.

"Can't I be here because I desire it?"

"No, you lovely little thing, there are greater mechanisms at work. Fate, luck."

Pheromones. That was the only explanation for the tightening of desire in her belly. Somehow, he was putting off a scent that lured her. But *people* couldn't do that. Not to this extent and not on purpose. For important missions, Red sometimes provided her with a few injection shots to ramp up her own appeal. Was this what those men had felt like? Drawn to her against their better reason?

"Luck," she whispered. No, not luck, something much more purposeful than that. Did he know? "Yes, our whole lives have led to this moment. But that can be said about any moment."

He leaned down and the touch of his lips jolted through her. Would this be what it felt like to kiss Red? The thought was not new, nor was indulging it. If her body wanted to play traitor, fine. Not like she'd ever get this from the man she truly wanted.

I am strong enough to resist Halis' pull. She wrapped her arm around his neck, lifting herself to her tiptoes. As the kiss deepened, she leaned into him, the firm muscle of his chest pressing against her. Tonight was the night.

All she had to do was get him back to her place, get the last of the information that The Agency wanted, kill him, and disappear. Everything was prepared; she'd leave no trace and no connection between Halis' death and The Agency. She'd turned on her net-implant just long enough to clear the waiting cache of communications. Her report on Halis' sex life should be back at The Agency center now. Her job didn't include questioning why they wanted the information, but she was thankful they had since watching him had warned her to be even more wary than usual. Her observations warned her not to go to bed with

Halis until the time came to end the dance.

But she needed to get him to her bed in order to obtain the last of the details they wanted. Since she also had to get him away from public places, it was time to funnel him to an appropriate place.

Few of the girls Halis met with survived; the ones who had lived came away pregnant.

"Back to my place?" Halis asked.

"No." Allison repressed a shudder at the thought of the dark mansion on the hill, Halis' frozen demoness of a sister lurking inside. No. His place wouldn't do. She'd been warned about Silvia by the chief of police, even if she didn't know what the warning meant, Allison didn't intend to go near Silvia. "Maybe..."

Allison had an invitation to her apartment on her lips when it occurred to her that was what Halis wanted her to say. She pressed her mouth to his again to give herself a moment to think.

A replay of the night was full of red flags. He'd chosen this park and then angled her onto a path that led them within a five-minute walk of Allison's apartment. He might have suggested his place, but he wanted her to contradict him. And if that was *his* plan, strolling in there on his arm was suicide. She couldn't hope to overcome him in a battle of strength.

He meant to kill her. The only advantage Allison had was that he thought her no more than a doxy under his spell. In an all-out fight, she couldn't master him.

Shit. Her concentration blurred as his hands slid up her waist and his fingers explored. Her fingers tightened in his hair and she pulled him harder against her. When they parted, her chest heaved.

"My place?" he repeated.

"No, your sister makes my blood run cold."

"She causes a lot of people to feel that way." His grin implied there were no hard feelings.

His hand reminded her that finding a bed was a pressing

factor. And the innocent chit he thought Allison was would be consumed with that desire.

"Here." She used her net-glasses to allow him access to her housing information. "Give me an hour? It's a small place. I just want to clean up a little. Maybe a bath too after work so I don't smell like grease."

"I don't care what you smell like."

She kissed him, enjoying the insistent feeling spreading from her belly. The brush of her breasts against him added to the pressure of his fingers and intoxicated her. Maybe they could consummate this relationship traditionally before... No. Get it done and get out.

"An hour," Allison said.

"An hour." Halis brushed his lips across hers one more time.

The contact elicited a moan from her. Maybe pull him into the trees?

Allison turned and deliberately walked away. Her body burned, and it wasn't the sunlight.

All I need to do is kill him. Then get back and somehow convince The Agency I'm loyal. One step at a time worked best. She'd worry about The Agency later. Would they make a second attempt to see her dead if she returned or let this serve as a warning?

The dingy apartments were lit against the oncoming night when she arrived. All of her neighbors had their curtains drawn tight, light leaking from the cracks. Allison grabbed the rusted metal railing and ran up the stairs to her apartment door. A glance behind her proved Halis wasn't following.

She pressed her ear to the door. After a few minutes, she swiped her key. If there was some sort of trap waiting, no noise gave it away. She nudged the door open with her foot, standing back as she pulled it wide.

Before stepping inside, Allison inspected the parking lot behind her. There was still no motion out there, just the usual junk vehicles. Was it possible she was wrong and he hadn't meant to trap her? Did he even know where she lived? Maybe he was so certain of his own victory, he assumed she'd fall on his knife. From their encounters alone, she would have gotten that impression, but the information she'd gathered suggested otherwise. The Agency was keeping secrets, excluding Red from her assignment. If not for the police chief's warning, would she have missed this?

"I'm paranoid," she said.

The entryway light turned on as she stepped inside and shut the door before stepping into the familiar room. Nothing was out of place. If anything had stirred, even a hairsbreadth, she would have noticed, but the kitchen and small living area were as she left them.

A spider scurried across the floor and Allison crushed it with the tip of her boot. Letting out a deep sigh, she went into the kitchen and pressed a button. The floor cleaning unit squeaked its protest as it emerged from the wall and tidied the spider's remains.

Allison ought to tidy herself up too after her excuse to Halis. The house was in perfect order, if a bit cluttered, but Allison did stink of the diner.

As she turned, she did a cursory inspection through the partially open door of the bedroom's dark interior. The door was precisely at the angle she'd left it, not a centimeter wider. The blanket on the bed was pulled back, revealing a triangle of red sheets. Too bad she wouldn't get to use that bed. Everything seemed in place, so she stepped inside.

The curtain fluttered against the window. The air blowing in was colder, and it chilled her arms as she inspected the room. If Halis had lain some sort of trap, she couldn't find it. With a shake of her head, Allison set aside thoughts of the impending conflict.

She tossed her net-glasses on the bed and smiled. A bath.

Allison stepped into the bathroom and grinned at the porcelain tub against the peeling wallpaper. That tub was the entire reason she'd selected this apartment. There were plenty of dirt-cheap rathole places a diner worker could ostensibly afford, but this was the only one with an old-fashioned bathing option. Quaint or not, Allison loved the feel of immersing herself in water. Often, she poured her bath cool, and when she closed her eyes Allison could imagine she was resting in her parents' pool.

As a child, she'd swum there under the watchful eye of her mother. She'd try to ignore her brother's splashing and imagine she was out in a vast lake. Of course, she'd never gotten to visit a lake, not the sickly daughter of a Lower Council senator. No, she might catch her death or drown. But swimming in the pool she hadn't felt weak.

The faucet gave a rusty squeak and turned, setting free a gush of water. She pressed the red button and dialed it up. This was no time for memories. Especially ones that involved her brother. Would killing Halis be as hard as it had been to plunge a knife into her brother's chest? Allison's body craved Halis, but no trace of attachment remained when he was absent.

This was not a time for regret, either. How long had it been since she'd felt the specters of her family haunting her? Decades? Centuries? But knowing The Agency was trying to kill her brought them back. The people she'd betrayed to gain employment at The Agency. Her admittance test had been standard practice for new girls, something vile to prove that the girl's only loyalty was to her new employers. For Allison, that had meant murdering her brother, framing her mother, and seducing key members of the penal system to push for an execution.

No ties outside The Agency. No going back.

She slid her fingers into the nearly scalding water so that little trails jetted off. After a moment, she shrugged off her uniform, letting it pool at her feet. Once devoid of her clothing, Allison stepped into the tub and lay back. The steaming water crept higher until it glided up over her belly. The white of her skin turned slightly pink in the stinging heat. The pain helped keep the memories at bay. With one foot, she turned the water off and sank until her face slid into the water.

When she emerged, something angular and white crossed her vision. Her hand fastened on the edge of the porcelain. The white-and-black blur across her water-clogged eyes streaked toward her. Allison gained her feet, her eyes and brain unable to work together to process the shapes, textures, and colors confronting her. An apparition of ghostly white and vivid black, too many limbs.

A spider. They come in through the window…

One white limb struck her wrist, slicing through flesh. Allison slipped back. A giant white spider, black markings on its sides.

Beautiful, like some ancient god made flesh.

Allison leaped back, years of training doing their work as she cleared the tub edge and landed on the tile. The blood from her wrist landed on the slick, white floor. *Where do I hit this magnificent beast to hurt it? Where are a spider's important organs?*

With a hissing sound, the spider sprang again.

Allison ducked down, sweeping up with her foot to hit the creature in its midsection. Thick, bristly hairs dug into her foot. The spider's leap carried it over her to knock into the wall behind Allison. Before Allison turned, one long leg shoved her forward.

Wet tile slid under her. She crashed into the tub, her head smashing into the porcelain, marking it a vivid scarlet. Pain blinded Allison. She sank into the water, her legs sticking awkwardly out of the tub. The water in front of her turned a vivid pink. Allison's vision blurred, and she saw her brother's gray face, his wide blue eyes accusing her.

You deserved to die.

Spider legs as sharp as blades wrested her from the water, then pinned her down on the cold tile. The creature's weight was not as great as she'd imagined. In fact, its hold on her was gentle, razor-tipped legs brushing against her, close enough that if she moved, she'd be speared.

Allison relaxed back against the floor.

"I died once, at the hands of a majestic demon sprung

from my own greed and hatred. What sort of beast are you?" Allison whispered. In all her years, she'd never even heard of something like this.

"*I am many things. Often, like you, I am a herald of death and despair.*" The voice entered Allison's mind, a rich feminine quality to the reverberations. "*Unlike you, I am never prey.*"

"And now? What mask do you wear now?"

"*I'll give you a hint.*" The spider leaned down until its glittering eyes were in front of Allison's face. "*I'll be the madness that eats you.*"

Allison heard the door open, and the spider waited, not moving its gaze.

"Well?" Halis' voice. "What do you think of her?"

That was hardly a surprise. Allison shivered. "Silvia."

"*This one is extraordinary, my love. As charming as you said. Perhaps you were correct all along.*" The Spider-Silvia's voice had a darker quality.

"I leave this decision to you, my queen," Halis said.

Allison laughed, unable to restrain the insane sound. "This is what that man warned me about. Berrick. What are you?"

"We are extinct," Halis said.

"*Soon, we won't be. She's the one, Halis. She is the mother to bear Havoc's companion. Yes, she's exquisite. You were correct all along. But we can't risk leaving her sane.*"

"A pleasing decision," Halis said.

The spider's mouth opened. A scream tore from Allison's throat, but Allison floated separately from it. The gaping maw fastened on her shoulder, sending a burning acid through her. The razors lifted from her body and Allison lay in a pool of cool water. Her limbs were unresponsive.

Halis' shuffling step approached and then, he formed into a lovely dark smear across her vision. Next to him stood Allison's brother. Pain radiated from Silvia's bite and her thoughts became hard to hold on to. Images flashed, the real mixing with the past and with demented imaginings torn from a hellscape.

An image of a rose being stripped of its thorns hammered into her skull.

"You deserved to die," she whispered to her brother. How many times in her youth had he entered her room and added that poison to her drink before The Agency had shown her the videos? All for an inheritance. Her entire youth lost to sickness, practically chained to her bed.

I grew thorns, the family's fragile flower, and I impaled you and snared mother.

"*They lied,*" the image of her brother whispered. "*I never hurt you.*"

Those were the last words he'd spoken before she'd plunged the knife and blood had welled up from between his lips. She couldn't be hearing them now. They weren't real. Allison struggled to concentrate.

Halis crouched over Allison, that smile no longer firing anything in her. Behind Halis, the spider.

"Red..." Allison whispered.

CHAPTER 14
THE SORCERESS & THE SPIDER

T he mirror reflected Silvia's cold eyes back at her. Wrapped in one of the pale girl's towels, Silvia sought humanity in her eyes. *Once I was human. I must still be.* The strange, painful thought had haunted her since their escape. The children born Drambish would all be like Halis. How would they view her when they grew? Yet no flicker of emotion ignited in her, listening to Halis impregnate Allison.

Shouldn't I feel something? I should pity her, but my heart doesn't stir.

The hive's voice crooned inside her, wordless but comforting. The voices there did not want her to feel for Allison. They saw no fault in these acts.

He doesn't need to harm her. We didn't need to harm her. I...

A tear escaped Silvia's eye at the jabbing sensation in her chest. But then the thoughts faded into a fog. She could not hold them. The hive voice came and drove away the misty remnants of doubt and sorrow.

"Hush, child. You are one of us. She is nothing. A meal, a receptacle. She matters only for the beauty she will produce. You are the living queen. She is only a fly in your web."

Silvia spun to the bathroom's other two occupants and smiled. Halis embodied perfection and watching him drove out doubts. Allison's white face and glassy eyes made her look like a doll. She wasn't real, never had been.

Halis stood and returned Silvia's smile. "Return home?"

"And leave her? The child she carries is precious. I'll not leave it to the fates."

"Local law inhibits us from snatching her easily," Halis said, crossing the floor, Allison's blood smeared over his chest. "They take disappearances seriously. So we'd need her to state she wished to go with us... or clearly be in a delirious state and not capable of making such decisions. If we were caught sneaking her, we'd both be detained and our grounds swept if they thought we were involved, and they would. We don't want that."

"That's a lot of research wasted if I'd said I wanted her dead."

"The top five places for an inconspicuous burial put in order by proximity and convenience from this apartment—"

"Save your breath for clarifying your plan for the existing situation. I will not kill her!"

"We just need her officially put in our care. If we leave her like this, someone will find her and send her to the state hospital. Her injuries may cause a fuss, but my DNA won't appear and assault is deemed a very minimal crime. With her declared insane, we can simply walk her offworld with us. I shouldn't have much trouble picking her up from the hospital once we have what we need. No one else will come for her. Even if they suspect me of harming her, without an accusation from her, they'll act on my presumed innocence."

"How are we to get this mess off-planet?"

"Leave that to me."

"Once our offspring is born, we grant her a swift death." *Allison deserves freedom after she's served her purpose. No more like Marim. No more fed to the hive without cause.*

Halis paused. "Why kill her?"

"Why do you care? You can't intend to keep her around as your little rape-doll?"

"Rape?" Halis glared at her. "That's a nasty accusation."

"What else do you call that!" Until Silvia had said the

words, Allison's prone form barely registered. As she finished speaking, panic rose in her throat, choking her. Her next statement died in her chest. *What am I? Death is clean, but this… I condoned this.*

Halis stepped forward, his brows drawn together, and the smile gone from his face. Silvia shoved him back and held her arm out to keep him at a distance.

"I call it fighting extinction. She's human—nothing."

She forced her next words to be softer. "Humanity has nothing to do with it. We didn't kill her like clean prey."

"She wanted to mate with me."

"Indeed, when you were courting her in the park. You aren't trying to tell me that threatened with death and insanity and poisoned, she remained willing?"

"Something is wrong with you, Silvia. Being around all these humans has warped your perception. They're nothing. She's nothing, just chattel."

"And me?"

"You aren't one of them. You never were like them. She's nothing but a lovely face to breed the continuation of our species."

But once Allison's body accepted the Drambish gene, she couldn't breed anymore. "Then why keep her?"

"Get dressed. We'll discuss this at home. If it means so much to you, we can be rid of her when the child is birthed. For now, we have more to worry about."

CHAPTER 15

THE BEGINNING OF THE END

G rease clogged his nostrils; the air was laden with it. Berrick leaned back in the seat and poked at the gelatinous pie in front of him. The waitress, a tired middle-aged woman, was busy on the other side of the diner. A stained rag in her hand smeared some clean-all substance across the tables.

Berrick looked at the files again. On top of the Drambish files lay another set covered in looping handwritten letters. Sometime after disembarking, the documents had been slipped in his bag. The intel had come from Allison—who else? The copious notes all detailed Halis' behavior patterns. Page after page of times he'd left the house, how long he stayed out, whom he saw, who he slept with, who lived after sleeping with him. That she'd written the notes on paper only showed she had always intended them to come to him. Surely, whatever report she'd sent her agency had been done electronically.

The house on the hill waited for him, but he'd come here first—to find Allison. He hadn't fully understood what Halis and Silvia could do, what they were, or the vendetta they had when he'd met Allison the first time. That was no excuse for not warning her properly. He'd only warned her about Silvia also being part of the equation, but after reading the government papers, he understood the full threat that Halis posed.

He didn't have to read the words anymore to see them. He could have recited all twenty pages. Allison stood about as much chance against Halis as Berrick's brother had stood against Silvia.

The secretions were designed with the intent of allowing the Drambish soldiers to gain access to dangerous areas in a covert fashion. Initial findings were all positive; the reaction of the opposite gender to Drambish secretions could seduce intended victims even when the infected test subject was deliberately belligerent. The chemical reaction in the unaltered humans resembles the chemical reaction of love. However, at this stage in the experiment, the secretions cripple any idea of a tactical strike at the population.

Would warning her have changed anything? When she'd left him in the station, the implication of her words had been that she'd foreseen her own death. Allison had already been caught up in the web, but that did not absolve him of his guilt.

As the waitress moved over, Berrick lifted his hand. Studying her notes here wasn't safe. Best get to the point and get to his newly rented room.

"I was told a girl worked here—pale, blonde, beautiful."

"Lilly? Yup. She did. Hasn't showed up in over a week."

So she was dead. "Any idea where she went?"

"Nobody tells me nothin'. Boss had a meeting with some lawmen. You a lawman?"

"No, just a friend."

"Well, rumor has it, just rumor mind you, she cracked. Had to send her away. Too bad. Rich handsome boyfriend and all. She was getting out of this place."

"Boyfriend?" That would be Halis.

"Yeah, handsome dark-skinned fellow. Lives in a mansion on the rise over the ocean with his bitchy sister."

Halis and Silvia.

"Well, thank you." Berrick turned to his unnaturally red pie and the waitress continued her tidying. The sticky red goo tasted like congealed cherry syrup.

Berrick turned to Allison's handwritten notes. Despite an urge to drive up to Halis and Silvia's house, waiting needed to fill the next few days. He'd study her notes, watch the house for himself. Only then could he start to take them out. One at a time until none of them remained. Annabelle last... first Silvia.

Doctor Drambish's notes on creating a central consciousness have disappeared from the computers. From what remains, his subjects were linked, much like ants to a central mind. This mind centered in Doctor Drambish. His early notes indicate this was to provide a stop measure should the experiment get out of control.

Since Drambish's disappearance, after slaughtering and partially consuming his aides, it can be assumed that Drambish has been contaminated. We have no data on how much of his own mind remains. The risk of him being at large and connected to these predators is unacceptable.

They won't hurt anyone else. The trail of death and insanity ends here.

△△△

Darith closed his eyes, but they opened moments later as a man in a business suit entered the dimly lit spaceship cabin. Energy pooled at Darith's fingertips as the craft jerked into flight. The blond, bearded man reminded him of The Brothel's agents. But after a closer inspection, Darith determined that couldn't be. The clothes were too expensive, the ring on his finger worth a small fortune. No. Whoever this man was, his presence on the shuttle to the moon colony had nothing to do with Annabelle, himself, Marim, or The Brothel.

The man seated himself on the plush seat opposite Darith. He didn't avert his gaze. Nor could Darith read any emotion there—looking into his eyes reminded Darith of staring into the abyss that had claimed Marim.

"You must be Darith Cortanis... No, no, don't even try your magic." The man held up his hand as if to display the small device in his palm.

Darith didn't recognize the machine but understood the

implication that it would affect his magic. It was enough to caution him.

The man continued. "It wouldn't work and I mean you no harm. At least for now."

"Who the hell are you? And why are you intruding on my privacy? How did you find me?"

"Oh, the pride of youth. I didn't find you. Our meeting is coincidental in that sense. We are both here because we became entangled in this Drambish mess."

"You are?"

"My name is Mr. Red."

"You're with The Brothel."

"No." Red's nose curled in distaste. "They're clumsy fools playing with fire. So are you."

Darith tightened his fist, cutting off Red's air supply. He felt the contact. *Apparently, the little device does nothing.*

His elation died quickly. The only reaction in Red's eyes was mild amusement. Rather than tearing at his throat, he reached into his pocket and pulled out a lock of red hair, tied with a stiff wire. Darith let go. His eyes fastened on the hair.

"Marim?" Darith asked.

"She's alive, and no worse off than at the hospital. Not pretty enough for The Brothel to use—"

"You shut up."

"Has anyone told you that you're a nasty little twerp? Wisdom works far better than brute force."

"I'm doing fine."

"I assume by that you mean your wife wasn't forcibly impregnated, driven insane, then kidnapped, your parents weren't brutally murdered, and you're not being chased by a powerful corporation or—"

"Enough." Darith's fingers dug into the chair. Who was this bastard and how did he know so much? "What do you want?"

"To tell you your wife isn't being tortured or raped." Red shrugged.

"Why do you care?"

"We're tangled in this together. Someone I care about is down on that colony."

"You're here to kill Silvia and Halis."

"You sound worried, boy. No. Not unless they get in my way. I'm here for my agent. Nothing more. I would've thought you'd be doing the same. You do realize your wife is on Yahal, correct?"

"Keep your nose in your own affairs."

"And I assume you believe that wisdom is driving you?"

Darith turned his face away from Red's smirk. They sat in silence as the shuttle sped away from the main spaceship toward the Veesp moon colony. It wasn't until the landing announcements sounded that Red spoke again.

"The Brothel is waiting for your 'spiders' to flee. Every shuttle departing this little outpost has attendants scanning for their DNA." With that comment, Red stood and left the compartment.

Darith lingered a moment before standing. Time to confront Silvia, find out if she knew as much as she implied. Any DNA scan would work on him too. Sounded like, getting off the moon colony would be an issue.

Once thing at a time. Silvia first.

△△△

Silvia shoved the suitcase against the wall. The bedroom was barren. What they weren't packing, Halis was burning out back. The only decoration remaining was the lovely woman curled up on the couch. Allison couldn't exactly be packed away.

At an insistent tugging at the back of her mind, Silvia crossed the room, looking out at Halis. He remained oblivious. Darith had figured out how to isolate Silvia. *Good, that means Halis doesn't know Darith is here.*

Silvia slipped over to Allison, the darkness forming an

invisible net around the pale woman. The air was thick and sweaty as Silvia's hand passed through it to stroke the girl's cheek.

What a wonderful member of the family Allison could have been, but Allison couldn't be trusted. She hadn't even been given a chance to be driven mad naturally by the gene... Silvia had planted the poison specifically to break Allison's mind.

"I'd do it again," Allison whispered to the ghosts in her mind. She lifted her head; a bloody hole was all that remained of her left eye. The right eye latched on to Silvia before closing.

Silvia lifted her new necklace, backed by silver and sealed beneath a magic time barrier. The violet color of the iris gleamed as vivid as a jewel.

Halis is a good man. He loves me, and that is all that matters.

But it wasn't. She knew the danger of sneaking off on her own now, when they had every reason to think The Brothel would keep coming after them here. Yet she didn't want him anywhere near Darith. If he couldn't even see the harm he'd done to Allison, not even feel it was wrong...

But it would leave them both crippled to be apart. Together as a unit, they were nearly indestructible. But alone... She shivered, remembering coming into that bedroom to find Berrick with a gun trained on Halis. And her love bleeding. Separate, they were weak.

The tug came again, and Silvia stood straight, feeling outward with her mind. Darith waited and through the murky vision of the web, Silvia recognized his location. *Darith's here and he's calling me.*

Silvia glanced out at Halis. The white blur of Allison at the corner of her vision made the decision for Silvia. She couldn't tell Halis. Love him or not, she couldn't trust him. Marim had rejected the Drambish gene and Darith was trying to overcome it. Silvia wasn't willing to risk Halis deciding they were enemies and destroying them. No. She needed to find out what Darith wanted on her own.

CHAPTER 16

BERRICK VS. THE DRAMBISH

L ike the shadow of a moonbeam, Silvia slid from the house. Berrick adjusted himself in his hiding place. Even compensating for her improved hearing and vision, she wouldn't notice him. Allison had fully vetted this spot to spy on the spiders. It was only luck that made the location she'd chosen a perfect layout for a sniper shot. He leveled the gun at her, setting her in his sights.

Words on paper told Berrick what she was. A contamination. A nearly unstoppable disease created in an attempt to build a super-soldier. No survivors. That was The High Council's decision, genocide was the only option, and because the Drambish gene was a contagion passed by prolonged bodily contact or sexual contact. It came down not to no Drambish survivors, but no survivors.

That sacrifice, all those lives, would be for nothing if Silvia, with her swaying hips and pouty mouth, wasn't eradicated. Berrick's arm shook.

We created them. Shot this into their veins.

Surprise was the only way to kill the sorceress. Halis he might be able to take by force, but Silvia had to be first. He'd waited for her to emerge, but now that she had, his finger stalled on the trigger.

Silvia pushed a floating stroller in front of her, dressed like a wicked queen from one of Marim's storybooks. Berrick followed her, every moment his mind commanding his finger to move. She rushed down the drive—deep red hair trailing after her like a stream of blood diluting in black ink.

Pull the damn trigger.

Berrick lowered the gun. She was too far away now. The chance was gone. Whether it was wise or not, he would have to go after Halis first. The spiders were preparing to leave the colony; he might not get another chance with them apart.

His back pressed into the tree behind him, Berrick watched the smear of Silvia's form disappear into the distance. He needed her far enough away that if Halis used the odd connection the Drambish shared, Silvia could not make it back in time to save her lover.

Berrick's understanding of the Drambish mental interconnectedness was minimal. Hell, the documents hardly seemed to indicate the researchers had even understood. They were just a mess of suppositions of powers the Drambish might have. But something connected them. Marim had rambled about it and Darith had tried to explain.

Get in. Kill Halis. Get out before the black widow returns. That was the plan.

I should have shot her. Why didn't I?

Berrick lifted his gaze to the thick black clouds that blotted the sun. "I love you, Marim."

All the windows in the house were dark and the streetlights barely penetrated the trees as Berrick crept toward the house. At any moment, he expected Halis to burst from the house. Turn to him and charge. Berrick adjusted his grip on the gun, twisting his hands around the comforting density.

He exited the trees and bent his knees, half-crawling forward. Smoke funneled into the sky. *From a fireplace?* Berrick wondered. There was a significant amount.

The long, grassy slope to the house provided almost no cover and his gaze never left the windows. At one point, he thought he saw a ghost of white cross the glass. He dropped to the ground. But nothing emerged, so he rose from the dirt and covered the last of the distance to the house.

The air was heavy with smoke and Berrick looked to the sky. A thick column of smoke peeled from the back of the house. It wasn't coming from inside at all.

"I'll probably be joining you, Polly," he whispered.

Gods, how he wanted to see Polly, to see Petyr. He closed his eyes and tried to picture them. Tried to conjure that part of his life, Polly in her rocking chair holding a cup of steaming tea. Marim laying in front of the fire reading a book to her brother, who, rather than sitting, still clambered all over her back. All of it was as distant and unreal as a dream.

He looked at the dark house and the rolling smoke, the weight of booze in his pocket calling to him. This was life. He couldn't touch those who had taken Polly and Petyr; they were too far up the governmental food chain. But the man who'd taken Marim and broken her was back there.

Berrick slid along the wall, stopping and listening after each step. He heard only the crackle of flame. At the corner, he listened longer, trying to distinguish footsteps under the sound of the bonfire. When he thought he knew the general location of Halis he stepped around the edge.

Thick and heavy, black flecks of ash colored the garden in gray and little bursts of orange. At the epicenter, a fire bloomed, sending cascading black clouds upward. Halis stood near it, tossing a chair into the flame, then watching it catch.

No playing hero. No warnings. Berrick lifted the gun and leveled it. If some invisible force had stayed his hand with Silvia, he'd be sure he wouldn't give it time to intervene for Halis.

Halis turned, his black eyes locking on Berrick.

Berrick squeezed his finger.

The gun recoiled against Berrick's shoulder.

A burst of red shot from the left side of Halis' chest. The scream that ripped from Halis began as a throaty human wail but transformed with him into a shrill screech.

Before Berrick could fire again, tiny spiders burst from the cracks of the house, from the trees and bushes, running onto the path at Berrick's feet. The swarm of black drove him back a step before his resolve hardened. Only one spider mattered.

Dripping blood, the giant black Drambish had stopped screaming. The noise it made now was more of a hiss. It launched itself into the air.

Berrick fired.

A shower of hot, sticky liquid shot into Berrick's face. Blinded, Berrick could only feel the spider's weight as it landed on him. Pain shot up his side as something pierced into him.

Thousands of pinpoints of pain covered him as the smaller spiders swarmed over his legs, arms, and torso.

Fumbling at his belt, Berrick searched for another weapon. His fingers crawled with arachnids as he crushed their small bodies in his search.

Halis reared up. Crimson coated his widened maw, but the liquid that dripped from his fangs was not blood. A drop fell to Berrick's shoulder, burning like acid.

Berrick pulled a second, smaller firearm from his belt. His eyelids batted against the red film blinding him.

The spider dove down, black eyes hungry.

CHAPTER 17
LITTLE GIRL LOST

B errick pressed the gun against the giant spider's thick hide and fired. And fired again. Teeth clamped spasmodically, the smooth surface pressed into Berrick's neck. A line of poison burned against his collarbone. He fired a third, fourth, and fifth shot.

The weight fell from him and Berrick lifted an arm to wipe his eyes. He kicked off the remaining legs of the spider and shoved himself back over the ash-strewn garden.

The Drambish looked pitiful, dripping red, scrawny legs thrown akimbo. Several of its beady eyes were reduced to pulp in its wrinkled face. Berrick shot one more time, dead center in its head.

His breath wheezed, and he sat frozen in shock, his gun still held aloft—until his fingers refused to hold the metal and let it clatter to the ground. Now only his arm held out toward the corpse. Could it really be done?

The pain in his shoulder brought him sharply back. Though it looked nasty, the wound wasn't deep. He tested his arm and found it moved. After fighting his way to his feet, Berrick grabbed a random item of clothing, which had been set beside the fire as tinder, and bound his side.

Get out, whispered the voice of reason in his head, *before Silvia returns*. He was several steps back around the corner of the house when he turned back. Was that movement? He'd seen the same thing before, a blur of white. Something or someone in the house.

Run. Run! He didn't.

He approached the window. Inside, facing him but seeing nothing, stood Allison. Her single remaining eye was as black as the night sky.

Run, the voice screamed. *You can't save her. She's gone.*

He couldn't leave her. Not again.

Going against the screaming warnings of his own mind, Berrick walked over to the patio door and walked inside the house. His boots crunched against the marble-tiled courtyard. Spiders scurried beneath his feet, a thick carpet of black. In his wake, a trail of footprints composed of tiny black bodies extended.

Allison didn't turn but remained facing outside. Berrick went to her, keeping his footsteps slow and his movements non-threatening.

"Allison?"

"There is no apple and I'll eat nothing," Allison said.

"Allison, come with me. We have to get out of here."

"Red, red, blood and love. I'll take the knife."

Berrick set his hand on her shoulder. "We don't have time. Silvia'll come back."

"The curtains aren't red."

Screw this. Berrick grabbed hold of her and tossed her over his non-injured shoulder. A bolt screamed through him at her weight. His knees threatened to cave and with her added weight, the room spun in front of him. The fall was slow, and he kept her perched safely even as he reached to support himself on the wall. Kneeling now, Berrick tried to regain his feet. Sweat from the exertion broke out on his brow, but the agony ripping through his side every time he tried to lift himself to his feet conquered him at every attempt.

Lowering her again, Berrick stared at the ragged hole where Allison's second eye had been. Nothing in the documents explained that. Whatever the original test subjects had been

—hungry, out-of-control, deadly—there was no indication that they had been intentionally cruel.

We created Halis and Silvia, not just with that damn compound. The government, The Brothel, and all of us like me who simply stood by, we did this. We created them by killing their entire race and then enslaving them. Had they watched as their race had been hunted down, slain and then, at last, the entire planet gassed? Where had the two surviving Drambish been when the planet had been bombed? How old would they have been, five, six, maybe ten? Children. Children watching everything they'd known and cared for wiped out in one careless strike.

The wreck of Allison's beautiful face brought back the feeling of regret that had momentarily kept him from firing at Silvia. As gently as he could, Berrick touched the side of Allison's face.

"I'd kill you again," Allison said, black swirling in her eye.

Berrick understood the spider's hatred, but it didn't matter who'd made the beast rabid. They still needed to be put down. But this girl? Like Marim, she was infected and like Marim, she was innocent of any crime perpetrated in the name of the Drambish. He couldn't kill her, and he couldn't leave her to them.

Allison giggled; her ragged, torn fingernails scratched against his neck.

The High Council had deemed those like Allison an extreme threat. The people he'd worked for his entire life would have him put her down, but wouldn't their judgment be the same for Darith? Marim? And what had their judgment ever given him but a dead family?

His hand fumbled at his pocket and came out with a flask. The liquid inside sloshed with the trembling of his hand and Berrick took a long drag. A burn slid down his throat and he focused on the bright, sharp flavor. There was no purpose to these thoughts.

Not for the first time, he recited the things that mattered. The things that must be done. The list could force away the litany of things that tempted him with their confusing spiral into ambiguity.

The spiders must die. The spider babies must die. Marim must be avenged. Nothing else mattered, nothing.

Still, he grabbed Allison under the arms and pulled her away from the window toward the front door. *Get her out of here and then come back for Silvia.*

The front door was in sight when Berrick heard the vehicle in the drive. Silvia hadn't left in a car. Didn't matter. He had to get out of sight. Car doors slammed.

CHAPTER 18

SILVIA

T he diner came into view, and Silvia smiled as the few scattered people on the street crossed away from her. Their fear petted the air around her, and she took a deep breath, letting the terror stroke her throat. There was no darker energy than fear and in front of her Havoc laughed, his bright, beautiful infant laugh, delighted with the dark wiggling around him.

Silvia could have found Darith with her eyes closed. He existed in a bright space absent of emotion. But she didn't deny herself the vision of the boy, sitting in front of the diner at a rust-tinted table. From the first moment she'd seen the boy, she'd known he was special. Even then, his energy had had a lack of emotion, a selfish darkness that complemented his pristine beauty.

He has met his potential. And he wants me dead. Just look at that hate. But something else burned in Darith's eyes. For the moment, she was safe. That look screamed need, and people don't kill those they require.

"Silvia," he said. His eyes flicked over Havoc in his stroller, but he made no comment.

"Boy," she said.

"I should slit your pretty throat."

Silvia sat down in front of him. The rickety table rocked, the cold metal of the chair reaching her through the thin silk of her black dress. Havoc had fallen asleep in the stroller and Silvia let him remain. It would be better to focus on just Darith.

"You won't," she said. "Because you've thought it through. You can't get to Marim on your own, and you begin to feel the crunch of time. How long will finding your answers take on your own? Every moment you delay, Marim remains in The Brothel's hands."

"None of that matters if you can't help me."

Silvia reached across the table and touched Darith's neck, right on the soft skin where she'd bitten him over a year ago. "We are distinct, Darith, in our abilities. Our magic mingled with the dark web makes us something different. Halis tells me no other before me could use the blackness as a venom. That is my trick, boy, and being the only one with the venom makes me the closest thing to an expert you have."

"Why would you help me, knowing I mean to cure myself and kill you?"

"For the fun of it? Out of familial love? Because I want Annabelle, and you can't cure her? Maybe I don't need a reason... and maybe I think I can change your mind." *Maybe I'm not at all sure anymore that I am in the right. That I don't need to be put down like a rabid dog. I helped hurt Marim, the least I can do is help fix her.*

Then the thoughts boiled out of her mind.

Darith's mouth moved, but the sound was lost in a sudden flare inside Silvia's mind. The web burned, and like an eclipse, the world went dark. The diner disappeared, the chairs and the sky faded to nothing. Only Darith remained against the flaming black.

Blood everywhere. Gunshots rang and blistering pain tore through her. The flame faded to a shower of dark blood. And then there was a hole, a crippling vacancy at the core of her being. The essence of him disappeared, smudged out, lost in a sea of bodies she couldn't recall. But she felt them, millions of still-cold legs, glazed spider eyes staring into a flare of agony.

Silvia screamed, unable to contain the suffering of the Drambish.

They wanted to walk.

They wanted their revenge.

△△△

"…and maybe, I think I can change your mind."

"You help me save Marim, I'll give you a chance to run. I'll give you a head start," Darith said.

Her eyes were black, and for an instant, a color like the flame of a dying sun rolled over them. Darith sank back and touched the web. Halis. Berrick must have found Halis.

Even as Silvia's mouth opened, Darith lifted his hands, pulling at the energy around himself and around the baby. He braced.

When her voice tore through the air, the shell of light around him shivered. Faces, black wisps of terror and pain, billowed against the shield. Individual faces looked at him, snarled at him. Many of them had spider fangs dripping venom. Then finding they could not reach him, they hurtled elsewhere. Each hateful wisp bit into his shelter, spider fangs and human teeth alike.

Several screams cut the air from the street. The shadows breaking out of Silvia seemed to seek bodies and bury themselves inside when they found them.

Darith shoved his hand forward, meeting the ghostly eyes as they faded or chased away from him. The street filled with Silvia's cry and Darith watched as an elderly man crumpled to the ground, blood trickling from his ears and red tears streaming from his eyes.

And then Silvia fell from her chair. Darith dropped his hand and dared a glance at the street. The old man was not the only form twitching on the ground. Inside the diner, the waitress screamed and pulled herself across the floor, blood dripped from her pores like sweat on a hot day. Farther up the street, a man howled, his hands pressed to his face.

For the first time since he'd been contaminated, the voice of the hive was silent. It felt empty and torn.

The baby's high infant wail rose and fell like a siren.

"Halis," Silvia whispered.

The vulnerability in her voice made it nearly unrecognizable. And looking at the sorceress spider sprawled on the pavement, Darith would not have known her if not for having seen her seated in front of him moments before. Her face was the sickly gray of death, the black drained from her eyes leaving them a clear icy blue, and her hair, toppling around her shoulders, shone a pale strawberry blonde.

Was this Silvia without the spider?

Tears streamed from her eyes and trembling fingers reached out toward him.

If it was Silvia without the spider... that meant she knew how to get rid of the spider. She wasn't lying or misleading him.

Darith threw himself beside the beautiful woman as her eyes fluttered shut. Her skin was cold and clammy to the touch. Her pulse was faint, hardly detectable. She would die without the black. If she died, how would he save Marim? Darith pulled her limp form against him and leaned down to her ear.

"Pull it back to you. Your son needs a mother."

A slight nod of her head was all the acknowledgment that Darith got. *No, no, she can't die.*

"Take us too, Halis? Please," Silvia said.

Darith lifted her and, with difficulty, carried her and guided the stroller to his hired car. If it was Berrick, he would be smart enough to leave the house, right? He'd assume Silvia would come for him.

No time to worry about it.

He laid Silvia across the backseat of the car. Some slight color had returned to her skin. Darith closed the door, a tight feeling in his chest looking at the bright blonde hair fanning out across the seat, and the long lashes, the color of fire that touched her cheek.

The stroller folded in, allowing it to rest perfectly in the front passenger seat. The black-eyed baby within sobbed, but the sound made no impact on Darith's heart.

Darith slid into the driver's seat and glanced over his shoulder at the woman and baby in the back.

Who is Silvia? Up until seeing her lying on the pavement, he'd thought he'd known, but did he? The words from the man on the shuttle, Mr. Red, returned. *Am I acting with wisdom? I thought I understood...*

He pushed aside the thoughts and drove up the hill to the house. There was no car parked in front. That was a good sign, though it was possible the killer wasn't Berrick or that he hadn't come in a car.

Darith parked and stepped out of the car. Behind him, the back door opened, Darith's head wouldn't turn. Which version of the Spider Queen would step out of the back? Did it even matter?

Silvia walked past him, leaving her baby in the car as if forgotten. Her hair was still the color of a pale sunrise, but for a few shots of darkness. Darith followed her into the house. Silvia dashed directly out back, but Darith moved more slowly. Blood marked the floor inside the house. There had been none outside. Or had he missed it?

Slowly, Darith followed Silvia out onto the patio and looked down, a grin spreading over his face at the corpse of the spider.

△△△

Allison curled on Berrick's feet; she might have been asleep for all the movement she made. He looked out the crack in the closet door, trying to make sense of the snippets of color and movement. Silvia's black dress and someone else, a man. *Another of Silvia's little slaves? Like my brother?*

When both forms had gone outside, Berrick opened the

door and crept forward. He needn't have been so careful. The woman on the patio made no note of anything. For a moment, he wasn't sure it was Silvia. Hair like springtime sun streamed down her back, and her posture was soft. Not at all the sorceress who'd left the house shortly before. But the face remained the same, the full lips, the high cheekbones, and the necklace that fell from her neck... by the gods, that was Allison's eye.

Berrick lifted his gun and aimed at the woman cradling the spider's mutilated head.

"Don't you dare shoot her," came a voice Berrick knew.

The boy stepped closer to the sorceress. Again, it took Berrick a moment to recognize the person he faced. Darith. Despite the lack of a wheelchair, the darkened skin, the black eyes, there was no doubt that the man next to Silvia was Darith.

"Move away," Berrick said. His eyes returned to Silvia. She had not acknowledged either of them.

"I can't let you kill her," said Darith.

Berrick's finger squeezed the trigger. A blast of air struck his arm, knocking him a step to the side. The bullet flew wide, lodging in a tree. Still, Silvia did not respond.

"I don't want to hurt you," Darith said.

The boy's hand was lifted, empty, with his fingers spread. Was Darith's desire to keep Silvia alive the effect of the secretions? There was no other explanation. Berrick had to kill Silvia. Nothing else mattered.

The gun pointed back at Silvia. He aimed carefully this time, centering on the eye hanging over her heart.

Before he could fire, Darith's fist closed. A cold, hard nothing squeezed around Berrick's throat and his feet lifted from the ground. Berrick fired.

Red spread out across Silvia's shoulder. This got a response from her. She gave a short, startled scream and looked back at Berrick with blinding blue eyes.

Fire again.

His chest burned. The pressure around his neck tightened and his vision contorted with red flashes of agony.

"Drop the damn gun, Berrick," Darith said.

Berrick pressed down again on the trigger.

Pain overtook everything and a loud snap traveled from his neck to every extremity. His body hit the ground, and he struggled to move his arms. The ceiling faded from white to gray, his airless lungs screamed, and up the back of his neck into the base of his brain, waves of all-encompassing shocks blotted out all else.

A face entered his vision. Darith's black eyes stared down at him.

"Sorry, old man."

The face came closer. Berrick could barely see it. Only shadows of light remained.

"I'll protect Marim, don't worry, and when this is done, I'll kill the bitch."

Berrick barely caught the last words over the buzzing in his mind. Then the buzzing faded and somewhere in the distance, he thought he heard a little boy's giggle. All was black.

CHAPTER 19

TIMING

T he hospital lobby was vacant except for a few banged-up teenagers and a withered woman coughing into a kerchief. Red's white leather gloves slid across the counter as he inspected the tinted glass separating him from the receptionist.

"Her name was Allison, but she might have come in under the name Lilly. You'd remember her if you saw her: pale, incredibly attractive."

"No last name, sir? Our records..." The woman trailed off as Red lifted a hand to his face, as if repressing a tear.

Playing emotions ran against his nature, but like he always told the girls, "In our line of work, you have to do everything perfectly, even the things that are repellant."

"I could ask. Hold on," the woman said.

Her heels clicked as she walked away and Red leaned against the counter. The lobby was sparse, lined with row upon row of white plastic chairs. Gods-awful choice of color for a hospital. He wondered how often they were smeared with red. Only a few moments passed before the clicking returned.

"She was here last week. Some sort of mental breakdown but no bodily injury. Her boyfriend took responsibility for her legally when he picked her up. I wish I could give you a contact number, I really do, but policy on that is strict. You understand."

Before he could debate with himself if he should bother

with getting the number, the doors behind him burst open, letting in a wail of both close and distant alarms. Emergency vehicles. A woman walked in, supporting a thin man with blood dripping from his eyes. Behind them, the previously vacant parking lot was busy with arriving people and several emergency vehicles with doors opening. One gurney was already being pushed around the side of the building.

Red stepped aside to make way for the stream of injured.

"The witch took my eyes! The witch did it!" someone screamed from a stretcher as it was pushed inside.

A story emerged from the screams and whimpers of those filing into the lobby. Red cursed to himself. Wrong choice. He should have followed the boy to find the Drambish. And now it might be too late. Something had happened with the Drambish woman.

Luckily, it didn't look sexual, which implied that none of these people would be infected. A whole dimension to the problem he didn't need.

At the very least, he could concentrate on finding Allison. He strode from the room into the lot and tried to calculate how long it would take to reach town. Too long. Whatever was happening would have reached its conclusion by then. So what? Go to the space-train station? No, he had to catch them before they reached the train or The Brothel would get them. They were the only chance he had at Allison.

A string of invectives left his mouth as he strode to his car and slipped inside. Once inside the cool interior, he forced a deep breath into his lungs. Allison was alive or had been. Whatever else, that was more than he'd feared. But before he went racing to town in a futile effort to find her…

Red tapped a red button on the back of his ring. A pleasant buzz denoted a connection had been made. "Glory?" he said.

A moment later, a voice made of sunlight invaded the sterile cracks of his mind.

"Mr. Red? Everyone's looking for you. Are you all right?"

Sweet, young Glory. The newest of the girls. He smiled at

the concern in her voice. He could have called any of the eleven agents. The Agency was kidding themselves if they thought a single one of the girls was more loyal to the corporation than to their trainer. He'd made damn sure of that. But Glory, lovely little Glory, was madly in love with Allison. She had been since the first day she'd set foot on The Agency's space station. More time in The Agency would have stamped that out of her. He'd been planning to rid her of that weakness himself, but she was still new, volatile and emotional.

"I'm in no danger, but Allison is in trouble. I can't stay on the line and risk them listening, so pay attention. They tried to kill her. They failed. You need to make them think they succeeded. Prepare the girls. Whether or not I return with Allison, I'm going to need all of you."

"*Of course, Red. Bring her home.*"

ΔΔΔ

"Silvia."

Blood coated her hands, sticky and half-dry. She moved her fingers, listening to the jagged, wet protest as her fingers pulled apart. *My blood and Halis'. I left him. I did this.*

A red, five-pointed print stared up at her like a star from the surface of the table. Silvia touched the bandage at her shoulder, her mind ceaselessly prodding at the hole of Halis' absence. She felt only a hungry numbness.

"Silvia," Darith said.

A day later and we would have been gone. The bloody handprint mocked her. Human blood. Human failure. She should have seen this coming.

Pale hair slipped over her shoulder, bringing back a half-forgotten face. A blonde woman with sea-green eyes, a gunshot wound through her skull. Silvia recalled the hungry numbness inside; she'd felt it then too.

"Mommy! Mommy!"

"Do we need the girl?" A male voice.

"Yes. Bring her. Shut her up first." Ymel, his voice even there, leaking like her mother's face into her consciousness.

Silvia made a fist with her sticky fingers.

"Silvia!"

A sharp tug on her chin brought Darith into view. How long had he been there? Tears filled Silvia's eyes, blurring her vision until his face could have passed for Halis'. He held Havoc in his arms and handed the child over to her.

"We must go," Silvia said, Havoc's warmth beside her in his carrier, a searing reminder that she had more to lose.

"Were you aware there's a one-eyed crazy woman in your closet?"

"Oh, that would be Allison." Silvia slapped the tears from her face.

"Gods!"

"Why was she in the closet?" Silvia asked.

"Who is she?" Darith's sharp, staccato words snapped at her like the jaws of a small dog.

Good. She needed the pain to focus.

"She came here to kill Halis. We neutralized her. We must bring her with us. She's pregnant."

"We can't go anywhere. There are agents paid by The Brothel all over the station, scanning for your DNA. If you'd gone, you'd just have walked into their hands."

"They would have taken us back. He'd be alive," Silvia said. Then the memory of her mother's brains splattered across the ground returned. "No, they would have killed us both. Our very existence is a crime they perpetrated."

"About that… How is it you lived when the infection left you?"

"It's not an infection. It's a gene… and because I'm human —or was once. Like you, I was blessed with the spider, not born to it."

"But you can change into a spider."

"Magic, in order to..." Silvia choked back a sob. "So I could be more like Halis."

"Do they know you can energy bend?"

"Mr. Ymel does. His men do. They couldn't tell anyone else for risk word of yet another illegal mutation getting out. Underlings won't know."

"So, I could simply alter the scanner?"

Silvia shrugged. She'd never tried something like that, but theoretically... it'd work. And what did it matter?

"If that's true, can you change into anything or just a spider?"

ΔΔΔ

On the screen, red hair spilled over Marim's shoulders in un- tamed knots. Strands cemented into clumps by drool slapped stiff and brittle against her face as she jerked erect. Dry lips parted and a throaty laugh emerged.

Ymel shrank back when she lifted her finger and pointed. Her black eyes, shot with swirls of brilliant fire, registered his movement and her lips curved up in a smile.

"*Your house of sticks will burn,*" she hissed, the sound com- ing out slightly fuzzy through the speaker. When she spoke again the voice that issued forth was clear and male. A nasal baritone filled with hate. "*Halis is dead and they are coming for you. Bloody eyes, bloody ears, bloody hands and red, red across the sky. You thought you'd get away with leaving us in chains, but we are coming. I will feast on your screams.*"

"Shut it up!" Ymel said.

Marim laughed again before lying back and closing her eyes. A red trickle ran, like a tear from her eye. A single drop fell to the table.

Ymel trembled as he stared in abject horror at the girl's prostrate form. One thing was clear. If Halis was dead, then his plan had gone awry.

CHAPTER 20
A DOG & A BABY

T he line looked endless. Lee-San half-listened to the people boarding the space-train as he scanned them, telling each it was a special security scan. No one objected, not since the topic on everyone's lips was the incident downtown a few hours earlier. Lee-San had called his wife when he'd heard, just making sure. She hadn't been downtown and neither had their children.

After that, he hadn't paid much attention.

A couple approached. They looked nothing like the descriptions of the criminals, but that didn't matter. His job was to scan everyone.

The woman, a pale sickly thing, was asleep in a wheelchair, a bandage over one eye. The man that pushed the chair was little more than a boy. Poor kid. From the look of it, he was strapped with an injured wife and a child. Too young for that.

Lee-San explained the scan, and the boy nodded his head. He even reached out and touched the scanner before Lee-San could jerk it away. Once safely out of reach, Lee-San ran the scanner over the pale girl, making sure to do so on the right side of the chair. Tied to the handle of the left side was a huge white dog. The creature looked foul-tempered if ever there was a foul-tempered canine. Beautiful creature, though.

The girl was clean.

He scanned the man. Clean.

For a moment, he considered scanning the baby in the

carrier on the right arm of the chair. But he decided against it as the dog snarled.

He waved the couple and their dog on board.

READ BOOK 2 NOW!

SPIDER'S GAMBIT

Join Jesse Sprague's Reader's Group for more updates and a free short story!

ABOUT THE AUTHOR

Jesse Sprague

 Jesse Sprague has been writing dark speculative fiction as a way of exploring ideas that don't fit neatly into our world since her college days as an English Literature major. She has previously published several speculative short stories, including stories in the Once Upon Now anthology by Gallery books, Seattle Crypticon's Decompositions, and stories in several anthologies which can be found on Amazon.

Jesse can be found on facebook at https://www.facebook.com/ JesseSpragueauthor/ and her website jessesprague.com.

BOOKS IN THIS SERIES
THE DRAMBISH CONTAMINATE

Spider's Kiss

Silvia is a spider queen without a throne. Having escaped the destruction of her race of shape-shifter spiders, Silvia has lived her life enslaved in the bowels of the galaxy's most infamous brothel. Her confinement keeps humanity safe from her powerful kiss, which brings death, insanity, or worse: contamination by the Drambish gene, converting the victim to one of her spider brethren.

Spider's Gambit

Silvia Black is pitted in a high-stakes game against the Brothel, and checkmate equals death. As one of the last survivors of a race of shape-shifting spiders, her will to survive and her lust for revenge both point to the same strategy—exterminate her enemies before they find her. For the Spider Queen, friends are hard to come by, and her one-time victim Count Darith may be her only hope

Spider's Choice

Coming soon!

Made in the USA
Las Vegas, NV
22 February 2021